'What use is it to be bea
here in Edinburgh? T
that,' she said mockingl

'I did not say you we
you were as alike as two peas, you and the other beauty of this city,' he said quietly.

The whole table seemed to move sideways in a grotesque lurch. The candles in the sparkling chandelier above them seemed to flutter in a ghostly breeze, and the rowan-berries glistened as red as drops of blood. In that chilling moment when the goose-pimples crept up her arms and rose even under her hair, Candida first became frightened of this other woman, so like herself. Then she had heard Ross correctly the first time.

'You have not been here five minutes,' she said, 'so how could you know such a thing? It is not true!'

'It *is* true, Candida,' he assured her, his face hard and serious. 'It is as I said. Your fame has gone before you.'

'Who is this other woman?' There, it was out, the question that had nagged at her for thirty-six hours.

'I don't know.' He smiled tightly. 'But after all this mystery, when mystery is not allowed in my scheme of things, I intend to find out.'

But not before I do, Candida vowed.

Inga Dunbar was educated in Dumfriesshire, at the Academy, and then at Edinburgh University and College of Education. She became a head teacher, living and working extensively throughout Scotland, from Edinburgh in the east to Ayrshire in the west, from Gretna in the south to the Shetland Isles in the far north. She now lives in Aberdeen.

One of her interests is astrology, especially the inter-relationships and compatibilities of the birth-signs, which she has touched on in this book.

She has written three other Masquerade Historical Romances, *The Rose of Redayre*, *Rose Royale* and *Dragon's Isle*.

SCARLET LADY, WHITE BRIDE

Inga Dunbar

MILLS & BOON LIMITED
ETON HOUSE 18–24 PARADISE ROAD
RICHMOND SURREY TW9 1SR

First published in Great Britain 1988
by Mills & Boon Limited

This edition 1988

ISBN 0 263 76127 4

Set in 10 on 10½ pt Linotron Times
04–0788–80,413

Photoset by Rowland Phototypesetting Limited
Bury St Edmunds, Suffolk
Made and printed in Great Britain

For my friends Ruby and Leslie Turberville

HISTORICAL NOTE

IF YOU VISIT the Chamber of Horrors in the Wax Museum in Edinburgh's Royal Mile, you will see the effigies of Burke and Hare and the beautiful Mary Paterson. Although Tanner's Close was demolished in 1902, you can still walk down Candlemaker Row and still visit the White Hart Inn in the Grassmarket, haunted by all three. Burke's skeleton is still on view in Edinburgh's Anatomical Museum, at the University.

Helen MacDougal (Nelly) was given police protection out of Edinburgh and as far as the boundary of Northumberland and Durham. It is believed she died in Australia in 1868.

Margaret Hare escaped with her life to Belfast. In 1850 she was employed as a nurse in Paris.

William Hare tried to hide all over the country. He was even seen in Shetland, but it was in London that he died more than forty years later, a blind beggar. He had been recognised and thrown into a lime-pit as soon as he arrived, and his eyes were burned out.

Dr Knox also got his just deserts. He was forced to leave Edinburgh, a broken man, and died in London aged 71 in virtual oblivion.

His assistant William Fergusson fared better: he became Sir William Fergusson, Sergeant-Surgeon to Queen Victoria.

Mary Paterson never had a twin sister. Candida and Ross and their families are fictitious, as is Paradise House in the Grange district of Edinburgh. If it really exists, I beg its pardon.

But all the other great figures of Scottish history live on into eternity: Sir Walter Scott, Lord Henry Cockburn, William Dick, Lord Monboddo, Sir Henry Raeburn, Susan Ferrier and Archibald Constable.

PROLOGUE—1809

NOBODY LOOKED at her. Nobody was paying any attention to the shadowy figure lingering in a doorway of Candlemaker Row.

'Holy Mother of God, preserve us,' she moaned.

Another ferocious gust of wind tore at her bedraggled cloak, but how could she put out her hands to clutch it back round her? The burden she carried inside it was becoming heavier by the minute, and she must keep it hidden. Turning slightly, she allowed the wind to blow the cloak back into place, shuddering violently all the while. She continued to watch. From where she stood she had a good view of everything—the White Hart Inn with all its comings and goings, the towering grandeur of Edinburgh Castle up behind like the backcloth on a stage, and straight ahead the whole length and breadth of the Grassmarket.

By three o'clock on that pitiless afternoon of Wednesday 16th November still nobody had spared her a glance, and she began to feel slightly and desperately encouraged. The few people who were out hurried by, their heads bent low before the merciless wind, scurrying for shelter, for warmth, for any kind of refuge. She could tell which of them had any money: they were the ones who headed straight for the White Hart. She watched it all, and waited.

The wind whipped a storm of leaves into a swirling dance of death, leaves that must have been blown down from Greyfriars' churchyard. Some of them stuck to the mud filming the cobbles. By dawn their brave scarlets and yellows would be grimed and blackened like she was becoming herself—like everyone and everything else here in the Grassmarket, dragged down into the surroundings.

But not all the leaves had stuck. A sudden flurry hurtled towards her, slapping her face and blinding her before they rustled to rest in the far corner of the doorway. Afterwards, blinking, she saw that the moment had come at last when the whole street was deserted. It was a moment she knew would not last long. Even now there was a cackling and a squawking as first a few geese and then more and more straggled down from the West Port. Soon the man who was driving them would be in sight.

'Mother o' God, forgive me . . .'

She bent down and laid a bundle on the heap of dry leaves behind her. A moment later the doorway yawned dark and empty. She was gone.

She was gone along the south road out of Edinburgh to Gilmerton, and battling against the wind and the bitter cold, the six miles seemed like sixty, as sure as God. She did not understand how the Blessed Virgin had ever allowed her to be in these straits, even yet—for had she not been a good Catholic girl?

But that soldier boy with his mass of golden curls and the twinkle in his eye had fair got round her, so he had, before he went off to fight and die in France . . . She should be proud of him, for hadn't they read out his name to her from the Lists of Missing, Presumed Dead, in the *Courant*? Sure, and it wasn't everyone got their names in the *Courant*, Ellen McGuire told her. After that there was only Ellen to help her, if you could call feeding her on scraps and berating her from morning to night about her sinful ways helping her.

'Would you just be looking at you! My God, when Father O'Malley rants and raves about the holiness of the virgin state to us poor Irish women, what's he goin' to say when he finds out the soldier was a Protestant, besides?'

Then, one evening not long ago, out of Ellen's watchful eye, she had met this new man over a glass of gin in the White Hart. Ever so nice he was, dressed posh, a travelling man, and like herself only out for a laugh. They were laughing when he said he loved her, but the funniest thing of all was that she believed him. She told him bits of her story, but not the bits that mattered, and he never suspected a thing, because Ellen had gone to the Jew's shop and got her this old cloak, stolen no doubt from some fine house, 'to cover yer shame'. He said to meet him at nine o'clock on the night of the 16th of November at Gilmerton—which was where he would have some business the next time he came this way—if she could give Ellen the slip, and then they would take the London coach to a fine new life together.

By Hallowe'en she was too big to go out, and all she prayed for was the birth to deliver her of her burden. Neither she nor Ellen could believe their eyes when she had the bad luck to produce not one, but two illegitimate children on the 9th of November, that bitter morning last week.

'That does it,' Ellen said. 'We might cover up the cries of one bairn, but never the two o' them! I keep a respectable house here, my girl. Sure, an' I'll give you a week to get back on yer feet, an' then out ye go!'

So here she was, struggling along the road to Gilmerton, for she knew in her bones this would be her last chance to be free and have a good time, and she had had all week to realise she could never have that, not with two babies in tow.

Dry-eyed, she peered through the darkness at the cottage nearest to the crossroads of Gilmerton. It was low and mean, but it was lamplit and there was smoke coming out of the chimney. Mercifully the wind suffocated suddenly, but it was in the grip of a deadly frost, and the moon shone hard and fierce. It lit up a bedraggled hovel indeed, although the lamp behind the rough orange curtain gave it a glow of homeliness. A dog barked and rattled on its chain, and she fled behind a bush. A minute later the door opened and a man came out and went across to the dog's shed. After a few minutes more the dog's barks eased and a woman stood framed in the doorway, tall and plump.

'What is it?' she called to her husband.

'There's nobody here. The dog's a wee bit restless, with her so near her time.'

'Och, you and your dogs, Joe Paterson! Come awa' in. The dog'll look after hersel'!'

It was a long time after that before everything had settled down again, while she said one Hail Mary after another right through to the end before she stole like a shadow up to the cottage door, terrified that every stealthy footfall would alert the dog again.

The child she had left in Candlemaker Row had been the second-born twin girl, the smaller and the weaker of the two. She didn't expect her to survive. But this one . . . She opened the newspaper wrapper a bit further, and then the thin shawl, and gazed in the orange glow at the tiny flower face. *This* one would be a beauty! She crossed herself and laid her first-born on the doorstep, and crept back behind the bush.

She felt dreadfully unwell. It had been cold all day, and she had been exposed to it for hours on end when she was not properly recovered from the birthing. She swayed and shuddered, and tried to summon up strength from somewhere. What time was it? Steadying herself, she examined the sky. Och, it was never nine o'clock yet! She would wait a wee while longer to see what happened now that the baby had begun to cry. Maybe her opening the shawl had disturbed her. The dog started to bark again, and the door opened.

'It was no cat, Molly,' the man called Joe Paterson said as he bent down to pick up the bundle. 'Come and see.'

'Och, the bonnie wee bairn! And only a week old too, by the look o'it! Now, who could leave a baby on a doorstep on a night like this? It's a wee lass, too, Joe . . . And me wi' four boys! Nothing but boys! Ay, the world is ill-pairted.'

'Well, you've got your wish now,' Joe said grimly.

'The mother will be miles away by this time. So what is it to be, Molly?'

'Another mouth to feed, Joe?'

'We've aye managed, lass.'

'Sent from heaven, so she is! We'll call her Mary—what else? Mary Paterson.'

'Well, get her in to the fire, woman!'

The door slammed shut, and the girl outside turned on her heel and ran without a backward glance, and all that remained were a few scarlet drops where she had stood to stain the sparkling frost.

CHAPTER ONE

LIZA CORCORAN smoothed down an already irreproachable white pinafore, settled her cap firmly on her head and entered the dining-room positively rustling with starch. She offered the silver tray to Mr Forbes first.

'Your letters, sir.'

'Ah, yes, Liza.'

Mr Atholl Forbes, Advocate, did not take his nose out of the *Scotsman*, and Liza laid down his pile beside his plate. As usual, the letters in it looked formidable and as dry as dust.

'Do you know what the Editor has written for his leading article today?' he asked, without raising his eyes.

'No, dear,' Lady Alison said mildly, taking her letters off the tray and riffling through them in an absent-minded fashion until she stopped short at one of them with a frown. 'What?'

'Here we are arrived at the 18th day of September 1827—1827, mark you—and he is still bemoaning the lack of bodies for the anatomists! When we all know, and have known these past two years and more, that nobody is safe lying in his grave! It would fit him better to ask why Edinburgh people must keep watch with lanterns over their loved ones laid to rest in the churchyards every time there is a death.'

'And one for you, Miss Candida,' Liza said, and Candida experienced the little thrill of hope that perhaps it was from Finlay.

She had been engaged to Finlay for some weeks, but still she had no idea what his handwriting looked like, let alone what thoughts his written words might express. In fact, there were a lot of things she had never shared with Finlay yet—too many, perhaps . . .

'It has the Thistle seal upon it,' Liza said, handing it over, 'so it might be from your Aunt Rose.'

'Did you hear me, Alison?' Mr Forbes rustled his newspaper agitatedly and finally lowered it sufficiently to look at his wife over the top of his spectacles. 'There is even a joke going around about it. "The surgeons make no bones about wanting fresh meat." Christopher North said recently that even the students are at it, especially the students of Dr Knox.'

'Did he, dear?' Lady Alison said. 'I fear I cannot take much interest in what Mr North said, this morning. There is something here much closer to home, I'm afraid. It is a letter from Ireland.' She paused delicately, and then dropped her bombshell. 'From Cornelia.'

She sat back with the air of one who must resign herself to weathering the storm while Mr Forbes gazed at her for some minutes in absolute horror. It was a storm that would break any minute now, with even the *Scotsman* cast aside.

'You cannot mean my most detested cousin, Cornelia Forbes? Mistress Alexander Laing?'

'The same,' Lady Alison said as firmly as her gentle voice allowed.

'But I thought we had got rid of her thirty years ago when they went off to Ireland?'

'*You* got rid of her, dear. I am the one who has been answering her letters all these years.'

'It is like a ghost come back to haunt us! Why, if you have said nothing about it all along, are you worrying me with it today?' Mr Forbes betrayed his growing suspicion. 'What can *she* possibly have to say?'

'She says she could not for the life of her spare a minute of the time she must devote to her golf and her husband's horses to come over here herself . . .'

'Thank God Almighty for that,' Mr Forbes said devoutly.

'Atholl!' Lady Alison frowned before she continued, 'But she is sending over two of their children, the eldest son and the youngest daughter, for a few months.'

There was a stunned silence in the dining-room while Mr Forbes struggled to digest this wholly unexpected and unwelcome information, and Candida seized the opportunity to speak. 'Which ones are they, again, Mama?'

'Ross Alexander Laing and Alanna Alexander Laing. It seems Ross wishes to do some research work at the University and Alanna is interested in the Outside Classes, and of course she cannot attend them unescorted.'

Candida had always known about these far-distant relations in Ireland but they were rarely discussed in the house in Charlotte Square, which made them even more interesting now.

'Do you mean to tell me, Alison, that they are actually coming *here*, to this house?' Mr Forbes spluttered. 'And what does that mean, Ross Alexander Laing and Alanna Alexander Laing? Is there a hyphen in it already? I can see that Cornelia is as determined as ever to have a superior name of some sort as well as her castle, since she could not marry a title.'

'No,' Lady Alison smiled. 'She did not manage that, after all. Thank goodness Cameron fell in love with Rose as soon as ever he clapped eyes on her, or it might all have been very much worse.'

'That's true.' Mr Forbes subsided a little, and Candida pricked up her ears.

She had always thought her aunt and uncle of the Thistle Courts had a romantic past, for them to be still so absurdly in love at almost sixty. Perhaps now she would find it all out, all the stories of long ago. Her parents never dwelt on stories of the past.

'It will only be for a very short time, my love,' Lady Alison said comfortingly. 'As soon as possible they will take up a residence of their own in the town.'

'Well, they will have plenty of money to do so. Alexander Laing must have been worth a fortune before he ever went over to Ireland and set up his own racing stables, and now he is a household name, even over here.'

'It is strange that Ross wants to study at the University,' Lady Alison said thoughtfully. 'He is a doctor already. He has been for years. He must be twenty-nine, if not thirty.'

'Perhaps he wishes to specialise in some branch of medicine, my dear, and there is no more renowned place in Europe for anyone to pursue surgery or medicine in depth than Edinburgh,' Mr Forbes said with gloomy pride. 'I suppose there is no help for it?' he added with a sigh.

'None, Atholl,' Lady Alison said firmly. 'We must do our Christian duty.'

Candida tried hard not to smile. Papa was indisputably head of the house, the one who read the prayers every morning as befitted the head of a staunch Presbyterian household, but Mama could always get her own way with just one quiet word.

'I have heard Cornelia's name mentioned before,' Candida hazarded, 'but I didn't realise she is your cousin, Papa.'

Mr Forbes took a square look at his daughter for the first time that morning. For him, it was proving a morning of one shock after another. 'Good God, Alison! The child's hair!'

'Now then, Atholl, I wish you would not think of her as a child—she will be nineteen in less than two months and a married lady in six! As for her hair . . .'

Lady Alison smiled lovingly at Candida, at her heart-shaped face surrounded by a glorious cloud of shining blond curls cascading almost to her waist, and into her clear blue eyes.

'Her hair has always been so beautiful as to be both a pride and a problem, I'm afraid. It is unthinkable to cut it, and it takes a very long time for us to coil it up in the ladylike way your daughter must be presented to the world. Therefore, from now on, I am allowing her to wear it undressed until after breakfast. Kitty can see to it in twenty minutes afterwards. She has become quite expert at attending to Candida's toilette.'

Together, Candida and Lady Alison beamed at him with such radiance and undeniable affection that as usual he was forced to retreat in the face of it. They were both as charming as they were beautiful, he had to concede, and more than that, as steady and as true-blue as their wonderful eyes.

Yes, Alison had made an excellent job of bringing up the baby, and if Candida's eyes had not been quite so brilliant, if they had been a shade more grey with the eyebrows a little heavier, he could have been persuaded for ever that she really was their own child, blond, blue-eyed and clever as any child of Alison's would be. He had not had such disturbing thoughts for many a long day . . . It was all his cousin Cornelia's fault, of course.

'Yes,' he sighed, 'Cornelia is a lady who has spelled trouble all her life, and she is still doing so, as you can see, to this very day.'

'Oh, she was never as bad as all that,' Lady Alison protested. 'She was a little foolish when she was young, Candida. Most of us are.'

'How can you tell what she has been?' Mr Forbes demanded. 'You have not been to Ireland to see what she has been up to all these years! How must her children have turned out, poor things?'

'We shall soon see. And they had their father, dear,' Lady Alison reminded him.

'Fortunately for them! Alexander Laing was a very decent fellow: a gentleman, in fact. How he ever allowed himself to be waylaid by Cornelia, I will never know. Still, Candida, it was at their wedding that your Mama and I first met, so I will say no more—for that above all was the most fortunate day of my life.'

Her parents smiled lovingly at each other across the length of the table and Candida considered that the little storm in a teacup was over, smoothed away as always by her mother's gracious ways and her father's total adoration of her. Once again she felt a little prick, almost of rejection, as though she had been eavesdropping, a stranger listening in to other peoples' lives. She supposed that everyone else felt the same, at least everyone else who was an only child. It seemed that a mother and a father as close as her parents led such a secretive, veiled life that it felt like an impenetrable fortress to their children. It was the reason why she did not confide absolutely everything either to Papa or to Mama.

From a very early age, Candida had always had a vague feeling that, surrounded as she was by all the material things of life and besides that, certainly by all the love in the world, she was at once privileged and yet at the same time one of the very underprivileged. It was an uneasy feeling, and quite ridiculous, one that she tried to dismiss by slitting open the letter that bore the Thistle crest. 'Perhaps I should read this out to you,' she said, after the first few lines.

To Miss Candida Forbes,
13 Charlotte Square,
Edinburgh
Candida, our dearest Niece,
As you will know, with all our own children now married themselves and gone into their own homes, some so far-flung that we have little consolation, we are sometimes very lonely out here at the Thistle Courts.

It would do our hearts good to have some young life about the house again, and we beg to receive you, and Mr Finlay Semple, of course, and as many of your friends as you care to bring, as from Friday the 19th for as long as you can stay, to comfort your Uncle,
Sir Cameron Kyle,
and your loving Aunt, Lady Rosalie Kyle.
P.S. We have looked after the little bird whose leg you bound up last time, and he is here still. He, at least, does not seem to want to fly away. R.

'Oh dear,' Lady Alison said. 'Your Aunt Rose must have been feeling very lonely when she wrote that! Perhaps you should go out and stay with them for a few days, dear.'

'Yes, of course,' Candida said. 'By a happy coincidence there are one or two little projects I want to pursue, and I may as well start them at the Thistle Courts.'

'What are they this time?' Mr Forbes asked. 'Horses, dogs, cats or birds?'

'No . . . No, Papa, it is human beings, this time.'

Perhaps now, at last, she would get to know Finlay much more intimately. The very thought of it brought a faint flush to her cheeks and a sparkle to her eyes.

'Well,' Lady Alison said, 'you cannot go on the morning of Friday the 19th, not if we are to welcome your Irish cousins, for that is tomorrow, the day they arrive. I suppose that is how she should regard them and address them, Atholl, my dear? As cousins, however distantly related?'

'Yes, tell me, Papa,' Candida smiled, 'for lately I have become so interested in relationships, especially my own connections. I had thought to make a small study of it—perhaps even to draw up a family tree. This is one of the projects I shall embark on at the Thistle Courts. It should interest Finlay, too.'

Long minutes hung suspended in silence over the table while her parents gazed at each other in consternation. Why were they so serious? What did it really matter? Ross and Alanna must be second cousins at least once removed, if not twice. Candida smiled encouragingly at them, but the little pool of silence while her mother and father spoke volumes to each other with their eyes deepened and deepened, and she could feel thrills of positive alarm in the air. Her curiosity was thoroughly aroused when Mr Forbes broke it with another clearing of his throat, always a signal of his distress.

'Ah yes, cousins indeed. But distant cousins, with very

little of the kin, only enough to permit you to call them by their Christian names, my dear,' he said strictly. 'We may allow that liberty, but in every other way they should be regarded as any other guests staying here for a short visit. We shall not be too familiar.'

'Exactly so,' Lady Alison agreed, but her face had gone quite pale. 'It need not interfere with your trip out to the country, either. Ross and Alanna would have to go out to see the Kyles anyway, so if they wished they could go, too, tomorrow. Of course you will invite Finlay to escort you?'

'And to stay with us, Mama, if his business will allow.'

'His *business*? I do not think his business will prevent him from social engagements,' Mr Forbes said.

'Then that is settled,' Lady Alison rushed on, with a warning glance at Papa. 'I shall send out word today to my brother Cameron to advise him and Rose that it will be late afternoon before you arrive.'

'Do you feel quite well, dearest Mama?' Candida asked anxiously, for by this time her mother's face had become quite ashen.

'The shock of all this has been too much for her,' her father said, rising swiftly from the table. 'Come, my dear, back to bed for an hour or two! I shall get Liza to come to you. No, Candida, you need not come. It is only to prevent one of her headaches. She will soon recover if she keeps very quiet.'

Candida was not deceived. Yesterday she might have been, but not today. Somehow a lot of things had changed, today. Once again she was being excluded, she thought, as she watched her father propping up her mother on their way out of the dining-room. All the quiet strength in the world lay in his dear shoulders, and she realised suddenly how much she and her mother depended on him, for everything—especially Mama, when she was indisposed like this, as she was so often, or when she wished to speak to him urgently and privately, which she was sure was the case this morning.

Her mother had seemed in the best of health when

they sat down to breakfast, before the letters arrived. Was it the letter from Ireland that had upset her? No. It had upset Papa certainly, but Mama had remained calm throughout, calm enough even to smooth his ruffled feathers eventually. Then could it have been the letter from the Thistle Courts? Candida read it again and could find nothing in it but the kindness Aunt Rose always expressed. So it all boiled down to something she herself must have said, and all she had said was that she was going to study the family tree. How could that possibly upset her mother?

Only if there was something to hide. Was that it? Was that why her parents never spoke of the past to her? Candida felt a strange prickle in her scalp as she wandered off thoughtfully to the kitchen to speak to Kitty, Liza's daughter, who had been brought up below-stairs in the house in Charlotte Square. Kitty was twenty-two, pretty and plump and cheerful, and Candida thought of her as one of her oldest friends as well as her personal maid. She found her looking out dusters.

'What are you going to do?' Candida asked.

'After I have done your hair, I am going to clean the windows, Miss Candida. It is a fine day for it.'

'Well then,' Candida sighed, 'we had better go upstairs and get the brushing and the combing and the horrible pins attended to.' Seated at her dressing-table, she pursued her theme. 'How happy I should be if only I could wear my hair down like this always, Kitty,' she said, for perhaps the thousandth time.

For the thousandth time Kitty smiled patiently and took up the hairbrush. 'Did I tell you about a girl I saw last week with hair just like yours looks now, Miss Candida? I was in the High Street speaking to Janet Brown . . .' The brush stopped momentarily while Kitty frowned into space. 'Janet . . . She's not the girl she used to be. Whatever's come over her? Anyway, the girl with the long fair hair stopped to say something to Janet, and oh what a sight it was, just a wild tangle!'

'No, you didn't tell me about her, Kitty.'

'Well, you would look just like her if I did not brush your hair, and brush it and brush it with the bay rum and cantharides sprinkled on it. It would never lie in those beautiful waves. On the other hand,' said Kitty, 'the girl was bonny, just like you, so I dare say the gentlemen excuse her.'

All this time Candida's head had been bent low while Kitty wielded the brush from the roots of her hair almost down to the floor.

'You may sit up, Miss Candida,' she said, and in the mirror they both surveyed the froth of curls critically. 'Now, it is the smoothing down.'

The brushing went on inexorably until the upraised ringlets were tamed. The bay rum filled the room with its aromatic scent, and once again Candida watched the miracle of its smoothing and polishing properties in the mirror.

'That was a strange thing to say, Kitty,' she said. 'What do you mean, 'the gentlemen will excuse her"? What was she like, that girl in the High Street?'

'Oh, just some painted taupie,' Kitty answered. 'A woman of the streets, by the look of her. And I wouldn't give tuppence for Janet Brown these days, either.'

'Kitty!'

'Pardon me, Miss Candida. It just slipped out!'

'We are not supposed to know about these things, Kitty.'

'No, Miss Candida.'

'But of course we all do. What was her name, since she is supposed to look like me?' Candida asked, her interest quickening.

'Oh, she is not like you at all!' Kitty said, shocked. 'You are a lady! It was only her hair that reminded me of you . . . I never found out what her name was. Janet Brown might know, though. Now that's finished,' Kitty said, as she slipped in the last pin.

'Isn't it a bit early to be cleaning the windows?' Candida asked, on the way back downstairs.

'The better the hour the better the deed!'

'You're up to something, I can tell. I know you so well, Kitty Corcoran. And you're blushing!'

'No, I'm not,' Kitty protested with a giggle, her face scarlet.

'Well then, I shall come with you and watch.'

'I can manage myself, Miss Candida. What would Lady Alison say if she saw you? Besides, you will make yourself late for Mr Finlay.'

'There's plenty of time for Mr Finlay. He will not arrive till twelve o'clock. I have something to tell you.'

Kitty studied her young mistress's face. 'Hm,' she said. 'Yes, I can see that something is in the wind. Come along then, Miss Candida, and tell me all about it.'

They began to polish the windows, Kitty sitting on the windowsill, one plump elbow with dimples in it bare to the passers-by as she pushed her duster energetically back and fore. Candida rubbed the inside of the glass absent-mindedly with another duster.

'I shall be going out to the Thistle Courts tomorrow,' she began, 'which means that you will be coming with me, Kitty.'

'Yes, miss,' Kitty said cheerfully.

'But before that, in the morning, some Irish cousins will arrive. They will be coming with us out to the country.'

'Ah,' said Kitty.

'There is something so upsetting about them . . . or something connected with them that Mama has taken to her bed.'

'Does my mother know?'

'Papa sent for Liza. She is with her now. Both Mama and Papa were acting strangely this morning at breakfast. It is either about the Irish cousins, or because I said I was going to find out about the whole Forbes family and make a family tree. These cousins are Forbeses too, on their mother's side. Is it something to do with them, after all, I wonder?'

Kitty took her curly red head back inside the window,

her grey eyes round. 'Oh, miss!' she said reproachfully. 'You never said you were going to poke about in the past! No wonder Lady Alison . . . Miss Candida, what does any of it matter now?'

Candida gazed at her maid confounded. She could not help but notice the stops and starts and almost guilty self-corrections she had just heard. She deduced at once that it all had a connection with the little incident in the dining-room. She had found out something else: Kitty knew something that she did not.

At that point a young man with broad shoulders, a tall frame and a plain face bursting red with anticipation and glowing with good intentions came striding past. His own grey surtout could not disguise his true calling in life. He walked with a heavy-footed measured tread, and when he saw Kitty he stopped short in feigned surprise.

Candida saw that he had stopped here before to speak to Kitty, and that was how her maid knew the time to be polishing the windows. Kitty's head ducked out again.

'So it's you again, is it, Frank Clarke? Do you always come this way on your Thursdays off?' she giggled. '*Constable* Frank Clarke, I beg your pardon!'

'Ah, Kitty Corcoran, cleaning windows again? They must be the cleanest windows in Edinburgh!'

The young man strode across the pavement to hold a more intimate conversation, and Candida stepped back from the red damask curtains, dropping her duster as she went. Kitty's attention was entirely devoted to Constable Frank Clarke, off duty, and she did not notice that her mistress had departed.

Liza did not find Lady Alison in bed, as she had expected. On the contrary, she was pacing about her bedroom in an agitated manner quite foreign to her true nature which was calm, and as far as Liza Corcoran had ever known it except once, completely serene. She took all this in at a glance.

'Now then, my lady,' she said, leading Lady Alison still fully dressed to the grey-blue silk chaise-longue before the fire, 'you will at least lie down.'

'I cannot,' Lady Alison said, with her slim shoulders bent and her beautiful pale hair streaked with silver shining in the light of the fire. 'How can I, Liza?' Candida is threatening to delve into our family roots. It will mean times and dates, death certificates and more especially birth certificates—and it is worse even than that! She says she is going to involve Finlay in the making of this family tree.'

'Yes, Lady Alison dear,' Liza said sadly, 'but calm yourself. It may never happen. *You* know Miss Candida better than anyone else. You know how many interests she has. One of them is sure to divert her.'

'Oh, do sit down here beside me, Liza! After all these years you must know the times you do not have to stand on ceremony with me, dear old friend. Sometimes I think you are the only one in the world I can talk to with complete understanding, woman to woman, for you were with me that dreadful afternoon eighteen—nearly nineteen—years ago. Do you remember?'

'I remember,' Liza said, and patted her mistress's cold hands. Then, putting a shawl round Lady Alison's shoulders, she sat down beside her and together they gazed into the fire. In its flames, leaping and dying, they both saw the same pictures of the past. 'Of course I remember, dearie. How could I forget?'

At four o'clock that same terrible day long ago, on Wednesday the 16th of November 1809, it was that last half-hour of daylight merging into dusk when the elegant coach with its gilded crests on each door began its cautious descent of the steep zigzag of Candlemaker Row. The horses were reined in and the brake half on as it groaned down the almost perpendicular road to the Cowgate. Only when it turned into the broad flatness of the Grassmarket did its occupants breathe sighs of relief, and the coach gathered a little speed.

'Is it not too late in the day, my lady? For this place, I mean?'

Lady Alison Kyle-Forbes stared bleakly around the inside of the coach. Perhaps she had made a mistake in choosing lime green for the upholstery. Between the slight worry of that and the overpowering smell of new leather and the unyielding stiffness of the seats, she was not enjoying her first trip out since her illness.

She had stayed too late at Mistress Henderson's Tea Afternoon. It was so very difficult to get away from Effie Henderson, but at least she had been spared the effort of talking. For a whole hour Effie's voice, recounting every item of the formidable list of gossip she had gathered together over the past month, washed relentlessly over her head. It was only when Alison stood up to go that Effie returned her attention to her.

'You are quite well again, Alison? Just one of your usual chills, I suppose? Well, if you *must* go, dear . . .'

And so Mistress Henderson never found out that her illness had been her second miscarriage in as many years, or that the fly-leaf on her large family Bible still remained obstinately blank below the record of her marriage: 'Mr Atholl Crichton Forbes and Lady Alison Kyle, married this day, June 3rd, 1804, in the Church of St Giles, Edinburgh.'

'That'll ha'e to be the finish, noo, Alison,' Dr Chisholm's words still rang in her ears, 'or I canna be responsible. I'll ha'e a word wi' Atholl.'

'He will agree with you entirely,' she had told him with a smile that was almost bitter on so gentle a face. 'He has been in a dreadful state. Having another baby so soon was all my idea. And, once again, it all went wrong.'

'Ye canna blame yersel', my dear. It's just that ye ha'e sic a delicate constitution.'

'I do blame myself, for being nearly forty before I found the perfect husband . . .'

'Nor for that, either. But there are plenty o' perfect babies—too many—thrown to the wall, abandoned in this city. Would ye no' consider adopting one o' them?'

'Adopting?' Alison gazed at her old doctor blankly. 'Never!'

Such a thing had never occurred to her. She wanted her own child, hers and Atholl's, and twice she had known exactly how her son would be—large and dark, with kind brown eyes just like his father. And, of course, very, very clever.

But now, it seemed, it was not to be, not ever. She had finally faced the fact, forced herself to accept it, but the ache and the longing for a child in her arms refused to go away. It made her feel so tired, every day. Painfully she dragged herself from her recent unhappiness back into the present, into the Grassmarket, which did nothing to uplift her. It was so dirty and so very depressing.

'Of course it is too late to be in the Grassmarket, Liza,' Lady Alison agreed with her maid, 'but mercifully it is almost deserted on such a day. We should not be here at all if anyone else in Edinburgh could boil a ham like David Rhymer. Ugh! The nearer we get to the West Port, the worse it becomes.'

She pressed her lace-bordered handkerchief to her nose, glad of its whiff of lavender, and returned her eyes to her maid and to Liza's three-year-old daughter she was trying in vain to subdue.

'Please excuse her, my lady! I said we should never ha'e taken her!' Liza said.

'Oh, don't hold her little hands so, Liza! She is only a baby, and she has so much energy! She has been trying to sit still for far too long. Kitty dear, you may come out with us when we stop at Rhymer's, if you are a good girl.'

'I know of no other lady who would ha'e taken in a widow wi' a bairn, my lady. Just so long as she doesna' run off,' Liza added pessimistically. 'It is her latest mischief.'

The coach bowled up smartly and stopped with a flourish outside Rhymer's shop. It gave the impression to anyone who happened to be looking that of course it did not belong here in the bowels of the Old Town. It belonged to Edinburgh's grand and elegant New Town, where the houses were made of honey-coloured sandstone and never more than three storeys high, to the most splendid street of all in fact, Charlotte Square. It gleamed richly green, spotless in the dying light except for the sparks of mud splashed up on it from the Grassmarket.

'You will wait here, Fergus,' Lady Alison instructed her driver, who was handing her out. He, too, was resplendent in dark green uniform. 'We shall not be more than ten minutes.'

'It will give me time to light the lamps, my lady. In ten minutes it will be dark.'

Lady Alison proceeded into Mr Rhymer's establishment, followed by Liza and little Kitty, and they crossed the threshold of an Aladdin's Cave brightly lit with oil-lamps and crammed with goods from the roof to the sawdust on the floor. A disembodied face appeared in a small space between the boxes piled on the counter.

'It's yersel', my lady,' Mr Rhymer said. 'Welcome back.'

'How do you manage it?' Lady Alison asked. 'You have packed in more than ever!'

'Ay. "Everything and a'thing", that's my motto. It has to be, my lady. I've got competition now, you see. There's a Jew opened up along a bit, selling second-hand clothes, next.'

'Well, I am relieved to see that your hams are wrapped and hooked up far away from *your* old clothes, Mr Rhymer.'

From somewhere on the other side of the counter the rungs of a ladder seemed to be moving along of their own volition before it was propped up and David Rhymer came into view, grinning, and his red hair on end. He wore a white apron and his hands were very clean, his customers noted thankfully.

'It'll be the smoked ham, my lady?' he asked, lifting one off its hook and climbing down again.

He cleared some of the boxes away and laid down the

ham on the counter. Under its paper skirt it was speckled yellow with breadcrumbs and wrapped in fine muslin.

'We will have the skirt off, and the ham wrapped in clean white paper, Mr Rhymer, if you please. There is nobody else in Edinburgh who can produce it like you.'

'Ay, it's the best, right enough, my lady. That's because it's from Irish pigs, born and bred, as you might say.'

'Surely not!' Lady Alison said. 'This has not come all the way from Ireland?'

'The pigs did, my lady. They have always lived here in the Grassmarket.'

Lady Alison shuddered delicately. She could well believe it. Mr Rhymer handed the parcel to Liza, and Lady Alison looked around for Kitty. The little girl was nowhere to be seen.

'Where is she, Liza?'

They looked at each other with the same dread in their eyes before they rushed out to the coach.

'Did you see her, Fergus?' Lady Alison asked anxiously.

'See who, my lady?'

'Kitty. Did you see her running off this way?'

'My bairn! Oh, my bairn!' Liza wailed.

'No, I did not, and that'll be enough o' that, Liza Corcoran!' Fergus said firmly. 'You're upsetting her ladyship. No, my lady, she didn't run this way, or I would have seen her. She must be back the way we came. We'll find her, Liza, don't worry.'

All this time he was settling them back into the coach, which had been turned about and lit and made ready while they had been in Mr Rhymer's shop. Now Fergus drove it slowly back along the Grassmarket, past the Bow Head and up the steep incline of Candlemaker Row. They had not gone far up when Liza's sharp eyes noticed a movement in one of the doorways.

'Stop, Fergus!' Lady Alison commanded, and before he could dismount they were out and into the dark entrance. 'Liza, have you found her?'

'Yes, thanks be to God! She's got something wi' her—a bundle o' some kind.'

'Take her out into the light, then. What is it?'

'It's a cat,' the child said, blinking in the coach lights. 'I heard it crying, Mam. Listen, it's crying again!'

Lady Alison's shocked eyes met those of her maid, and for a moment neither of them could speak. Then Liza pulled Kitty's head into the shelter of her skirt, and Lady Alison came to herself suddenly, and took charge, trembling.

'That's no cat, my lady,' Liza whispered.

'We shall just go home as fast as we can. Mr Atholl will know what to do,' Lady Alison said shakily, tucking the bundle inside her fur-lined cloak. Then, with a warning glance at Liza, 'We will say nothing about it, not to anyone.'

'No, my lady,' Liza said, lifting her dazed half-sleeping child into the coach behind her mistress. No, it certainly did not belong to a cat, that little blue foot they had both seen dangling from a corner of the bundle . . .

They shivered when they bestirred themselves, although the fire glowed red now.

'Ask Candida to come and see me before she goes out, Liza,' Lady Alison said.

Up in her own room, Candida was inspecting the dress of white French lawn with its buckled sash at the waist and the same intricate stitching down the skirt and each sleeve. She had always liked white. She had even chosen a white stone for her engagement ring to Finlay. But the moonstone surrounded by pearls had been a great disappointment. It was supposed to change colour with her moods, and so far it had never done so. Of course that was probably because Finlay got so little chance to be alone with her since, if she was not otherwise chaperoned, Kitty had to accompany her everywhere.

An engagement should be more exciting than this, Candida was sure, and if an exhilarating moment in it ever did occur, she would remember to glance at her ring. If *she* had been a man, if she had been in Finlay's shoes, she would have given Kitty the slip long ago. But, then, Finlay was too much of a gentleman to do anything of the sort. He had kissed her only once, and that was over before she had had time to notice.

She had despaired of the eligible young men in Edinburgh before she met Finlay. She had dismissed all her suitors, one by one. There was not a spark among the lot of them. Only Finlay had that little air of mystery about him to challenge her—but was a little air of mystery enough to base a marriage on? And what was his secret? Candida thought about it while she was dressing with Kitty's help, but resolved to say nothing to Mama when she went to show her the results of one of their shopping expeditions.

'How are you, Mama?' she asked anxiously, for if she loved Papa immoderately, that was nothing to what she felt for her mother. She searched her face minutely, relieved to find that some of the strain had gone out of it. 'Are you better?'

'Much better, dear. That blue is very nice with your white dress. Is Kitty ready to accompany you?'

'She is putting on her cloak. Did you know she has a follower, Mama?'

'Constable Frank Clarke? Yes, Liza asked me yesterday if he might be permitted below-stairs some time, so that she can look him over.'

'He looks serious to me.'

'Courting is a very serious matter, Candida. Now, do you have everything with you?'

'I suppose the most important thing is my ring,' she said, taking the blue doeskin glove off her left hand.

'I was never sure of that ring,' Lady Alison said doubtfully. 'Pearls are for tears, my Candida.'

'Oh, the pearls are only incidental, Mama. It is the moonstone that is the thing!'

'I am sure I hope it proves so,' her mother said sadly.

Her words niggled, and as Finlay Semple handed her

into his carriage, Candida glanced at Kitty, who withdrew into the furthermost corner. As if Kitty could ever become invisible! Candida smiled at her, and then began to think about their last scraps of conversation just as they were ready to go. They niggled at her even more.

'That shade of blue is exactly right, miss.'

'Yes.' A glance in the mirror confirmed it. 'We can always trust Mama's taste. It is accurate.'

'Well, we all know it has to be perfect,' Kitty smiled, 'to be seen out wi' Mr Finlay. He's the greatest catch in the whole o' Edinburgh!'

'Kitty!'

'All the lasses say so, Miss Candida. They all think him so very good-looking, never mind bein' rich.'

'Which lasses?'

'The ones in the High Street, anyway.'

'So we are back to Janet Brown again? How could all the girls in the High Street know Mr Finlay, Kitty? He belongs over here in the New Town.'

'It must be because of his Club, Miss Candida. After the Clubs come out, all the young men go into the taverns in the High Street. I suppose that's where they see him.'

Well, Candida thought, as Finlay seated himself beside her and the carriage moved forward, all the lasses in the High Street were certainly right. His fair hair nestled in waves and curls close to his head, his features were those of a Greek god, and his broad shoulders were exquisitely clothed in sage green velvet.

The drive out to Prestonfield House, their luncheon while they watched the peacocks strutting about the lawns from the window and then the drive back were all very pleasant—pleasant, but completely uneventful in any way.

She looked forward to Madame Tussaud's Travelling Exhibition, where they arrived at three o'clock, and for the first half-hour Candida was silent and awe-struck. All these famous people: John Knox, Robert Burns,

Napoleon, Mr Pitt, Mr Compton and his 'mule', Mary Queen of Scots . . . She looked around in bewilderment. How could she believe that they were not real, but only made of wax? Her breath was taken away to be standing in the presence of His Majesty King George IV, and in his kilt, too, just as he had dressed to please his loyal citizens on his last visit to Edinburgh, his famous birthday visit of five years ago. She did not allow herself to smile even if the King was as fat as she remembered, and his legs were encased in pink stockings which clashed so comically with the Royal Stewart tartan.

It was a little eerie in the crush of silent figures. Gradually Candida realised that all the other visitors had gone, and she and Finlay were the only two human beings left. His arm went round her and she looked up in time to admire his golden sideburns before he kissed her on the lips for only the second time since she had known him. As before, his kiss was slack and brief. Perhaps he was nervous. Perhaps he felt guilty. Candida did not feel guilty in the least.

'I am going to the Thistle Courts tomorrow for a few days,' she told him in a low voice. 'Aunt Rose has invited you as well, Finlay. Will you come?' She moved her eyes deliberately to a spot beyond his left ear so as not to appear too forward. 'We may have the chance there to be alone together much oftener.'

She had the satisfaction of seeing that he was tempted. His colour, already heightened, turned brick-red, and he licked his lips.

'It would be delightful,' he said.

Candida waited while he considered the matter. She could not imagine what there was to consider, and the longer she waited the more impatient she became.

'We may see each other in the evenings,' she murmured daringly, 'even when it is dark.'

She had never been in his company later than six o'clock on any day since she had accepted his ring in this strange engagement. Finlay Semple courted her in the mornings or the afternoons only.

'It would be delightful,' he repeated, and kissed her again.

This time she had the presence of mind to keep her eyes open and to glance at the ring on her hand, placed as it was against his neck.

'But, you see, Candida, on Friday evenings I must attend my Club. It is the Friday Club, you know.'

The moonstone remained as milky white as ever. She was not surprised.

'I could try to come out on Saturday, if that is convenient,' he added.

'Oh, it would be quite convenient.' Candida smiled quietly, and inside began to boil with indignation. How could the Friday Club, or any Club come to that, be more important to him than his future wife? There was a little acid in her voice when she suggested, 'Or Sunday, if you prefer?'

'Sunday might be better still,' he agreed, looking unconcernedly into her outraged eyes.

She was still fuming next morning when Kitty helped her into her new violet velvet pelisse with its lace ruff. In silence they placed upon her head the bonnet to match, trimmed with white feathers between the double brim. The violet kid boots went on next, and after that the Limerick gloves. Last of all, Kitty handed her the large ermine muff and she set off unhappily with her mother to meet her Irish cousins.

'I am so glad you have chosen those quiet colours today,' Lady Alison said, herself attired in restrained dark blues. 'We must remember they are from a remote place, and hardly likely to be able to keep up with the fashions.'

They were approaching the Tron Kirk, where the Glasgow coach always came to its final stage. They were early, of course. Mama was always well before time. The Glasgow Fly was well in time, too. They had scarcely descended from the carriage before it roared round the corner from the South Bridge and came to a lathering halt, and after a small delay its passengers straggled down the steps and stood about in groups waiting for their boxes and baggage to be unstrapped.

Candida's eyes were drawn to the roof of the stage-coach, to what seemed to her an uncommonly heavy load of luggage. Piece by piece it was handed down until she saw it had all been built around the largest box of all. To her horror, she saw it was a coffin. There could be no doubt about it. Even from here it obviously measured six feet by two.

'Dear me!' Lady Alison said. 'I never saw such a thing—a coffin on the roof of a stage-coach?'

By the time it was man-handled down, all the other passengers had gone and four people were left standing by the coach, three men and a girl.

'That young lady must be Alanna,' Lady Alison said. 'Go and see, dear.'

The nearer Candida got to the little group the more clearly she saw that Alanna was not only in the fashion, but strikingly in its forefront. Tall, sandy-haired and plump, her ample curves were most becomingly clothed in black and white satin stripes, and on her head was poised positively the most interesting bonnet ever seen in Edinburgh. It was made of white satin, trimmed with long black plumes and yards and yards of black and white striped ribbons.

But even this could not stop her attention moving to the three men behind Alanna, especially to the tall one in the middle who seemed to be giving orders to the other two. He had his back to her, and this gave her time to admire the work of his tailor in fitting his pale blue frock-coat so perfectly over his broad shoulders and then bringing it to a narrow waist before it flared out again over moleskin trousers of the same shade. He turned his head slightly, and Candida considered that it was fortunate for him that curly hair such as his should be so fashionable for men, but in the same instant she doubted that it should be unruly enough to make him wear his top hat on the back of his head at such a rakish angle, or continue in such extravagant jet-black sideburns.

A wicked little thought flitted through her mind. If this was the man they had come to meet, he could give Finlay Semple—who considered himself the dandy of Edinburgh—a run for his money. This afforded her immense satisfaction. On the other hand, if he was her cousin, what business could he possibly have with those two terrible men he was speaking to so rapidly as she drew near?

'Mr Knox, the Surgeon, prefers his subjects fresh,' he was saying. 'Therefore,' addressing the less sinister of the two, 'I require this to be delivered immediately to No. 10 Surgeons' Square. Here is a guinea for your services, and you will be paid another when you get there. A card will be sent to me within the hour as my receipt.' He spoke with authority, and with the very faintest Irish burr.

'Indade, yer honour, it is right now this very minute we'll be taking it,' the man said, gesturing to his companion to shoulder the coffin. 'Is that not so, William?'

The other man grunted as he settled the long box on his shoulder, and turned his face their way. It was brutal. The deep black eyes, set wide apart, did not match. One was higher than the other, above cheeks that were sunken and scarred. But it was the black eyebrows and the pointed chin that made him look like the Devil. Never in Candida's whole life had she seen such a face of black evil before.

William, the smaller man had called him. William who? Whoever he was, nobody should treat him lightly . . . She stared after the little procession, rooted to the spot.

'Miss Candida Rowena Forbes,' the man in blue said as if there could be no doubt about it.

His statement ended her speculations abruptly, and reminded her not only of the task she was supposed to be carrying out but also of her manners. 'Yes.' She smiled, and gave him her hand.

'Then what our Irish students have come home and told us is true, after all. Your fame has gone before you,

you see,' he said cheerfully. 'They said you are one of the two most beautiful women in all Edinburgh—as alike, according to them, as two peas in a pod!'

He was certainly from out of the Emerald Isle, Candida decided. Only an Irishman could pay such a back-handed compliment. It had the effect of making her deeply resent this other woman, whoever she was. She was shocked by the message of his words. She was shocked by her next reaction, which was that she would rather be the *only* beautiful woman in Edinburgh so far as he was concerned, no matter how angry the thought was making her.

In fact, Candida was shocked by the entire events of the morning so far, and further stunned to find she could not tear her gaze away from the brilliantly green eyes in the hardbitten face of the purveyor of human flesh . . . Her distant cousin, Ross Alexander Laing.

CHAPTER TWO

'THIS IS the old part of the town,' Lady Alison explained as they settled themselves into her carriage at the Tron Kirk. 'Edinburgh is in two parts. When we turn this corner we shall cross the North Bridge into what we call the New Town.'

'Oh, dear Aunt Alison, we have been told so much about the Athens of the North with its houses built like Greek temples!' Alanna exclaimed, her eyes sparkling with excitement.

The stark black and white lines of her dress pointed straight to her eyes, as green as her brother's, but a soft and dancing green. Not only was Alanna very fashionably dressed, she was also very cleverly dressed, Candida observed, glad to have someone else to focus her attention on rather than the man opposite, of whom she was uncomfortably very much aware. Deliberately she directed her eyes to Alanna, to her even white teeth, to her pink and white complexion as flawless as fine porcelain, and to her smile which was infectious if not downright wicked. Candida warmed to her from the start.

'It is quite mild even on this windy bridge today,' Lady Alison said calmly. 'Now we are turning left into Princes Street. I'm so glad the weather is fine for you, my dears.'

Candida expelled a breath of pure relief. Then her mother was unaware of that terrible transaction at the Tron. She must never know! But at the first opportunity her father must be told, and she dreaded to think how he would react, when his whole energies were directed towards stopping the diabolical activities of the grave-robbers, to discover something—or someone—as sinister under his own roof. Ross Alexander Laing was bound to create havoc one way or another, she could feel it in her bones.

'We have been looking forward to this, have we not, Ross?' his sister laughed.

Candida allowed her eyes to flicker over him briefly before she turned her head to look out of the window at her side. It was safer, somehow, to look out of the window. He had such thick black eyebrows. Much though she took an immediate and passionate dislike to thick black eyebrows, especially when they were drawn together in a frown like that, she was aware of a delicious quiver of excitement running through her. Everything about him was strong and black and powerful, quite different from the open-faced youthfulness of her male acquaintances so far. In other words, he was a man. In the space of two seconds, Candida discovered to her horror that she was comparing Finlay Semple quite unfavourably with him.

'For once it has been better to arrive than to journey hopefully.' She heard his voice saying one thing and no doubt meaning totally another, again.

She scarcely noticed that they were now bowling along the wide straight mile of Princes Street. She did not consider herself a vain person, but whatever vanity she had ever possessed was quite deflated now, thanks to this man. First for Kitty to tell her that there was a common girl in the High Street so very like her, and now for this Ross Alexander Laing to have attacked her with such a two-edged sword: 'You are one of the two most beautiful women in all Edinburgh!' What did that mean? Who was this other woman? Her eyes swept blue and unseeing over the others, and clung to the one person she had always been able to trust.

'Well,' Lady Alison was saying, 'you two will be the first of our guests to try out the most recent of our innovations at No. 13 Charlotte Square. Candida and I have been enjoying ourselves all summer. We have had the workmen in to make over the whole top of the house for the convenience of visitors.'

'Yes,' Candida murmured politely. 'You have arrived just in time.'

'But, perhaps, not soon enough?' Ross eyed the ring on her left hand.

Alanna took up his cue. 'You are engaged to be married? What stone is that in your ring?' And then, without waiting for an answer, 'Oh, what is that magnificent building at the foot of the hill? It looks brand new!'

The Alexander Laings were far too outspoken, both of them, Candida decided. She thrust her hand back into the ermine muff, feeling that she and her ring had been dismissed.

'It *is* new,' Lady Alison replied. 'It is the Royal Scottish Academy, and the hill is called the Mound. You must remind me one day to tell you its story.'

'There is a strange contraption trying to climb up the Mound,' Ross said, leaning forward to watch it.

'That's the "Noddy", a cab balanced on two wheels, as you can see.' They watched the passengers inside the cab tilted backwards at an alarming angle. 'Now you will understand why I have never disposed of our sedan-chair, although it is very out of date, I'm afraid,' Lady Alison sighed.

'But if they were going down instead of up, the passengers would all land on the horses' backs,' Ross said, and began to laugh.

His laugh was as infectious as his sister's smile. It transformed his face, its expression up to then so grave and serious, in a flash of pure magic. It was as though the sun came out after days and weeks of black clouds, a cheeky urchin ray of sunshine to light up her heart, all Princes Street and the whole city of Edinburgh. There had never been an experience quite like it in all Candida's life—never in her childhood, in any of her flirtations, even in her engagement—and it alarmed her more than words could say.

'Ah, now I see the resemblance, Ross,' Lady Alison remarked. 'You are so like your dear mother, and *she* could always charm the birds off the trees! We are turning up into George Street now. Charlotte Square is at the far end.'

Well, here was one bird Ross Alexander Laing would never charm off her perch, Candida vowed. At the same time she found herself wanting No. 13 Charlotte Square to make a particularly good impression today. She had always taken it for granted, but now she was seeing it with new eyes. In fact, she was seeing everything with new eyes. She could swear that the whole world had turned upside-down in the light of that devastating smile. It was a relief when Alanna confirmed that it had returned to its usual place.

'Oh!' she exclaimed. 'The entire side of the Square looks like one long elegant house!'

'You are looking at the north side of it,' Lady Alison said, 'designed by Robert Adam. No. 13 is in the middle.'

'And we may occupy the whole top floor?' Alanna asked in amazement.

The carriage came to a halt. Ross descended from it first and extended his hand to help the three ladies out.

'Yes, dear,' Lady Alison said as she alighted. 'You can be self contained; quite independent, if you wish.'

'It is a good idea.' Ross helped his sister down next. 'Alanna, you may engage our own staff as soon as you like.'

'Your own staff?' Lady Alison gasped. 'But we have a whole army of servants here!'

'Dear Aunt Alison, Ross means it will all be most suitable until we find a place of our own!' Alanna beamed. 'It may be too confined for him here, you see. So I may as well look for our own servants to take with us when the times comes.'

'Too confined?' Candida stood up in the carriage and looked around the most spacious square in northern Europe. 'Here?'

'My sister is too direct,' Ross said. 'We have always

lived in the countryside. We shall be looking to the outskirts of the city eventually for a house.'

The blue doeskin gloves lay discarded inside the muff on so mild a day, and so it was her bare hand that he took in his to help her down. She was to regret for many months to come that she had ever removed her gloves that morning, for the touch of his hand on hers sent the same thrills through her that his hard green eyes were doing now. It even felt indecent, but in that white-hot moment Candida would have given all her world only to allow it to stay . . . Of course it was indecent! For a lady engaged to be married to someone else even to think about it—to stay and touch all that was reprehensible, evil and despicable in Edinburgh? She came to herself with a start and snatched her hand away.

They followed Lady Alison and Alanna up the stone steps and into the large square entrance hall of No. 13, where the old sedan-chair still occupied a corner, their footsteps sounding staccato on the mosaic of brown and yellow floor-tiles.

'Oh! I have always wanted to see a real sedan-chair!' Alanna squealed, and ran across to it, while Lady Alison opened the little door to show her the seats inside and the tiny curtains looped back now, and out of use.

'You were like a doll,' Ross said under his breath, 'a pretty china doll, until we made you angry. You are prettier still, now that you have come to life.'

'And you have kissed the Blarney Stone, sir,' Candida whispered coldly. 'You are Irish, after all. Just like the two terrible men you entrusted with that coffin.'

'Jesus Christ was born in a stable,' he retorted, his penetrating green eyes stripping away everything but the truth. 'That did not make him a horse.'

'Oh dear,' Lady Alison broke into the conversation, 'I should not have referred to Ross and Alanna as "your Irish cousins", Candida. Of course they are Scottish, born of Scottish parents. You will excuse her, Ross?'

Candida muttered an excuse, and fled up the broad

stone staircase that rose so gracefully with its decorated iron balustrade from the hall. She left her cousins speaking to Mama, who remained as calm and pleasant as ever, and reached her own room, flinging the ermine muff to the wall. She hated Cornelia's children as much as Papa hated Cornelia, especially Ross Alexander Laing!

She was further agitated to discover by the clock that after all that had happened it was still only eleven in the morning, and the moonstone for the first time in its career had changed colour. It had assumed a definitely angry purple glow.

Further west, in Moray Place, in another gracious terraced house, Finlay Semple was only getting up at eleven o'clock, feeling very much under the weather. He struggled into his chintz dressing-gown and Turkish slippers with a groan and with the help of his valet, James.

What, he asked himself with another moan, was I doing yesterday to feel so weak today? There had only been the luncheon with Candida at Prestonfield, those few stolen kisses afterwards at Madame Tussaud's—which had fizzled out so disappointingly—and later in the evening a meeting with some of the young fellows of the Hell-fire Club quite by chance in Swanston's. That must have been it . . . He tried to tear away the veils of drink, and remember.

'Yesterday was only Thursday, was it not, James?'

'Indeed, sir. Today is Friday.' James looked down his nose at him as usual.

For a second, Finlay brightened. Then tonight again he would be in the High Street, after his own Club, the Friday Club, came out. He would be in the taverns, Swanston's in particular, and he would see Mary Paterson again, that delectable creature. But in the treacherous see-saw of the morning after the night before his mood plummeted once more. He was engaged to be married to Miss Candida Forbes, and Candida's kisses could not compare with Mary Paterson's. Why did the world have to be so very unfair?

'I am going down to the stables, James,' he said, eyeing himself in the cheval mirror in his long underpants topped with a clean white ruffled shirt. Even so, he still looked unattractively jaded. 'What shall I wear?'

'Your colour is raised a little this morning,' James said, looking at the bright red veins on his master's cheeks, 'so perhaps the dark green again?' He helped Finlay into his pantaloons of glazed white ticking tight to the knees, white waistcoat and the green coat with its broad velvet collar. 'Your breakfast, sir?'

Finlay looked, and felt, worse than ever. 'No breakfast,' he said, and departed, feeling rather than seeing his servant's disapproving eye.

He reached the stables thankfully. Here, at least, he could be truly happy, no matter how bad he felt. The horses took him as they found him, and they looked at him with the same brown and shining eyes, the same aware eyes, as ever, and offered no criticism. He loved the horses more than anything in the world, more than anyone, more even than Mary Paterson.

There, it was out! Oh God, if only he could steady up, if only he could think straight! He staggered down the length of the stables until he reached the stall of his own horse, and scrabbled in the straw for the bottle he had left hidden there.

'Oh, Bruno,' he said, and took a swig with one hand on the horse's neck to steady himself, while the great brown eyes swivelled round at him. 'Thank God for a hair of the dog!'

He would never, could never, make a husband for Candida Forbes, he told himself in what felt like the cold grey light of dawn while the stables and the world gradually came to a standstill around him. She had been all his father's idea, not his, and besides, she had not the slightest interest in horses except to draw them, whereas horses were his only passion—except for Mary Paterson, of course.

He thought of Mary Paterson, and took another bracing gulp. Blondes, or better still red-heads, they were the only women for him. Candida in her very refined way or Mary Paterson in her completely opposite way personified the blondes, good and bad. Separate them in his mind, he could not, and the result was that when he was with either one he felt very confused. Once he had caught a glimpse of another loose woman in the High Street, and his imagination had been fired for ever more. He had another drink to refresh his memory. She had had very fair hair too, but tinged with a wicked red. She, above all, might have been his finest hour if only he had ever seen her again, but she had proved a will-o'-the-wisp.

'Finlay Semple, I just thocht I would fin' you here!' The strict tones of his parent bellowed down the stables, and he hastily thrust the bottle back into the straw. 'An' what time did ye get back last night?'

'Latish,' Finlay admitted.

'The worse o' drink again, nae doot! Ye'll no' be fit to come to the business, then? Another day lost!'

Finlay hated 'the business', no matter if it *was* the grandest emporium of fashion not only in Edinburgh but in all Scotland, no matter if it *did* look like a brand-new mansion house on the South Bridge. Worse still, he hated the way his father called it 'the beesiness'. It was so old-fashioned, and so Scottish.

'I'd rather work with the horses, Father,' he muttered drearily.

'The horses? The horses?' Francis Semple shouted, while his offspring winced. 'Wha's goin' to run the beesiness after I'm gone, can you tell me? Of course, at the rate you're goin', laddie, ye'll be dead an' buried afore me!'

Finlay could well believe it, judging by the way he felt. He looked dolefully at his father, a thin wiry man of fifty, spry on his feet, and became convinced of it.

'You're right, Father. Die I surely will, out of sheer boredom in the business.' He sighed deeply, for he was very fond of his father. 'It's only for your sake that I even try. I'll start again on Monday,' he said, and meant it sincerely.

'Weel, Friday's no day to make a fresh start,' Francis Semple softened slightly. 'I suppose it's the Friday Club tonight as usual?'

'Ay, Father. Are you coming?'

'I canna manage it. But the Friday Club will never harm you. Not wi' Lord Henry Cockburn in the chair. Ye found Miss Candida well yesterday? Now there's a young woman I thocht would be interested in the beesiness, wi' her taste for fashion.'

Finlay shot his father a hard look. 'Then you were barking up the wrong tree. But yes, she was well enough.'

'Ye dinna sound verra enthusiastic, laddie.'

'Six months is a long time to wait,' Finlay said shortly.

Francis Semple examined his son shrewdly. 'Aye,' he sighed, 'a young man must sow his wild oats in the meantime, I suppose. I was young once mysel', ye ken. Once ye're married, that'll be the end o' that. Just see ye dinna get into ony scrapes in the interval, my lad.'

Finlay walked with his father out to the mews behind Moray Place, where the stable lads were settling the horses into the shafts of the new carriage which so far he had never seen. Francis Semple had kept it a secret.

'What do ye think o' it? he asked his son now, as proud as a peacock.

Finlay inspected the shining chocolate brown carriage from one end of the other, its white window-blinds with their tassels like little snowballs, and the gilt edgings and gilded crests upon the doors. Their coachman sat ready to go in his dark brown livery to match, with gilt buttons and white gloves.

'The new delivery vans are all in the same colours, with "Semple and Son" on the sides in gold letters, laddie. Think aboot it.'

'I will, Father,' Finlay promised, as the coach rolled away.

But think about it he did not for the rest of that morning while he worked off with the grooms the effects of his drinking-bout, getting the horses ready to leave in pairs. He managed to while away the rest of the day in his usual idleness until at last he could go to the Friday Club.

Lord Henry Cockburn rounded off the meeting with a speech lamenting the ruin of everyone's friend, Sir Walter Scott. It had been a cruel casualty of commerce. All the members shook their heads in sorrowful agreement while they sipped their champagne.

Then on to Swanston's, feeling on top of the world again, to eat a few oysters served on their own deep shells, and to drink some ale while he waited for Mary Paterson. At long last she arrived, a sensation in scarlet, with a pretty dark girl of about her own age whom she called Janet.

To Finlay Semple, Mary was the most tantalising creature in the whole world, with the exception of his will-o'-the-wisp. He loved the wild golden mane of curls cascading down to her waist, no matter how crudely dressed her tiny waist, no matter if it was always shown off in garish scarlet. All the better . . . She was the cynosure of every male eye in the place.

He waited, and drank with his friends until she had downed a few gins, and then she began to sing one of the bawdy songs of the day in her high, trilling soprano.

The strawberry stuck
To a raspberry tart,
For they were in love
Heart to heart . . .

'Oh God,' Finlay said, 'she's the raspberry tart to end all raspberry tarts in that red dress!'

He could not believe his good fortune when the sparkle in her eye was undeniably and continually directed at him again that evening. At him, above all others! He could hardly wait until he got her out into the dark close to kiss her again, violently and deeply as though parched with thirst. He was unable to stop. He knew he was drunk, although not as drunk as usual. He was on fire.

'Don't torment me again tonight with just a few kisses, Mary,' he begged.

Mary Paterson pulled herself away from him. 'I dinna do it for nothing, ye ken,' she said, her little face sharp and her voice sharper still in the gloom.

For answer, he pulled out all the money he had with him. He remembered that there were at least two guineas among it.

'Ah, well,' she said, 'it's no' far to where I live. Come!' And she pulled him willingly away.

It was Saturday evening before he crawled back to the house in Moray Place, half-sober, totally unrepenting, and in his own estimation, at least, completely his own man, a real man, at last. He found his father conveniently absent.

'You may get me ready a bath, James,' he told his astonished manservant, 'and fill it with Cordova perfume. I need a complete overhaul.'

James had never seen his young master so imperious, so sure of himself. He snapped to attention.

'And then pack my bags. I shall go out early in the morning to the Thistle Courts,' Finlay added. 'Well, get on with it, man! A bath first and then a night's sleep, and I can take on the world!'

'Yes, sir,' James said. An hour later, in the clouds of steam, he asked, 'What shall I pack?'

'You have been with me long enough to know! I shall stay there tomorrow night, and on Monday morning I shall require the correct dress for business,' Finlay growled, a cigar between his lips as he lay back in the cooling water and contemplated the beauty and the power of all womankind; God bless them all, especially Mary Paterson, his saviour!

'Yes, *sir*,' James said, and scuttled off.

On Sunday morning, groomed and scented, dressed to perfection, Finlay presented himself at the Thistle

Courts. Lady Rosalie Kyle was the only one who happened to be indoors to receive him at the time.

'Finlay, how nice of you to come,' she said. 'We were hoping you would manage it, although we know how preoccupied you must be with business. We have all been to the Kirk, and the others went out in the gardens on such a fine day.'

As she spoke, a shadow fell across the floor.

'I've come in for a wrap,' said a young woman.

'Oh, it's Alanna,' Lady Rosalie said. 'Miss Alanna Alexander Laing, Candida's cousin, lately come from Ireland. Allow me to present Mr Finlay Semple to you, dear.'

Finlay bowed over her hand, thunderstruck. Here was the woman of all his tortured dreams and imaginings come to life! Here was the woman with the wicked red in the gold of her hair, his will-o'-the-wisp woman he thought he would never see, least of all in the statuesque and expensively dressed form before his very eyes! She smiled her brilliant smile and he went completely weak at the knees. His first distracted thought was one of bitter regret for the events of Friday night.

'Alanna?' he said in a dazed fashion, voicing the second thought to come into his head. 'That is a beautiful name, one I have never heard before.'

'Oh, that is because it is Irish,' she laughed into his eyes. 'It means "the darling one"!'

He stood smiling at her foolishly for some minutes. 'The darling one . . .' The smile was still on his face when he turned round to include their hostess in this conversation. Finlay Semple was astonished and not a little put out to discover a frown on the face of Lady Rosalie Kyle. Why must everything in the world be so dashed complicated? Why could it not be as straightforward as he was himself?

Left to her own devices when Alanna left the garden, Candida walked over to the kitchen door at the back of the house, wondering what so many birds were making all the commotion about. It was the handful of crusts flung out, and right in the middle of them was the little bird she was hoping to see again. There was no stick bound to his leg now. He stood straight on both of them, looking healed and strong again, and utterly disconsolate.

She scooped him and the crusts into her skirt and carried him fluttering out to the spot in the meadow where she sketched from one season to another in her diary, a secret book she showed to nobody and kept specially for whenever she was out at the Thistle Courts. She headed for the large sycamore. Round about it the hedges of hawthorn and thick impenetrable beech were her especial interest. She knew intimately all the little creatures who lived in them. They were all there in her diary, in pictures and in words. She took out her miniature box of paints to capture her swallow now for the last time. He sat there on the grass drooping and shivering, emitting occasional tiny cheeps of complaint.

'Oh dear, you are not a happy little bird,' she said, as she sketched quickly and then moistened her paint-brush.

'No, he is not,' agreed a masculine voice behind her.

Candida snapped shut her book. 'Oh, it is you,' she said ungraciously, when Ross came to sit beside her. 'You know what is wrong with him, of course, since you are a doctor?' She edged away.

'Ah . . . So you don't like doctors, Candida?'

'That depends on the doctor,' she countered, 'and more especially on his field of interest.' There was a short silence while she wished she had not brought up the subject of the coffin so soon. 'And,' she added hastily, 'you have not answered my question.'

She turned to look at her Irish cousin. His eyes were the same hard green as when she had first seen him and his manner was cool and dispassionate. Then it was quite safe to continue the discussion.

'My field of interest? At present my interest is entirely directed to this field,' he said, 'and to the two birds I see in it, the one drooping and unhappy and the other determined to capture his misery on paper. Should we not be trying to find out what is the matter with him instead?'

'I know what is wrong with him already, even although I am not a doctor. Why women should not be allowed into the University I have never understood! Our brains are the same size as yours, you know. Anyway, I shall know what to do with the little bird when the time is right. It is all to do with instinct.'

'Indeed it is,' Ross said, and to her horror she saw the ghost of a smile in his eyes.

'I meant the bird's instinct,' she said, before she realised that was enough to let him know she followed his meaning, and to her annoyance she could feel her blush beginning.

'All animals have instincts, Candida. Human beings are animals too, you know.'

She was sure she should not pursue this line of conversation with the sort of man Ross Alexander Laing was, if all her suspicions were correct. 'If this little swallow does not fly with the flock, he will eventually try to fly alone, and then he will surely die,' she said instead.

'Then what are you waiting for?' Ross asked, lazily chewing a blade of grass and watching her out of his green eyes.

'That's what I am waiting for,' she said, when the agitated twittering of many birds came from beyond the hawthorn hedge. 'It means they will soon be going.'

She stood up and began to scatter crumbs before the swallow. He pecked at them uninterestedly, shivering when the flock flapped and twittered again. Inch by inch, foot by foot she urged him on to the hedge with the crumbs, and peering through a gap saw that the field beyond was black with birds. With a hop, the swallow reached the gap himself and stood looking fearfully out. Gently and silently she threw the last of the crumbs a few feet in front of him and he entered the field at last, running and fluttering to join his family, who were rising up a few feet and sinking again, more noisily now.

'That was well done,' Ross said, smiling at her. 'It is not everybody who would have known what to do.'

As she picked up her diary and her paintbox, Candida was conscious of a glow of pride, and not only that, but a strange battle going on inside her. Why was it that when she had met a man who for the first time in her life she could have admired, he had to be a possible criminal? He was so very handsome in a frightening sort of way when he was serious, and outrageously attractive when he smiled like that.

He stood up to join her and they turned to go back to the house. They had only taken a few steps when a black whirring, shrilling cloud of birds rose from the field behind them, darkening the sky and deafening their ears. In the very instant that she stumbled and fell Candida wondered if black wings, or the vision of black wings overhead, was the bad omen it was always supposed to be. She was given no time to think about it. The next minute she was upright again, held fast in her cousin's arms with his face close enough for her to see the faint blue of his beard beginning to appear when it was still only midday.

She felt like a rabbit hypnotised by a snake. So he must have to shave twice a day! She stared into his face while such an immodest thought—which she had certainly never cast in Finlay's direction—turned her knees to water.

'You are all right?' Ross asked, with those eyes which she was sure could see into the minds of other people examining her critically. 'You have not hurt yourself?'

'No,' Candida said. 'I am perfectly all right.'

But she wasn't. She knew she would never be the same again.

'Of course I believe some women are intelligent,' he said, as they walked along again. 'But, as you see, they are the weaker sex, Candida. Still, if you stick to your instincts and the prejudices of all women, and I stick to facts and figures as all men must do, we shall understand each other and get on famously, given time.'

For two complete minutes her breath was taken away by what she had often noticed was this typically male superior attitude. Apparently, in Ireland, men had no diplomacy either, with which to disguise it.

'Oh, I always trust my instincts,' she said with a sweetness anyone who knew her would have found very dangerous. Indeed, she thought, what had been her first instincts about Ross Alexander Laing? 'They are never wrong.'

'Never?'

'Never,' she repeated coldly.

'One day I shall hold you to that,' Ross said in a tone that almost frightened her. But that, too, was ridiculous here in Edinburgh, here among her family and friends. 'I swear that, too.'

He looked at her so oddly, almost sadly, that she felt her heart fluttering like the swallow's wings. Her uncle would be in the stables, perhaps. She hastened towards them.

'Are you interested in horses?' she asked, to cover her confusion.

'More interested than most,' Ross replied, 'and for very different reasons from most people.'

'Why?' she asked boldly, now that Uncle Cameron was within earshot.

'They are very worth while,' he said enigmatically.

'Well, they are certainly worth more money than some human beings,' Sir Cameron laughed.

Money. So that was it. He would do anything, sell anything, for money. She had no doubts left now. It was a body in the coffin he had been selling to Dr Knox in Surgeons' Square. And he had the audacity to be speaking in quite a normal ordinary way to her uncle now, as one rich man to another.

'She is in foal, I see,' he said, with his hand on Lady's neck. 'It will be born in seven or eight weeks?'

'In the middle of November,' Sir Cameron confirmed,

'if all goes well. Lady o' Thistles belongs to Candida, but we look after her here. I am afraid we have been unlucky with her so far. She has lost two foals already.' He shook his head sadly.

'This one will be different,' Candida said. 'Third time lucky.'

'You heard that, did you, sir?' Ross asked, while the two men gazed at her gravely. 'It is what I have been telling her! Women are full of superstitions and fancies.'

'Of course they are,' Sir Cameron agreed. 'My wife is the expert at it. But the strange thing about it, my boy, is that they are almost invariably right!'

By five o'clock it was already becoming dusk, and the sky was a quiet melancholy purple when Candida leaned out of her bedroom window. She loved the Thistle Courts, and she could never decide in which season she loved it best; for spring, summer, autumn or winter it had always seemed a fairytale house to her, dreaming among its lawns and parks. Now a few stars had begun to sparkle, and with a sigh she turned back into her room to dress for what Aunt Rose called 'supper'.

Kitty lit all the candles, for out in the country there was none of the gas lighting newly installed in Charlotte Square.

'What shall it be tonight, miss?'

'The turquoise, Kitty. While you are attending to the hot water, I shall look out the ribbons and feathers for my hair.'

'It must be important, then, if you are going to wear your new dress, Miss Candida.'

'I suppose it is, Kitty. At least, it will be the first time I have been in Mr Finlay's company in the evening.'

'Hm,' said Kitty. 'Mr Finlay is very good looking, right enough. I even thought so myself until I saw Mr Ross, that is.' Her eyes in the mirror became quite dreamy as she washed Candida's back. 'So tall, so dark, so mysterious, Miss Candida! If only he would smile! Have you ever seen him smile, miss?'

'Oh yes,' Candida admitted grimly, her heart lurching.

By the time Kitty had laced in her waist, settled the broderie anglaise of the deep neck trimming and secured the turquoise ribbons and feathers in her hair, Candida had subdued herself, and at six o'clock she went downstairs to join the others in the dining-room. The table was set on gleaming white linen, the glasses were all of different colours and the epergne in the middle rose high, laden with autumn fruit from which trailed sprays of rowan-berries. She did not like the red berries on the white cloth and, furthermore, she did not like the cosy way Finlay and Alanna had their heads together over a book. They only glanced up and smiled when she came in.

'Alanna is so busy with Mr Semple that I think you must allow me to escort you to the table,' Ross said crisply. 'She is showing him pictures of our horses at home.' That explained it! Finlay's whole interest seemed to lie in horses, to the exclusion of everything else. He could really be quite tedious at times. 'But we shall sit opposite them, at least,' he said, steering her firmly to her chair.

He was once again clean shaven, and as crisp as his words in his evening dress of mauve tail-coat and white embroidered waistcoat with long white trousers; his frilled shirt was topped by a high cravat, the ends of which were tied in a bow, flat and impeccable. Candida glanced at him from beneath lowered lashes, at once thankful she had dressed accordingly, while at the same time deploring the circumstances that were throwing her so much in his company.

It was ironic, she thought, that the long-awaited occasion with her husband-to-be was quite divided by the tall epergne. She could scarcely see Finlay, much less hear what he was saying to Alanna. And this 'promiscuous seating', when the gentleman must serve the lady at his side, made it all a hundred times worse. Once the servants had laid down the hot plates she was forced to accept the soup Ross was ladling out from the tureen nearest to him.

'One will be enough,' she said, waving him away.

'I do not dispute it,' he said coolly, 'laced in as you are. You could not possibly contain any more. It is a very unhealthy fashion.'

To her annoyance, Candida privately agreed with him. Many a time she would have eaten more to satisfy her healthy appetite, but it was too uncomfortable to do so. 'We all eat more than we need to survive,' she said. 'The poor people exist on very much less.'

'And you are concerned for the poor people, Candida?'

'Of course. For them, and for the animals of this world. They do not have a voice.'

'Well, whether you eat sparingly or not, the result is very beautiful, I assure you.'

She looked at him sharply, but his expression was perfectly sincere. She believed he really meant it. She toyed with an idea while the servants cleared away the soup-dishes and laid down the oval steak-plates of bone china with its translucent body and sparkling glaze of white decorated with flowers and sprigs of darkest blue. She plunged her knife into the steak he served her. It cut as easily as butter, and as she speared a morsel on her fork, she decided on her line of attack.

'Beautiful?' she said mockingly. 'What use is it to be beautiful if you are only one of many here in Edinburgh? There is nothing remarkable in that.'

'I did not say you were one of many, Candida. I said you were as alike as two peas, you and the other beauty of this city,' he said quietly.

The whole table seemed to move sideways in a grotesque lurch. The candles in the sparkling chandelier above them seemed to flutter in a ghostly breeze, and the rowan-berries glistened as red as drops of blood. In that chilling moment when the goose-pimples crept up her arms and rose even under her hair, Candida first became frightened of this other woman, so like herself. Then she had heard Ross correctly the first time.

'You have not been here five minutes,' she said, 'so how could you know such a thing? It is not true!'

'It *is* true, Candida,' he assured her, his face hard and serious. 'Alanna and I are not the first two students to arrive in Edinburgh from Ireland. Others have come and gone, and one of my closest friends is here still, studying divinity. It is as I said. Your fame has gone before you.'

'Who is this other woman?' There, it was out, the question that had nagged at her for thirty-six hours.

'I don't know.' He smiled tightly. 'But after all this mystery, when mystery is not allowed in my scheme of things, I intend to find out.'

But not before I do, Candida vowed.

There was no mystery exercising Mary Paterson's mind, none at all. Counting out her money carefully to the last farthing, she knew exactly how many beans made five. With that fool Semple's three guineas she had more than enough now to go down to the Jew's shop and get that fur tippet she had had her eye on for weeks, now that the cold nights would be coming in. The cold nights were uncomfortable, but not if you had enough gin in you, and who was she to complain about the long dark evenings? Och, that's when she had the most fun, and always had been.

It all reminded her of Gilmerton and Joe and Molly Paterson. Dearest, kindest Joe! That is, until he caught her with young Joseph in the barn, and after that he began to look at her sideways. Mary smiled at the memory. She had been only fourteen at the time, but well aware of men. She liked them, young and old.

Molly had looked after her, helped her through her 'difficult times', and had always seen to it that she had a decent gown of some sort to wear, which wasn't easy because they were so poor. The plain fact was that everybody in the Paterson household loved her, the men because she was so pretty, and Molly because she had been left a baby on her doorstep.

She had thought she could always deceive Molly, who had sung her to sleep as a child with that old, old song—how did it go?

> Oats and beans and barley grow,
> Oats and beans and barley grow,
> But not you nor I nor anyone know
> How oats and beans and barley grow.

And then she would stroke her forehead, stroke back the long golden curls and call her 'her little angel Mary, sure as God'.

It all went on until she was fifteen, and then young David and the other Paterson boys were always tormenting her. They would not leave her alone, but they weren't really her brothers, so it wasn't so bad. But from the beginning she had always liked Joe himself best. In fact, she loved him, and in little ways she was winning him over when Molly suddenly took a hand. She turned as cold as ice, and the next Mary knew she was on the road to Edinburgh, thrown out in what she stood up in, and that was all. She would never forget that long walk through the night, when she wondered briefly who her real father had been, and then dismissed him. Her real mother was scarcely more interesting, except that at least she had had some sense. In Mary's opinion she was quite right to get rid of an unwanted child. It was what she would do herself if ever she were that unlucky.

But so far, at least, she was not. She reached Edinburgh, and before it was properly light felt herself pulled towards the High Street, she didn't know how. It had not taken her long to see that she had landed up in the right place. The smells did not worry her, although they were worse than those the little farm had ever produced. She forgot them in the wonder and excitement of the tall, crowded tenements, twelve stories high on both sides of a street which was soon teeming with people—people who shouted, and ran, and pushed her about. She knew none of them, but she loved them all, and she loved this wonderful town. She was in the right place for her.

She pressed her nose up against a bake-shop window. Ah, if only she could eat those delicious smells! She would die soon if she didn't get something to eat. She had eaten nothing since the three o'clocks the day before. There was a thin, middle-aged woman presiding over the breads and buns inside. Mary eyed them avidly while the woman eyed her. Eventually she came out.

'Well, what do *you* want?' she asked. 'Dinna press yer nose against my window unless you want the goods.'

'I do,' Mary said, 'even a crust, but I ha'e no money.'

'You could work for a living,' the woman said, looking her up and down closely.

'I would, and willingly,' Mary said, 'if someone employed me.'

'I'll give you a try. You can sit here in the window. Watch over the bread and put all the money in the till. The prices are on the tickets, and I've got it a' coonted, so you needn't try to cheat me, my lady.'

Not until ten o'clock that night did the shop shut, and Mary, plagued all day by the appetising smells, was left with a two-day-old scone to chew, with the rats for company on the bake-house floor, and it was three months later that she realised the woman's profits had multiplied by ten, and all because of her form and figure in the window. It was about then that she met Janet Brown, one day when she was out in the High Street for an errand.

'I've seen you in that shop window,' Janet said. 'I look at you every day. You're so pretty.'

Mary was used to gentlemen telling her that, especially the students from the University, but women only looked at her in a nasty way. She decided to make a friend of Janet. It would be fine to have another woman to talk things over with.

By then the bread and buns and cakes were all disappearing long before closing-time, and some of the gentlemen customers were making exciting propositions. She could take her pick and charge her own price, and she could never get over how easy it was to make all this money. She took up lodgings in Mrs Lawrie's, and because it was a big room, asked Janet to go with her. A few months later they both gave up their daytime jobs, Mary hers in the bake-shop and Janet hers helping out on a fish-stall, and began devoting all their time to their new profession.

They were down in the Grassmarket, Mary buying her fur tippet, and Janet trying to decide whether to buy blue or pink garters from the Jew, when Janet suddenly remembered something she had been meaning to tell her all along.

'There's another girl like you in Edinburgh, ye ken, Mary.'

Mary's face hardened. There couldn't be another girl like her! 'Like me?' she asked sharply. 'Where?'

'Oh, they say she lives over in the New Town, far away from us.'

'And have you seen her, this other woman?'

Anxious to make amends, Janet nodded her head. 'Ay, I've seen her. But she's not nearly as bonny as you, Mary. Her hair is all twisted up, not like yours.'

'Ay,' Mary smiled, quite mollified, 'it's queer how many women dinna ken what a man likes.' She swaggered along the Grassmarket in her new fur tippet, swaying her hips, and Janet copied her as best she could. 'But she'll be one of those high-ups from the likes o' Charlotte Square?'

'She'll never bother us,' Janet assured her as they climbed up Candlemaker Row and back into the High Street. 'Forget I ever told you.'

But Mary had forgotten already. There was the exciting prospect of the evening's work, and the even more exciting prospect of the rest of her life. She was not even nineteen, not for another two months, and she calculated she could carry on for twenty years at least, by which time she would be a very rich lady.

'Let's go to Swanston's, Janet,' she laughed.

Candida climbed out of the turquoise gown with a sigh, while Kitty took the ribbons and the feathers from her hair, and then the pins, and laid them all on the dressing-table in a little heap.

'Just let it all down, Kitty,' she said tiredly. 'I am going to bed.'

'Yes, miss,' Kitty said, removing the warming-pan. 'Is there anything else?'

'Not tonight.'

'Then I'll bid you good night, Miss Candida.'

'Good night, Kitty dear.'

Left alone in her room, Candida was a worried woman. She had scarcely spoken to Finlay all evening, in spite of her plans—which had included a great deal more than just speaking to him. There was some sparkle missing between her and Finlay, a sparkle she could not define, but she recognised that such a thing existed. It was grating on her nerves to be perfectly aware that it existed in the sharp edge of her conversations with Ross Alexander Laing, on the other hand—of all people! She felt very uneasy.

As a result, she slept uneasily and was totally unprepared and still half-dozing when Alanna knocked on her door early on Monday morning and came in.

'Oh, Candida!' she stopped on the threshold. 'Oh, Candida, your beautiful hair! I have never seen it down like that before. Why do you wear it up all the time?'

'It is Mama's idea,' Candida said. 'She thinks it is tidier. But I hate it.'

'Let me arrange it,' Alanna said, gently taking up the hairbrush. 'Come over here to the mirror, and see if I'm not right. I have a way with hair.'

Candida did not doubt it: Alanna had a way with most things! Within ten minutes she had brushed and combed her golden curls into so many loose ringlets and lifted them up with white ribbons that they stood up round Candida's face like a crown.

'Isn't that pretty?' Alanna asked.

When they all met at breakfast, Uncle Cameron looked startled, and then smiled, and Aunt Rose was quite vehement.

'Oh, Candida,' she said. 'Dear child, you look positively brilliant this morning! Your hair is so becomingly arranged—what a pity Finlay and Ross did not see it before they went into Town. Who did it?'

'Alanna,' Candida said, completely disappointed.

'Then you must instruct Kitty. Today,' Aunt Rose said firmly, smiling at Alanna.

The conversation went on over her head while Candida ate her kippered herring and considered the two men missing from the table. Finlay would have gone in to the business, no doubt, since now and again he must justify himself at it if ever he was going to inherit it for her sake as well as his.

Ross was another matter. Why had *he* gone away so abruptly? It could only have been in connection with that wretched coffin and perhaps with the two men who had despatched it. All she knew was that her new hair-style was entirely wasted, and, for the first time in her life, the Thistle Courts actually paled in her interest.

CHAPTER THREE

DOWN IN Tanner's Close, off the Grassmarket, the two men who had taken the coffin to Dr Knox in Surgeons' Square regarded each other solemnly. So early in the morning, the ashes in the fireplace still had enough heat to make the peats thrown so carelessly on top of them reek and smoke through a room that was evil-smelling enough already, for it was to the rear of the house, and faced the pigsty. They sat on stools and shared the last bottle of whisky, and the lower the level of the whisky the more downcast they became.

'That old man moaning and groaning kept me awake all night,' the younger and more presentable of the two grumbled.

'Sure, and it's dying he is,' the other leered cruelly. 'That's what's on me mind, Wull. I was after thinking, when he does, why shouldn't we be selling him to that Dr Knox? The one we took the coffin to?'

'The other lodgers will know he died, William. They'll be expecting the undertakers, and a coffin and all.'

'Ay. They'll screw down the coffin right enough, and for the look o' the thing we could even have a proper Irish wake—but then what's to stop us unscrewing it and filling it up wi' tanners' bark? There's plenty o' it lying about in the tanyard outside.'

'Take the last belt oot o' the bottle, William, you deserve it! It's a brilliant idea! How much d'ye reckon we'll get?'

'Whatever it is, we'll split it,' said William. 'I've got other plans, but I'll need your help.' He stopped there to glare ferociously at a thin, raddled woman edging round the door. 'And what would your wife be wanting?'

'What's wrong, Nelly?' Wull asked.

'He's dead, that old Donald. They're all shouting about it; all the lodgers.'

'Dead?' William said, springing up from his stool. 'I'll go and see.'

God help the old man if he was still living, Wull thought, for he would surely think he was dead and gone to hell, and this was the Devil himself come to take him, if he looked up into William's face. And now here was Nelly, dying for a dram by the look of her.

'Jesus, Wull, an' it's the shakes I've got, something terrible,' she said, wringing her hands together to try to steady them.

'Cheer up, Nelly,' he said. 'You'll have whisky again tomorrow, and maybe a rabbit as well from Rhymer's.'

'How's that?' She stared at him suspiciously.

'Never you mind. Just leave it all to me and William. We've got plans.'

It all worked out better than they could have hoped. The undertaker came with the coffin, and when he had got old Donald properly laid out inside it, he hammered on the lid and went to get a man to help him carry it to the paupers' graveyard.

As soon as his back was turned, the lid was chiselled up again, old Donald was hidden in the filthy straw on the bed, and the coffin the undertakers respectfully removed was filled up with bags of bark. The two Irishmen waited until it was dark to carry the sack to Surgeons' Square, and when they knocked at the door of No. 10 a tall young man opened it, the same student to whom they had delivered the coffin the first time for Mr Ross Alexander Laing.

'I've seen you two before, have I not?'

'Indade you have, Mr Fergusson, sir,' Wull said, cap in hand. 'We have here, in a manner of speaking, another body for Dr Knox.'

'Fresh?' William Fergusson asked eagerly.

'Newly dead. We found him in a close off the High Street, sir.'

'Bring him in, then! Follow me.'

He led them to a large airy room, where there were more students in white coats and a large marble slab, and the two Irishmen understood they were expected to desack old Donald on to it.

'I'll see if the doctor wants it.' William Fergusson strode off, and left the two standing nervously beside the corpse.

'Now,' Wull said to the other students, 'the way that we found him . . .'

'Never mind that,' one of them said. 'Here's Dr Knox now.'

Dr Knox's appearance was quite arresting. His face was heavily pock-marked, his scalp glistened through his fluffy pale hair, and a black patch across his left eye lent him the air of a terrifying pirate. But black patch or no, he wore a pair of gold-rimmed pince-nez perched in a deep notch on his long nose. He was not a man to cross lightly, the two carriers thought uneasily, and they watched in dumb agony while the great doctor made a brief examination of the corpse.

'Seven sovereigns, ten shillings,' he instructed Mr Fergusson, and without another word, without a single question, he departed in a flurry of coat-tails.

Mr Fergusson handed over the money from a heavy leather purse and conducted them back to the door. 'When you have other bodies to dispose of, we will be glad to see you,' he said. 'A good night to you both.'

'Did you hear *that*, Wull?' William turned his brutal face to his companion on their way back down the South Bridge. '"When we have other bodies to dispose of . . ." That was my plan. I told you!'

'But how can we?'

'I'm after thinking,' William said.

So when Constable Frank Clarke was on his midnight rounds that night and heard the noise of the jigging and the reeling and the drunken bawling coming from Tanner's Close, he paused only to think how cold and thirsty he was and how merry they were in there. He swung his lantern into the darkness of the next wynd where the rats scampered, and mused wistfully on how unexciting had been his career so far. He would never get promotion at this rate, and above all he wanted to be promoted—and quickly—so that he could ask his Kitty to marry him.

Out on the street again, the idea of Kitty shone like a beacon through fog thick enough to suffocate a man. If they had been the brightest lamps in the world instead of the dim little lamps they were, they still could not have held a candle to her. He cheered up into good humour when he remembered that tomorrow was his Thursday off, and this Thursday he was invited to tea in the kitchens of No. 13 Charlotte Square.

'It looks as though our Irish visitors have taken Mama at her word, Kitty,' Candida said fretfully after a whole week since the visit out to the Thistle Courts. 'They are certainly being independent, upstairs. We hardly ever see them.'

'That should suit you then, Miss Candida, since you don't like Mr Ross.'

Did she, or didn't she?

'No,' Candida sighed. 'But I did think Miss Alanna would have made an amusing companion. What does she do? Where does she go?'

'I can soon find out!' Kitty smiled confidently. 'I know her maid, Elizabeth. She is running up and down to the kitchens all the time.'

'So Miss Alanna has got her own servants already?'

'Ho! That one doesn't let the grass grow under her feet—if you will excuse me, Miss Candida.'

'May I come in? Candida, are you there?'

A knock sounded on the door, and on her way to open it Kitty bent her head to whisper.

'Speak of the Devil!' she said, and curtsying demurely when Alanna came in, closed the door behind her on her way out.

'My dear!' Alanna strode across the room, attired today in startling shades of orange and yellow. 'I have found out about the Outside Classes! There is one we simply must attend at the college, conducted by Dr Thomas Charles Hope. It is in chemistry, and ladies are permitted—escorted, of course.'

'Escorted by whom?' Candida asked. 'Our maids?'

'Oh no, dear. By gentlemen. But that is an obstacle already overcome,' Alanna said sweepingly. 'I have instructed Ross, and you will easily persuade Mr Semple to come with us.'

'Ross?' Candida said. 'I cannot believe he would allow himself to be instructed by a lady, Alanna, even you.'

'Oh, that was a little exercise learned long ago at Mama's knee. It all depends on the bait, you know. Men can be like donkeys, but dangle the right carrots before their noses, and off they go!'

'And what carrot did you dangle this time?'

But Alanna only laughed, and in spite of herself Candida found herself laughing along with her. She was very hard to resist with that Alexander Laing smile of hers.

'Of course I will come with you, Alanna. It will be something to occupy my mind, as Papa would say. He will certainly approve. When does this Outside Class start?'

'On Monday afternoon at three o'clock. But this afternoon I am going on a different excursion, out to look for a house! Will you come? I can think of no other person I would rather have with me, Candida.'

'Papa is in his study now, Kitty told me. There was another little matter I wanted to discuss with him, anyway,' she said, 'so I shall mention that and the Outside Classes at the same time.'

But on the way downstairs Candida dragged her feet. The 'other little matter', the matter of the coffin, hung over her in a heavy black cloud, but she could not go on without alerting her family about it. She knocked at the study door and went in, to find her father at the far side of the fireplace almost entirely enveloped in one of the huge high-lugged chairs, a glass of sherry in one hand.

'Papa,' she said, walking over to him, 'there is something dreadful I must tell you about Ross Alexander Laing . . .'

Too late, she came up alongside the chair facing her father's, and there, with his long legs stretched out, sat the subject of her conversation. He rose to his feet politely, in time to gaze down at her in the worst moment of her life so far.

'Fools rush in, my Candida,' Atholl Forbes said. 'Come and sit down here beside me! Ross, sit down again. Now what is all this?'

She thought she detected a twinkle in her father's stern eyes, and her discomfiture changed to indignation. 'You will not think me such a fool when I tell you, Papa. Do you wish to stay?' she addressed Ross.

'I would not miss it for the world,' he replied, and his face gave nothing away.

'He arrived in Edinburgh with a coffin,' Candida said scornfully. 'With a dead body, Papa! I have had nightmares about it ever since.'

'If it worried you so much, what a pity you did not speak of it sooner, my dear,' Mr Forbes said. 'Of course I knew about the coffin. Your Mama told me. Now, what is this dreadful thing?'

Perhaps the whole world was turning upside-down, after all. Here was Papa next, apparently unperturbed. 'Isn't that enough?' she asked.

Mr Forbes addressed Ross calmly, almost in sorrow. 'No, she is not a fool, no matter how it looks. But it is a demonstration of how the untrained mind works. Candida does not stop to consider every aspect of a given situation, as you can see, my boy.'

'I have already told her that ladies rely on their instincts,' Ross said lazily. 'But, with your permission, my sister and I will remedy all that. Alanna has fallen mad to go to the chemistry class, and if Candida will go too, I should be happy to escort her. A little scientific instruction should be of great benefit.'

Candida felt a rush of a colour, which seemed to come

from her feet and spread up over her whole body to settle hotly on her cheeks. What had Alanna said to Ross? Was that the carrot?

'A capital idea! Capital! I have often thought it not only a pity, but a waste of a female's life that the universities do not admit them. But, of course, we must observe the proprieties.'

'Indeed, sir,' Ross was quick to agree.

Candida gazed at them both, speechless. It all felt like a nightmare come true. The harder she ran after the truth the further it receded. Mr Forbes put a small oblong card into her hand, on which was the grisly likeness of a corpse and some writing that blurred before her eyes.

'That is Ross's passport into Dr Knox's lectures, Candida. He received it today. It is true he brought a body with him from his hospital in Ireland, the body of an old soldier with no relatives, who had expressed the wish that it should be donated to the research of medical science. That is why Ross and Alanna arrived almost without warning. Dr Knox's classes are so popular that it was the only sure way of obtaining a place.'

'But he is a doctor already,' she objected.

'And I intend to be a surgeon as well,' Ross said. 'There is no more brilliant anatomist than Dr Knox to train under. He lectures all morning, every morning, which will allow me to escort you to the chemistry classes in the afternoons.'

'I shall ask Mr Finlay Semple to do that, sir.'

'I believe he has already offered, in the circumstances, to escort Alanna. It seems that their conversations about horses keep them both spellbound.' Ross smiled. 'Perhaps our conversations will be spellbinding too, Candida, on our way to and from the Outside Classes?'

She flounced out of Papa's study far more indignant, if that were possible, than she had gone in, without one shred of remorse for her mistake. But she was more uneasy than ever, although her uneasiness was taking a new turn. Given that Ross Alexander Laing had very neatly exonerated himself from one sort of blame, she could now point her finger at him in another. He, and his sister along with him, were trying to separate her and Finlay. Why must he accompany her to the Outside Classes? She wanted Finlay, who might be dull and (she even admitted it) quite boring, but at least he was safe in that he was entirely predictable.

Candida made up her mind to get in touch with Finlay again as soon as possible. She loved him, didn't she? And, without doubt, he loved her. He had asked her to marry him. Ross Alexander Laing was not to be trusted, no matter what Papa thought, and in spite of his clever green eyes, in spite of his tall elegance, and most of all in spite of the many tentacles he seemed to be putting out all around her she had no intention of being trapped.

He was just like an octopus, she thought angrily, and that was without moving from his seat. In any case, it was Finlay she had started off to think about, and not him. With great difficulty she dismissed Ross from her mind, so that she set forth with Alanna dressed in her favourite white, tipped this afternoon with gold, with golden ribbons in her hair, quite recovered.

'You look enchanting!' Alanna told her with all the charm of the Irish. 'Of course, we have kept to green for our new coach, in deference to Aunt Alison. It would not do if we had coaches of different colours coming and going from No. 13 Charlotte Square. Ross insisted on it.'

'It is very pretty,' Candida said, trying not to sound doubtful, for she could not help noticing that green it might be, but it was a very dashing green adorned with canary yellow shamrocks echoed inside in its bright canary yellow upholstery. She knew full well that Mama would think it far too vivid. 'It has character, anyway.'

'Oh, well, that is because I chose it all!' Alanna beamed. 'I like bright colours, and everything new. It is so exciting!' Then, instructing her coachman with her head out of the window, 'We will go to the south side of the city, Oliver. I told you where!'

'To the south side?' Candida asked, while Alanna

rearranged the feathers on her hat which had become a little askew. 'You do not think that may be a little unfashionable, now that everyone who is anyone is flocking to the New Town on the north side?'

'Unfashionable it may be,' Alanna said vigorously, 'but it is warmer. I have never been in such a cold, windy place as this Edinburgh of yours, and there is still the winter to face. In Ireland it is so much milder.'

Candida laughed. 'You are on the east coast of Scotland now, Alanna, where the weather is notorious. You will have to buy some warmer mantles and pelisses, for now that it is October you cannot go outdoors much longer without them. Which address are we going to today?'

'One that I do not understand. In fact, I cannot make head or tail of it, it sounds so odd. We are going to the Land of Canaan.'

'Oh, to Canaan?' Candida laughed again. 'There are lots of stories about it.'

'What are they?'

'Sometimes the district is known as "Little Egypt", and one story is that long ago Christians were expelled from Egypt, wandered through India and Europe and finally came here, known by that time as "the gypsies". Another story is that rich Jews migrated to Edinburgh, paid for all these lands, and that is how the Jordan Burn came to have its name, and Goshen, and Eden and Hebron.'

'I believe the second story,' Alanna said. 'Look at the orchards and gardens we are passing, and the beautiful large villas! Oh, I was quite right to come here! It is a large house along here in Canaan's Lane we are going to look at, the only one for sale in this district. We are expected, so the gates will be open.'

The carriage stopped beside a ramshackle wall. So many of its stones had come away from the plaster and rumbled sadly to rest in piles on the ground that it was only a travesty of an old wall, like an old man's teeth with very few remaining, and the gates were so rusty after years of decay that it was not hard to imagine how they must have creaked back excruciatingly as if in pain. As the Alexander Laings' carriage bowled brashly up the meandering drive, Candida thought it must resemble a brilliantly green dragonfly darting gloriously up some muddy stream, oblivious of the overgrown weeds, for nettles were everywhere, trailing about the paths, and the heads of the dandelions had long since lost their fluff.

Yet, immediately, she was aware of a strange magic, of happy voices on once-velvet lawns, and of dreaming music—music that had so beloved a tune, so bitter-sweet, if only she could pick it out, if only she could remember it, perhaps. And then the house came into view, sad, forlorn, and in Candida's eyes the house she had always known existed, somewhere in paradise.

'Oh,' she said, and caught her breath, and fell silent.

'Well!' Alanna stepped down briskly from the carriage with the help of her coachman. 'This has been a perfect waste of time, Oliver! Still, as we are here, we may as well look through it. Wait here.'

'Can we get inside?' Candida asked.

'I have the key,' Alanna said, 'but I doubt if it will turn. The lock will be too rusty, like everything else here.'

But the key turned and the door opened silently, almost graciously, and an atmosphere of long ago enveloped them.

'I do not know where to start in this sprawling place,' Alanna complained.

'Follow me,' Candida said, and as if in a sleep-walker's trance she led her cousin through all the rooms, along all the corridors and unlocked the long windows out to the gardens, to the stream, and over the bridge to the fields beyond until they found themselves at the edge of a lake.

'Children skate here in the winter,' Candida said. 'In the winter it freezes over.'

'How do you know that?' Alanna demanded. 'You

have been here before? You must have been here before!'

'Of course I have never been here before! But I just know it. I feel I know everything about this house.'

'Well, it is not for me,' Alanna said decisively. 'It is too old. And it will not do for Ross, either. We require space, but not this kind of space!' She took up her skirts and headed back through the house to the coach, with Candida trailing in her wake and gazing to right and to left soaking up all the sights and sounds she could in such a rapid retreat.

They arrived back at No. 13 Charlotte Square in time for dinner.

'There is plenty of time to change,' Lady Alison said, 'and I have invited Ross and Alanna to come downstairs and join us. Put on your pink, Candida dear. You look a little pale. Are you all right?' There was a note of anxiety in Lady Alison's voice. 'You look as if you had seen a ghost. The pink will lend you some colour.'

The talk at the table that evening was all of the expedition to Canaan's Lane. Alanna was in dark green shot through with glittering gold. Her hair was dressed aslant, asymmetrically, with a glorious, floppy green-gilt bow to one side of her head. She was too beautiful to be true, a dragonfly woman, if it had not been for those two faint lines running down from each side of her mouth. Candida had never noticed them before, but perhaps they were there only because Alanna was upset that the house for sale had not been to her satisfaction.

'And what did you think of the house in Canaan's Lane, Candida?' Ross asked lazily. 'Was it really so terrible?'

'It was beautiful,' she said, under cover of the rest of the conversation. 'I thought it was the house of my dreams. But my dreams are neither here nor there.'

'They are enough to interest me,' he said. 'Will you come out to it again with me tomorrow morning and show me, since we still have the key until mid-day?'

Perhaps this was what it was like to be intoxicated,

Candida thought, although she could not have told why this strange thrill ran right through her. Of course, it must be the prospect of seeing the house again.

'I shall ask,' she answered guardedly, and then longingly, 'But yes, I would like to see it again and feel the peace and contentment within those old walls. You may not feel such an atmosphere, though.'

'Your father was quite right in his assessment of you,' Ross said. 'You do not study every aspect of a situation, and you certainly do not listen to everything that is said to you.' His eyes looked very directly into hers, and once again a thrill ran from the top of her spine to the bottom. 'If you are interested in the old house, then so am I. I will soon tell you about its atmosphere.'

Mama should not have insisted she wore the pale pink, Candida decided in that moment. It was too young, and she had grown up suddenly during the course of this meal. In fact, her parents had kept her too young and far too vulnerable as a result, to judge from the way her heart was leaping inside her—and all because Ross had presumed almost on the intimate. She would have to be careful, most of all with herself.

Next morning turned out to be one of those October mornings in Edinburgh when everything was touched by gold. The shafts of mellow sunshine pierced the soft mist to gild the railings before the houses in Charlotte Square. The leaves in Princes Street Gardens glittered and danced, and on the drive up Lothian Road towards Canaan's Lane the yellow inside of the coach reflected it all.

If Ross was a little overpowered by his sister's choice of colour scheme, he made no comment. Instead he made a careful study of the two girls sitting on the seat opposite.

'Powder blue becomes you, Candida,' he said at last, and smiled his heart-stopping smile. 'And as for you, Kitty, you are very scrubbed and shining today—especially so.'

'Yes, sir,' Kitty giggled. 'Thank you, sir.'

'Canaan's Lane is special, is it?'

'Miss Candida says it is, sir. And . . .'

'And?'

'And Constable Frank Clarke's beat is out there this week, sir, as it happens.'

'Ah!' Ross smiled again, and said no more.

Perhaps all the criticisms of her were quite true, Candida thought. Of course she had noticed the pains Kitty had taken over her appearance today. It just had not occurred to her to wonder why. The coach slowed down as it came alongside the house, its gates mysteriously open wide again.

'Odd,' Ross said. 'How could anyone have known we were coming back today?'

They moved slowly forward again, and from behind one of the tall gateposts a solid figure emerged.

'I've checked the house from the outside and the grounds, sir,' Frank Clarke said cheerily. 'All's well.' He grinned at Kitty, who had the grace to blush violently.

'So it is a lovers' meeting?' Candida accused her maid. 'Very well then, Kitty. Fifteen minutes, and then you must come looking for me. You will remember?'

'Oh yes, thank you, Miss Candida,' Kitty said breathlessly as the constable helped her down. 'I'll be there.'

Once again the door yielded to the key, once again the house came to life, not an empty shell, but living and breathing as it had lived before, and once again Candida led the way through it.

'This was the library,' she said, as their eyes took in the empty shelves which once were stacked from ceiling to floor with books whose very bindings swam blue and red and dark green before them. The curtains blew softly at the empty, tight-shut windows, and a little table materialised beside an armchair, bearing a bowl of roses. They could almost smell the charred embers of a log fire they could imagine still smouldering in the hearth.

'You love this house, Candida.'

It was not a question. It was a statement that Ross made as they went upstairs, and in that instant a wild idea entered her head. Papa had always said that she was a very rich young lady. How rich? she wondered. Rich enough to buy this house herself? She felt her head reeling in the excitement of it, before cool common-sense returned. Of course, she realised with the excitement draining out of her, as if it was her heart's blood draining out of her, it could never be. No properly-brought-up young lady in Edinburgh would ever be permitted to move out of the family home into an establishment of her own, unless with her husband, no matter how rich she was. She tried to imagine such an affront to Mama, and shuddered with horror.

'It is a special house,' she sighed. 'But not to Alanna.'

Ross did not rise to the bait. 'And what room do you think this was?' he asked as they entered an upper room, long and low and rather like a ship's cabin with its small windows all around.

'It lets in a lot of light. It is the north light, too. The people might even have built it for some purpose which required so much light. Perhaps one of them was a painter.'

'Yes. Perfect for you to illustrate your diary, for example? Oh yes, you would be happy here, Candida, lifting your head from time to time to gaze out over the gardens. I can picture you here.'

She knelt on the window-seat and looked out upon the morning. The sun shone misty gold still, and there was a brisk high wind now to toss the trees. In half an hour they would be gone again in the coach, the view from the windows and the house itself once more only a happy memory.

She sighed and turned away from the window, only to come face to face with Ross, his eyes still dreaming green but now fixed on hers a mere two feet away with a secret, inscrutable look. Panic began to rise inside her. 'I want to go home,' she said, her voice perilously near to trembling.

'You are home,' he insisted.

But her happy mood had gone, and at the thought of it her face froze, and despicable tears welled into her eyes and strayed upon her cheeks.

'Finlay would never live here,' she managed to say.

'What has Finlay to do with it? What has Finlay to do with anything—now?' Ross asked, pulling her to him, with his arm about her shoulders. 'And that is something else I have been meaning to tell you. That moonstone ring is as wrong for you as he is. Take it off, Candida, and never wear it again.'

They were suspended in time, in a moment that would not pass, while his lips touched hers softly, and all the solidity, the safety and the security of her life lay in ruins around her.

'There you are, Miss Candida!' Kitty chose that moment to find them.

Ross's arm fell from her shoulders, and their little procession moved back through the house, back into the coach, and under the watchful eye of Constable Frank Clarke back out through the gates.

'They are very stiff, sir,' he shouted up to Ross, who immediately sprang out to help him.

The two men forced the gates shut and locked them up again. Ross paused to push back the ivy winding around the gateposts. 'Come and see this, Candida,' he said.

Afterwards she could not believe it was she who had responded. She was not there at all that bright morning. Some other woman got down obediently and looked at the name he had uncovered, half-blurred and indistinct —PARADISE HOUSE—while somebody dealt Candida Rowena Forbes a terrible blow to her stomach.

'What else could it ever be?' he asked.

'What else?' she agreed sadly.

A week later the Outside Classes began, and armed with notepads and pencils and dressed in their best, Candida and Alanna paid scant attention to their escorts. It was all too new, too exciting, and in one short hour Dr Thomas Charles Hope bombarded them with so much information that when they got back home again they spent hours together comparing notes and trying to decipher them.

For three weeks they were entirely engrossed, and the month had changed into November while they were finding out that the whole word was made up of chemicals which could in different combinations produce other chemicals, and that there was such a thing as the chemistry of the blood, of animals and even of human beings.

It was on the 2nd of November, at four o'clock on a dank miserable afternoon, that Atholl Forbes came home and went at once to Lady Alison's sitting-room, just in time for tea. As usual, he had timed it to perfection. Kate had put down a finely embroidered tea-cloth on the low table beside a glowing fire, and set it with her ladyship's delicate china. Polished silver reflected the dancing flames, and there were hot buttered toast, freshly baked scones and home-made cakes.

'This is the best time of the day,' he said, sighing with satisfaction as he sank into his chair. His wife handed him a cup of tea. 'Where is everyone?'

'Sh! Don't ask! They can all tell the time, you know, Atholl, and it is so pleasant to have you all to myself for once in the dusk. This hour before we must draw the curtains and light the lamps is my favourite time, too. Were you busy today?'

'We were all too taken up with the new heating system in the Signets' Library and much too comfortable to be busy. What a wonderful invention, my dear! I wonder if I could install it in this house? They have run great thick pipes of hot water all round the walls, and they give out such a heat! Henry Cockburn and I went down to examine the boiler-room in the basement, and became so interested that we almost missed the Meridian.'

'Dear me!' said Lady Alison with her gentle smile. 'It must be wonderful indeed, at that rate. But I trust that you and Henry remembered after all to have a glass of brandy and something to eat at mid-day?'

'We went to Ambrose's and ate several varieties of fish. It was over the oysters that Henry's comments on the considerable incomes to be derived by the teachers of the Outside Classes became quite caustic.'

'Dear Henry,' Lady Alison said. 'He is so very conservative!'

'He says that Dr Hope is in an absolute ecstasy with his audience of veils and feathers when he lectures to the ladies on chemistry. It seems he receives three hundred of them by a back window which he has converted to a door. Each of them brings a beau, and the ladies declare that there never was anything so delightful as these chemical flirtations! Henry hopes some of Dr Hope's experiments will blow him up, and then each female student would get a bit of him.'

'Oh dear,' Lady Alison laughed, 'we had better not tell Candida or Alanna that! Henry Cockburn would naturally think women to have only one place, and that is in the home. But times are changing, Atholl.'

'Thank God for that! Candida is far from ready to settle down by her own fireside.'

'I made a mistake about that coffin,' Lady Alison sighed. 'I should have discussed it with her at the time. In fact, we have made a lot of mistakes, looking back. Is it right to allow her to marry Finlay Semple under this veil of secrecy? He and his father should be told the truth.'

'First of all, Candida must be told the truth, Alison, and the sooner the better. I have always said so.'

'I know you have, dear, but when will the right time to tell her ever come? How would you—or anyone else—like to find out you were a foundling, a baby left to die in a shop door? Oh, I cannot believe a woman could be so cruel to her tiny daughter, even yet!'

'Well, it will be her birthday in seven days, on the ninth. That would seem most appropriate to me.'

'She will not be here, Atholl. You know she is never well, for some reason, in Edinburgh on her birthday.

Cameron and Rose are determined she will become nineteen at the Thistle Courts, and they have invited all the young ones to go out with her. I have agreed, providing there is no party and no excitement.'

The 7th of November dawned with a thin grey light which hardly altered even in the early afternoon. Candida shivered in her furs when she stepped inside the coach to go with Alanna to look for something new to wear. She was even grateful today for the canary yellow of their surroundings. At least it was bright, and gave the illusion that somewhere in the world there was a speck of colour, even sunshine.

'There is no finer emporium of ladies' fashions than Semples' on the South Bridge, Alanna,' she said, 'and that is not because it is my fiancé's business. It is a fact of Edinburgh life.'

'Then that is where we shall start,' Alanna replied with all her usual enthusiasm, 'although I shall buy nothing unless it appeals to me! And for that, only the very latest will do.'

Ten minutes later they alighted into the dazzling foyer of Semple and Son, to be met by the commissionaire in his chocolate brown uniform leading the way and opening doors before them.

'Oh, it is all so tastefully done!' Alanna exclaimed, pointing to the brown carpets, white curtains and the little gilded cubicles discreetly curtained for the ladies to try on the gowns.

'Yes,' Candida sighed, bored already.

Alanna flitted from one fashionable clothed bust to the next in a fever of interest until a small wiry figure appeared from behind one of them.

'Allow me to introduce Mr Francis Semple to you, Alanna,' Candida said. 'He is Finlay's father. Mr Semple, this is my cousin . . .'

'Miss Alanna Alexander Laing! Pleased to meet you, my dear,' Mr Semple said with an agonised look behind him. 'My son has told me so much about you. If you would be so kind as to wait here, ladies . . .'

He darted back, and in through a little door of what was obviously an office. The two girls could plainly hear his voice. 'Tak' your feet off that desk, Finlay Semple,' he hissed. 'Miss Forbes is in the shop, and her cousin wi' her.'

'Alanna?'

'The same. A fine figure o' a woman if ever I saw one.'

'What did I tell you, Father?'

Finlay came out and bowed over their hands, and after smiling into Candida's eyes with a roguish sort of innocence, he turned to Alanna with quite a different expression.

It was one of adoration, pure and simple, and in that instant Candida realised that it could change her life. While the others were talking she discovered she felt no pain, only impatience that it was too soon yet to wallow in relief that, whatever her future, she would not be sharing it now with Finlay Semple. If she had any regrets at all, they were for her mother, and for the disappointment she would be sure to feel about the exquisite wedding gown, ready now for months and hung away in a wardrobe of its own swathed in tissue paper.

'It is quite wonderful,' Alanna was saying. 'I have never been in a shop like it before—so big, and so luxurious! It makes me feel I could stay here for hours and just spend money!'

Francis Semple looked at her with startled respect. 'Ay,' he said, 'that's just what I set oot to do. Finlay, ye'll maybe conduct the ladies aroond the place?'

'You showed me around already,' Candida said swiftly. 'I'll just stay here with you, Mr Semple.'

'Well, well, lassie,' he patted Candida's gloved hand, 'it's no' often I get the chance to ha'e a wee chat wi' you.' He beamed at Alanna. 'I can see you ha'e an eye for beesiness, Miss Alexander Laing.'

'My father always said so,' Alanna said modestly. 'He keeps telling my mother it's a great thing to have children to follow in your footsteps. You are so lucky in your son, Mr Semple!'

'Ay,' he agreed drily.

Finlay took Alanna's arm with alacrity as they set off on their tour of Semple's emporium, and the old man was left with Candida. It was painfully obvious he did not know quite what to say next, facing his son's fiancée. She made it easy for him.

'Would there be a cup of tea, Mr Semple?' she asked. 'It looks as though they may be some time.'

'A fly cup! The verra thing!' he agreed gratefully, and they were shortly sitting in the office sipping tea while Finlay's father expounded the intricacies of business and finance, all double Dutch to Candida.

'There is the business,' she said during a pause, 'and there are the horses, Mr Semple. Except for my own horse, these things do not really interest me, unfortunately. I must be frank with you.'

'Dinna fash yersel', lassie,' Mr Semple patted her hand again, still on the upsurge of enthusiasm over Alanna. 'Ah, here they are, coming back deep in talk. Nae doot it's a' aboot the beesiness. Dinna worry, my dear, it'll a' work oot.'

On the way back to Charlotte Square in the carriage Candida sincerely hoped so. Both girls were silent, shivering after coming out of the warm shop. The night had darkened, and the twinkling street lights went past with monotonous regularity which only intensified their secret thoughts. Eventually Candida roused herself.

'Did you buy anything, Alanna?' she asked.

'Oh dear! Would you believe it?' Alanna laughed. 'I shall have to go back another day. In all the excitement I quite forgot!'

What excitement? Candida wondered. Had there ever really been any with Finlay Semple? She felt silent again, convinced there had been none, and now she was in the impossible position of being engaged to be married, when the marriage would never take place. What could she do about it? Nothing at the moment. She would just have to wait and see.

CHAPTER FOUR

IT WAS nine o'clock when Sir Cameron Kyle flung the last log on the fire. It brought the orange arc behind it crashing down in a flurry of sparks, spitting busily and shooting up in flames. It was the most exciting thing that had happened the whole day, Candida thought, now she was nineteen. Everyone had been at such pains to keep things calm.

'I believe Lady's foal might share your birthday, yet,' her uncle confided. 'Your horse is very uncomfortable at this minute. But you must not worry. This new groom, Johnson, is very good.'

'I'll say good night,' Ross said abruptly, standing up dark and tall one minute, and leaving the room the next.

'Perhaps in a little while we should all be thinking of bed,' Lady Rosalie smothered a yawn and smiled. The relief in her voice to get this day, the 9th of November, over and done with without mishap was not lost on Candida. 'It is so nasty and cold tonight, but there will be fires lit in all our bedrooms.'

One by one they left the drawing-room and made their way upstairs.

'Oh, you are here, miss,' Kitty said, sleepy-eyed, when Candida reached her room.

'I shall not need you after all,' she told her maid. 'I shall sit awhile by the fire. You may go, Kitty.'

But when ten o'clock rang out, boomed out in the hall downstairs, echoed in chimes all round the house, and the tiny silvery strokes sounded on her bedroom clock, Candida could stand it no longer. She knew it was ridiculous, but she felt so well that something must be wrong. Where was it wrong? she fretted. At home, in Charlotte Square? Were her mother and father all right?

But then she knew with a dreadful certainty that what was wrong was precisely here, at the Thistle Courts.

Still dressed in the warm blue woollen dress her mother had given her for her birthday, Candida stole along the passages and downstairs, and then along more passages until she found her way outside into a hard, breathtaking frost crunching under her feet. There was a dim light in the stables, and picking up her skirts she ran towards it, a few little snowflakes stinging her face as she went.

Outside the door she heard the cry of her horse, half a neigh and half a scream, and her heart twisted in sympathy. The night grew colder and whiter every minute while she dredged up the courage to open the stable door. What she saw inside turned her heart to ice altogether. Lady was on her feet, her head thrashing from side to side in pain and terror. A young stable-lad cowered in a corner, and Ross's face was black with anger.

'There should be buckets of hot water here,' he said, beginning to strip off his clothes. 'How can I help this animal in these circumstances?'

Candida remained utterly calm. It was as though her whole mind froze down to concentrate only on the immediate emergency. 'You mean boiled water,' she said, 'and some purification even of that? Soap is not enough, is it?'

'No, it is not.' He looked over his shoulder at her, his expression a little surprised. 'Before you fetch me the water, go up to my room and look on the dressing-table among the little bottles there. One of them contains a yellow powder.'

Lady screamed again in agony, and before Candida fled she had time only to hear Ross berating the stable-lad.

'Get up and tie her head!' he commanded. 'Tie it to that post, boy, and hold her tight!'

If any bedroom was designed for a man, this was it, she decided as she burst open Ross's door and rushed through the severe greys and blues of it to the dressing-table. What met her gaze were little phials all like specimen bottles ranged on the right-hand side of the long mirror, while small boxes with clear lids were lined up in precise order on the left. Even in this extremity she could not resist looking into them at the pretty stones, some glittering, some coloured. There was one huge pearly one which even as she looked seemed to change colour. She snatched her eyes away and searched for the phial containing yellow powder. Down in the kitchen there was enough light from the dying fire to empty the hissing kettles into two pails, and she calculated that by the time she had carried them down to the stables on this bitter night the water would have cooled down so that Ross could put his hands in it. With a steaming pail in each hand, she set off into a welter of whiteness, for it was snowing heavily now, and it took her all her time to arrive back at the stable without slipping into disaster.

'Bring them here,' Ross said unceremoniously when she appeared.

She set them down, wondering indignantly if he realised that she had risked life and limb on her errand. At the same time she was struggling with the question of whether she ought to be affronted by the sight of his hard, muscled shoulders, rippling arms and chest of black hair, for by now he was stripped to the waist. She handed him the small glass bottle while she debated the matter.

'Do you know what is in this?' he asked as severely as a schoolmaster.

'Of course,' she said, stung. 'What do you think we did at the Outside Classes? It is a bleaching powder of some sort, probably chlorine.'

'And how much would you put in each pail?'

'Very little?'

'All right, so you know a little about chemistry. Now we shall see what kind of nurse you are. The head is twisted the wrong way,' he said, with one arm straining inside the mare. 'The foal cannot be born alive like this. I must bring the head round and tie its feet at the same time. But the rope must be cleaned first, soaked in one of the pails.'

He flung a coil of rope at her and turned again to the mare. Why was he being so strict and intimidating all of a sudden? she wondered, bending over the pail and pressing the water into every strand of the rope, while he toiled and grunted with effort.

'Is it ready?' he asked.

She handed the end of the rope up to him, and while he sweated and strained, the stable-lad moaned and turned his head the other way. The lad was no use, and the groom not even there, Candida thought. In fact if Ross had not been here and known what to do, Lady would have lost another foal, if indeed this one was not lost as well. Of course, he was a doctor! Then she realised he was behaving as he would do in his own hospital, when he must keep his mind on his work and instruct his nurses at the same time. He was thinking of her as one of his nurses now.

'I've got it,' he said in quiet triumph a few minutes later. 'Now, to tie its feet.' He made a loop somewhere inside Lady. 'Now—pull!'

She went behind him and pulled on the rope. Two glistening little crescents appeared first, and she could not understand what they were. Then came the tiny head of a horse, its mouth lying on the crescents which she recognised now as its front hooves. Then, slipping through a slithery transparent bag of skin, came the outstretched front legs, then the body and at last the hind legs of Lady's foal.

Ross deposited it on the straw, cut the cord, washed the orifice and then his own hands in the other pail while they watched Lady first weakly and then wholeheartedly lick her baby, and in a few minutes she was urging him up on his feet.

'It is a miracle,' Candida said unsteadily, hardly able to believe that the litlte horse was standing there, pure white like his mother, and perfect.

At that same moment the stable door burst open, a cloud of snow flew in over the straw, and Sir Cameron Kyle stood in the doorway. His eyes took in the whole scene at a glance. 'Where is my groom?' he demanded.

'He only went out for a minute, sir.' The stable-lad found his voice at last.

'It has been a long minute! Go and fetch him here, boy.' When the terrified lad ran out, he turned to Candida. 'Well, you have got your foal now, my dear. You must name him.'

But she could not speak. She could not move. She felt a horrible sensation of swinging. It was a nightmare. Nothing was real. Lady was licking the last drops of blood from her foal, and her tongue darted them onto the snow Sir Cameron had brought in with him in the flurry. Drops of blood on the pure white snow . . . in November . . . Candida knew no more before she fell to the ground.

It seemed hours later that she came back to life, with Uncle Cameron fussing over her, hemming her in. In the distance she heard Ross's voice.

'I don't understand it, sir. She helped me magnificently all through the birth without a tremor. Something distressed her, certainly, but it was not that.'

Fresh air, to be able to breathe, was all she wanted. She could not understand why she had fainted in the first place. She had never done so before. If she had air, she could try to think. She shook her head and Ross put his arm round her and dragged her outside. He seemed to understand. As she gulped in the fresh air, she felt that, after the snow, the bitter edge of the temperature had softened a little, and the wind had eased.

'They will not leave you alone until you have named the foal, Candida,' said Ross. 'Some people think it unlucky not to do so at the birth. So you had better think of a name now, and I will convey it.'

'I cannot think,' she said, looking up at him, her blue eyes enormous with distress, so that he drew in his breath sharply, and his grip on her intensified. 'Help me.'

'He is white,' Ross said steadily, 'as white as a candle, and he was born by candlelight. Your name is Candida, by coincidence, and that means "white" or "pure" or "truth".'

'Candlelight, then,' she said, while uncomfortable ripples ran through her again.

White snow, red drops of blood, red berries on a white cloth, Candida for whiteness, Candida for the truth. She felt pushed to the edge of a great precipice of truth, but she was in the dark, she could not see, and her steps faltered as they entered the house.

'Is Kitty still up?' Ross asked, as they went upstairs.

'No. I sent her to bed.

'Well then,' he said, 'I must be your maid tonight. Nobody is up except Sir Cameron, and he will be hours admiring the new foal and dealing with his groom, I shouldn't wonder.' They reached her bedroom, and he half-carried her in. 'You are in no fit state to undress, but we will take off your gown.' He whipped the blue woollen dress over her head. 'And as for that corset! Turn round, Candida.'

She felt his merciful hands loosening the strings Kitty had tied so tightly in the morning, and then her petticoats were coming off, one by one, until she was down to her last.

'No,' she said. 'No more, no more!'

She felt her breasts exposed, all her figure exposed. She might as well have been naked. She came back to earth with a thud. What was she doing undressed in her bedroom with a man who was not even the one she was going to marry? And why did she suddenly want him, more than anything else on earth, to strip off all the rest of her clothes? That was what she should be feeling for Finlay, and the sad fact was she had not even thought of Finlay for hours.

'No,' she said again, and made vague gestures of fending him off.

'Oh, Candida!' Ross laughed, and scooped her up in his arms. 'You are a very beautiful nurse as well as a very capable one. Did you think, in the face of all that, that any doctor would harm one hair of your head?'

Then suddenly she was deposited on her bed, he was gone, and she had never felt so bereft or lonely or so let down in her whole life. It was towards morning before she finally closed her eyes.

It was a subdued party that arrived back in Charlotte Square the next day. Candida felt tired, and the effort of avoiding Ross's eyes during the entire journey had been a further strain, so that she was grateful when Alanna and Finlay chatted quietly between themselves without involving anyone else. In the afternoon she went to visit her father in his study, as she always did on the days he was at home.

'I suppose it is not proper for a young lady to buy a house—a young lady who is not married, I mean?'

Mr Forbes paused, pen in hand, and gazed over his desk at his daughter in astonishment. The expressions that passed over his face ranged from horror to mystification before his lawyer's mind came to his rescue. He set down his pen carefully in its groove and struggled to give the matter his full and considered attention, failing miserably in the attempt.

'Good God, Candida! What next?'

'Surely she should have some say about the house she would live in after she was married?'

Mr Forbes remembered his wife's words, 'Times are changing,' but even they did not restore his composure, and said, 'In the company of her future husband, perhaps. But what is all this about, Candida?'

'It is about Paradise House in Canaan's Lane, Papa.'

'But . . . Yes, what is it?' he asked when a young housemaid knocked and put her head round the door.

'Someone to see you, sir. He would not come in. He said he would not detain you more than a few minutes.'

Her father left the study, and Candida roamed around

it, familiar with every piece of furniture and every book since childhood. It was strange that her father had not locked away the large family Bible, as he usually did every morning after household prayers.

It was such a beautiful book, its pages gilt-edged, and one she had never herself handled before. She opened the leather cover and turned to the fly-leaf written in Papa's clear copperplate writing, and read through the first entry, the record of her parents' marriage, But it was the words beneath that leapt up into her face with such a smack that she felt her heart actually missing a beat. She held on to the desk, her knuckles white, until the swimming letters steadied enough for her to read them again:

Adopted,
Candida Rowena,
found in Candlemaker Row, parents unknown.
Date of birth, probably 9th November, 1809.

All she knew was that she was over the edge of the precipice now, well and truly, while she stared at the words, every careful loop of them. Behind those four terrible lines she found the sadness and the mystery she had always known were there, and which she had been waiting for, it seemed, all her life.

So this was why her parents had always denied her nothing. They must have felt they must shower everything they possessed on the foundling, to make up for the fact that she was a foundling, of course, and once that became clear to Candida, so many other things simply fell into place. She would need time to come to terms with the enormity of it all in her own way, and try to recover from the shock. Carefully she closed the Bible again, and went back to sit on her chair before her father returned.

'Yes, my dear,' he said. 'About the house in Canaan's Lane. I was just about to advise you to forget it. It has been sold, you see, to some gentleman. Your mother knows more about it than I do. You must ask her.'

To all outward appearances Candida remained calm in the face of this second tremendous blow. It was easy to do. Everything else paled beside the record she had just read in the Bible. She knew by her father's face that she had deceived him, anyway, when she merely smiled and left the study. As she closed the door, he picked up his pen again as though nothing very much had happened.

From then on and for many days to come she could think of nothing else every waking moment. How Mama had never spoken about her birth, for example. There had never been 'the day you were born' or 'the nurse who came when you were born', or any reference to it. She had often wondered why.

Then who was her real mother? Or her father? Were they still living? In Edinburgh? There could be no peace for her, and certainly no wedding, until she found out. It would be marrying someone under false pretences. How many people knew she was adopted? Candida became more and more convinced they were very few, or else someone would have let it slip long ago. As time went on she persuaded herself that she had deceived everyone, even Mama, with whom she discussed nothing except the most mundane matters of what to wear on which excursion out. After each one, she delivered a full report and hoped that her mother would not question her too closely—not yet.

Only Ross looked at her quizzically on the way to and from the Outside Classes, for by this time it was an accepted fact that he accompanied her, while Finlay accompanied Alanna. 'You were disappointed about the house, I hear?' he said.

'It is out of the question. Someone else has bought it already. Finlay never saw it, anyway,' she added as an afterthought.

'Then you will look for another house?'

'No. If it is not Paradise House, then it is nothing. I am no longer interested in houses, in any case. Besides . . .'

'Besides?'

'Besides,' she said after a pause, while the tears stung

her eyes, 'I doubt very much if I shall marry Finlay or anyone else, after all, and so I shall not require a house. Only that is between you and me, if you please.'

She looked up at him, in time to see that although his face remained calm and composed, two little devils of laughter danced in his eyes. Why on earth had she confided such a thing to Ross Alexander Laing, of all people? She could have cut out her tongue.

'You can trust me,' he said, and she smiled bitterly. 'But what has happened that you have come to such a momentous decision?'

'Nothing,' she said flatly, and too quickly, so that his green eyes searched her face as though to diagnose an illness. She shifted uneasily beneath them, but could not escape. 'Ladies are permitted to change their minds.'

'I always said our conversations would be spellbinding, and so they are proving. But I do not believe you have changed your mind so suddenly about Finlay Semple. You did that weeks ago, before you and I ever met,' he said with deadly accuracy, 'although you probably did not realise it at the time. No, I have seen a big change in you in the last few days, Candida. It is as though you have suffered a shock.'

She turned her face away, willing the tears not to well up in her eyes.

'You should have been treated for shock,' Ross went on. 'Did Aunt Alison never think of consulting your doctor?'

'She does not know . . . That is, she knows, but she does not imagine . . .' Candida's voice trailed off unhappily.

He put his arm around her unexpectedly, and gave her shoulders a sympathetic squeeze. 'I do not mean to pry, and I would not hurt you for the world. You do believe me, Candida?'

She almost told him the whole story then. His eyes were soft, and his words so gentle that she was sorely tempted to pour out all her fears. But she could not stop loving the only parents she had ever known, no matter how much she felt they had betrayed her by their silence, and she thought her heart would break unless she could speak to them first about it.

'Yes, I do believe you,' she said, 'and you are quite right. I have had the greatest shock of my life so far. I have not spoken to anyone about it. I cannot speak about it. Not yet.'

'It sounds to me as if you had uncovered a secret, and an unpleasant secret at that,' Ross said. 'But perhaps it is only in your mind that it is unpleasant. Another opinion may chase away the black clouds.'

'I hope that may be true in the end. But I haven't uncovered a secret. I only wish I had. I have only scratched the surface of it, so far.'

'Candida,' Ross turned her round to face him, now they had arrived at the Outside Classes, 'remember I will help you if I can. A trouble shared is a trouble halved, you know.'

But not this one, she thought. 'Yes, I'll remember,' she said out loud as they parted.

She did not doubt that one way and another, he was a very good doctor.

'Come with me for a walk, Kitty.'

'Yes, Miss Candida. But it's awfu' early. Where to?'

'Over to the Old Town. We shall walk there, but not back. I have ordered the carriage to pick us up at a quarter past ten, because Miss Alanna wants me to visit a new coffee-house in Princes Street with her later. When I leave you, the carriage will take you home again.'

They set off briskly, wrapped up against the weather, Candida in her fur-lined pelisse and Kitty in her dark hooded cloak, and before long their cheeks were rosy pink and their spirits uplifted that windy sunny morning.

'We will go up the Mound, Kitty,' Candida said. 'It's the shortest way to the Royal Mile. We need not go all the way round by the North Bridge.'

'Yes, miss,' Kitty said, as she puffed up the hill beside

her. 'I see they have made this a proper road at last, after all the mud and rubble of so many years.'

'It could not have been anything else, dear, when they were draining the Nor' Loch and needed somewhere to pile the rubbish.' Candida looked along the dry bottom where the Nor' Loch had been. 'They are going to make that space into another Garden for Princes Street. It will be a beautiful street, so wide, with gardens all along one side. And in the meantime the Mound can take carriages now. I believe it will become a very important Edinburgh road.'

'Yes,' Kitty said doubtfully as they laboured on up until at last they reached the Lawnmarket. 'Where now?'

'I am interested in a street called Candlemaker Row.' Candida tried to sound casual. 'If we go down to the Grassmarket, we will find it.'

'Oh no, miss, you are never going down there!' Kitty exclaimed. 'It is full of poor people, and pigs, and the fever!'

'It is early in the morning, Kitty. The poor people will be sleeping off the drink of last night.'

'Well . . .' Kitty agreed grudgingly. 'When will the carriage arrive?'

'In half an hour. That should give us plenty of time.'

'Plenty of time for what?'

'Oh, just to look in the shop windows, Kitty. There are shops here I have never seen before, but I have heard a lot about this one! Come!'

Followed by her maid, Candida entered a small shop in the Grassmarket lined all round by rows and rows of walking-sticks, a great many of them silver-topped. But the racks she made for were the ones with the parasols.

'Parasols are the thing for the summer,' said the old shopkeeper in very broken accents. 'But it is the umbrella you want now, mademoiselle. *Un parapluie*, as we say in France.'

'The umbrellas are all black, monsieur?'

'They have to be, *ma petite*, in, how you say—Auld Reekie? There is so much soot coming out of so many chimneys, no? The rain, it rains black here!'

Kitty accepted the awkward parcel philosophically and the old Frenchman bowed them out. They were no sooner out on the pavement again than Kitty recognised a woman walking towards them. Her clothes were too tight, with too many frills, and all rather grubby, and her moth-eaten muff did not quite cover the bottle she was trying to hide. But her face underneath last night's paint had once been quite pretty.

'This is the Janet Brown I was telling you about, Miss Candida,' Kitty muttered with her head down.

'Oh dear! I see what you mean, Kitty. Perhaps we should just hurry on by.'

But Janet Brown stood in their path, blocking the way, and gazing at Candida to Kitty's great discomfiture.

'Get oot o' the road, Janet Brown,' she said, 'and let my mistress pass.'

'Oh, pardon, miss.' Janet shook her head in disbelief. 'I've never seen you close up before, only from a distance, and ye're that like Mary Paterson ye could be sisters!'

The Grassmarket and Candida's world swirled around her head as she remembered the first words Ross had ever said to her. 'You are one of the two most beautiful women in all Edinburgh—as alike as two peas in a pod!' A week or so ago she would have considered such a remark from the likes of Janet Brown just as impossibe, just as insulting. Now, she thought it might be a clue to the mysteries that seemed to be heaping up, one on top of the other.

'Mary Paterson?' she managed to ask. 'Who is Mary Paterson?'

'My friend,' Janet said. 'We share the same lodgings, and she's a bit under the weather this morning. That's why I've been for some medicine for her. We . . . go about together in the evenings. Mary's the toast o' the town,' she added proudly.

'Are your lodgings far from here?' Candida asked, suddenly inspired.

'Oh no, miss, not far.' The girl's eyes narrowed. 'Why?'

'I wondered if you would take this parcel and keep it for us until this evening? This evening a gentleman will be with us to carry it. It is so awkward a shape.'

There was a startled gasp from Kitty, but Candida ignored it and continued to smile steadily.

'It's like talkin' to Mary, as sure as God,' Janet said. 'I canna say No to her either. Ay, I'll keep it for you, miss. D'ye ken the address?' she shouted after them, as Kitty marched her mistress away.

'Ay,' Kitty scowled.

'*Do* you know the address?' Candida asked, as they hurried off.

'Of course not, Miss Candida!' Kitty was scandalised. 'It will be a house of ill-repute, if you ask me. All the Edinburgh policemen will know it, though. They'll be keeping an eye on it. Frank'll know, and he won't like you asking about it any more than I do!'

'Now, then, Kitty, not another word, not to anyone except him! It's all part of a secret, all part of a plan of mine.'

'Oh no, not another of your little schemes!' Kitty tried hard to sound disapproving, but she had been a partner in so many of them, over the years. 'What is it this time?'

'I must see this Mary Paterson, Kitty, and if possible speak to her. I cannot tell you why, not yet.'

'No, miss,' Kitty sighed.

'You're a good girl, Kitty. One day I shall explain all this to you, but in the meantime I need your help, and no questions. Somehow we've got to get out of the house tonight.'

'I'll see what I can do,' Kitty promised, as they came to another shop where more people were beginning to stir.

'David Rhymer,' Candida read the name about the door. 'He appears to sell everything.'

'Rhymer's?' Kitty's nose wrinkled. 'I'm sure I remember that name from somewhere, but it was a long time ago . . . Yes, I was here. I found a parcel, I'm sure. Something wrapped up in a newspaper. I thought it was a kitten,' she laughed.

'Where?' Candida asked, her heart leaden, and dreading to hear the answer.

'Not here, miss. Up there,' Kitty pointed up another steep winding road out of the Grassmarket. 'In a shop doorway.'

They read the street sign, 'Candlemaker Row', in silence.

'Mother o' mercy!' said an elderly woman who had bumped into Kitty and stood staring at Candida. Then she crossed herself. 'Who are you, lassie?'

'Dinna tell her!' Kitty came to stand between her mistress and the old woman. 'Come,' she said, and put her hand into Candida's arm and pulled her away. 'If you had told her your name, you would never have got rid of her! She would come begging. I know her sort.'

'Which doorway, Kitty?' Candida asked, as they toiled up Candlemaker Row.

'That one,' said the flustered maid. 'No, that one, maybe. Oh, I canna mind, Miss Candida!'

'It doesn't matter,' Candida smiled sadly. 'Anyway, here is the carriage.'

They got into it thankfully, and first it set down Candida at Ambrose's and then it continued back along Princes Street until it turned off into Charlotte Square. Even by that time Kitty still had not recovered from her morning's adventures, so that she did not notice the sedan-chair that had been following and was now parked on the other side of the Square. Its curtains were pulled back, and an old woman watched where she went.

'Thirteen?' she sniffed. 'It was aye an unlucky number. Well, I've seen all I wanted to see,' she informed the chairmen who had carried her there. 'Ye can tak' me back, noo.'

She twitched back the curtains and began counting the coppers in her purse.

Candida could smell Ambrose's even before she came to it. The wonderful aroma of freshly-ground coffee pervaded everywhere, even to the pavement outside. From the tea and coffee shop on the ground floor she was ushered up the wide gilded staircase. All the little tables and chairs were gilt up here, too, and the seats round the walls padded with crimson velvet. Lighted chandeliers sparkled over and over again in the mirrored walls. She found Alanna, and Alanna was not alone. A young man was with her, a very young man, eager and round-faced, and, as she saw when he stood up, very short. But his courteous smile and shining sincerity made up for any deficiency.

Alanna made the introductions, looking even more flamboyant than usual, in scarlet. It must be wonderful to have such freedom, Candida sighed to herself, to be able to dress in such very bright colours and to meet young men without a chaperon. What other men did Alanna meet alone?

'This is our very dearest friend in Edinburgh,' she said. 'Donald Lonegan, from back home. He has just qualified in the ministry and is only waiting for a Call. Is that not so, Donnie?'

'That is what I was going to tell you, Alanna. I have received one from the congregation of St Catherine's-in-Grange.'

'Grange? Isn't that the district where Canaan's Lane is, as well?' Without waiting for an answer, Alanna rushed on off-handedly and, if Candida had not known better, she would have said almost nervously. 'Finlay may appear. He said he might.'

Mr Lonegan seemed to know who Finlay was; perhaps Alanna had been speaking about him before Candida arrived. Perhaps Alanna could not help speaking about him. She had often noticed that about people in love. Was that how the land lay? Had she been so busy about her own affairs that she simply had not seen what was happening under her nose? Candida realised with a savage pang of guilt that she had not thought of Finlay for days, far less spoken to him.

They were drinking their first sips of coffee when he arrived, and the glances between him and Alanna confirmed all her suspicions. The great difficulty, Candida thought as she toyed with the miniature spoon in her saucer, was how to speak to him alone. But when she rose to go, it seemed there was a conspiracy to solve it.

'You must leave?' Finlay got to his feet, while Alanna looked anxious and admiring. He had never looked so resolute before. 'I shall take you home, Candida. Mr Lonegan has promised to look after Alanna.'

He marched her masterfully down the stairs and into the brown carriage drawn up waiting. It was the first time she had ever been in it, and she could not help wondering how many times Alanna had occupied this same seat she sat in now, looking straight into Finlay's face. His eyes slanted away, and she detected a film of sweat on his brow.

'Candida . . .' he began, and took out his handkerchief.

'Dear Finlay, I know what you are going to say. Don't say it.' She took off the moonstone ring and held it out to him. It remained as obdurately milky as it had always been except once, and that had nothing to do with Finlay Semple—and everything to do with Ross Alexander Laing. 'Let me say it, instead. Our engagement is at an end. Our marriage is off. Is that what you wanted to hear?'

'Oh, Candida! Keep the ring, please. The strange thing is, I never felt fonder of you than I do now.'

'And I am fond of you. I always will be. But that is not enough for marriage, is it?'

'No.'

'It is Alanna that you love in that way.'

At the very mention of her name, the colour flew up

into his cheeks. She could almost feel his heart thud. Finlay did not argue.

'She has taken such an interest in the business, Candida! She has made it another world for me. Now I *want* to go to work in the mornings, to continue the name of Semple, bigger and better than ever! I am finished with my old way of life!'

Such enthusiasm *she* had never inspired, never hoped to see!

'You have all my good wishes, Finlay, both of you,' she said. What he had said was very true. She had never liked him better. 'And we shall remain friends?'

'Of course,' he said, clasping her hands in his. 'But what of you?'

'I have so much to do,' Candida said. 'Perhaps that was the trouble all along.'

It was one huge worry off her mind, at any rate. She felt almost light-hearted when she smiled and waved goodbye from the steps of No. 13 Charlotte Square, and the brown carriage bowled jauntily away. Now she was free to work out her own destiny, whatever that was and wherever it lay. She did not give Finlay Semple another thought.

Constable Frank Clarke was preoccupied, not to say worried, as he paraded down into the Grassmarket on his usual beat at about the same time. For weeks he had not seen Abigail, the old woman who usually came into the town from Gilmerton every Thursday with her little basket of shoe-laces and stay-laces, and Frank believed in finding out everyone's business and keeping a sharp eye on it.

He confided as much to Kitty that afternoon when they were walking out. She looked so pretty with her white cap frilling out over her auburn curls under her hood. He clasped her hand where it lay in the crook of his arm.

'It is very suspicious,' she agreed. 'How long is it since you last saw her?'

'Three weeks.'

'Oh, Frank!'

'Is she still living? That is what I ask. There have been so many people disappearing lately from the Royal Mile, and all unexplained.'

'Oh, Frank!' Kitty gazed up at him, utterly horrified. 'You don't mean somebody did her in?'

'You must not worry your pretty little head about it. I love you, Kitty,' he said, and his arm clutched her tightly to his side.

'I love you, Frank,' Kitty said, her insides melting.

'Will you marry me?'

'Like a shot!'

'Come in here.' He pulled her roughly into one of the closes and kissed her thoroughly. 'Say it again. Will you marry me?'

'Yes, please, Frank Clarke,' Kitty laughed between kisses.

'The only thing is, I don't know when it can be,' he sighed, as they continued their walk.

'I don't care! We can wait. Are we engaged now, Frank?'

'If only I could afford a ring,' he groaned.

'What about this one?' Kitty showed him the moonstone ring. 'Miss Candida gave me it only this morning. She said she didn't like it. But I like it. Do you, Frank?'

Frank put it on the third finger of Kitty's left hand, where it glowed with a soft pink light.

'Yes, it is very pretty, but the wedding band is the thing, Kitty. I shall buy you that. It will be pure gold,' he said proudly.

'Between us, every problem will be solved. I feel it,' Kitty said happily. 'So, now, help me with my latest. Miss Candida is determined to be in the Royal Mile tonight to meet Mary Paterson, and I must go with her.'

Frank Clarke looked at his intended with undisguised horror. 'Whereabouts in the Royal Mile?'

'Wherever she lives. Where is it, anyway, Frank?'

His face looked stern. 'She was thrown out of her

lodgings in the Royal Mile,' he said. 'She is in an even worse house now, at the top o' Leith Walk—Mrs Worthington's. I suppose it is your duty to go with Miss Candida, but you will certainly not go there without me, my girl! Do you hear me, Kitty?'

Liza invited her mistress below stairs, for once, for the four o'clocks.

'It is a special occasion, my lady,' she said, producing a white and pink iced cake from nowhere. 'My Kitty is engaged to be married to Constable Frank Clarke here.'

Frank stood stiffly to attention, and cleared his throat. 'It would make us even happier, my lady, if you could see your way to approve of it.'

'Of course I do, my dears! And I am sure Mr Forbes would wish me to add his congratulations.'

Lady Alison settled herself by the kitchen fire, accepted a cup of tea and a slice of the cake, and observed Candida's ringless hands and Kitty's sudden acquisition of the moonstone with apparent equanimity. But later, upstairs, it was a different matter.

'You will explain yourself, Candida.'

Candida had prepared herself. 'It is quite simple, Mama. I broke off my engagement to Finlay when he told me he was in love with Alanna.'

Outrage followed shock across Lady Alison's expressive face—that any gentleman should prefer someone else to her beloved daughter!—and while she struggled to speak, Candida forestalled her.

'Finlay was not very exciting, Mama. I do not believe I ever really loved him. It was far better to find it out now, rather than later.'

But her mother was not so easily diverted from the subject of Finlay. 'Your father was worried,' she admitted. 'He did not think Finlay was spending enough time in the business. He thought he was too fond of his pleasures.'

'Oh, Mama,' Candida laughed, 'let's have no excuses! You and Papa will both see that Finlay will become a model businessman in the future. Alanna is showing him the way. I just was not interested enough. Besides, now I prefer gentlemen with lean waists, and you must agree that Finlay's has become quite thick, lately.'

'Isn't that just a little flippant, dear?' Lady Alison asked.

'Perhaps it is, Mama, because I feel so relieved. The only thing I bitterly regret, more for your sake than for mine, is that wonderful wedding gown you got ready for me. I am truly sorry,' Candida said sincerely.

'It will just go on hanging there in its wardrobe until the right time comes, dear—and the right man.'

'Until the right time comes.' Candida looked at her mother, and wondered why with all her education and her common-sense Lady Alison had never told her the circumstances of her birth, or at least how she was found and then adopted. Now would have been the perfect opportunity to ask, if only Mama had not had one dreadful shock today already. As a result, the last thing she could discuss with her mother now was that she felt she was not a fit person to marry anyone.

'Finlay was not the right man for me, anyway, Mama.'

'Why?' Lady Alison asked sharply. 'Have you found another?'

'Another?' Candida's voice was startled. It was reflected in the sudden flurry in her heart. The only other man of any significance she had met lately was Ross, and to speak about him and marriage in the same breath was out of the question. 'Of course not, Mama!'

'I cannot say I am sorry to see the moonstone ring off your finger, Candida. Pearls are for tears. But was it quite right to hand it over to Kitty, do you think?'

'Why not, Mama? Finlay and Alanna are too taken up with each other ever to notice, and Frank and Kitty are delighted. They could not afford to buy a ring.'

'What now, dear?' Lady Alison asked.

'Now?' Candida smiled cheerfully. 'Kitty has invited me out to meet a friend of hers this evening. Frank will go with us, so it is bound to be all right.' She edged out of her mother's room, thankful to have got off so lightly after all.

'It's all fixed,' she told her maid at seven o'clock.

'But you will wear my best cloak, Miss Candida,' Kitty insisted. 'It is fuller, and Frank says you must be well covered up. Pull up the hood so that no one will recognise you.'

'Anything he says,' Candida agreed, putting it on and impatient to be off. 'He knows the Old Town. We do not. Where are we going?'

'It is to Mrs Worthington's lodging-house at the top o' Leith Walk.'

But when they got there at nearly eight o'clock, the place was in darkness.

'Perhaps we are too early,' Kitty said.

'Too early?' Candida could not hide her disappointment.

'These ladies do not usually go out until nine o'clock at least,' Frank informed them. 'But follow me. I'll knock them up.'

He entered the close first, swinging his lantern, and what they had mistaken for a bundle of rags rose up and faced them. Candida and Kitty clung together in terror.

'Och, now, Jamie, you gave the ladies a fright! Are you not at the taverns after a dram?' Frank asked kindly, and when a silly grin came to the man's face, they realised he was simple.

'I'm waiting for Mary,' he said. 'I aye wait for Mary.'

'Wait outside, then, that's a good lad,' Frank said, and when Jamie shambled out good-naturedly, they saw his bare feet were twisted. He was a cripple.

'That was Daft Jamie,' Frank said. 'He follows Mary Paterson wherever she goes.'

He hammered on the outside door, and hammered again. Janet Brown opened it after a long wait.

'So early?' she grimaced, the paint on her face cracking. 'Come in.'

They followed her up a creaking, shabby stair into one large room which contained two ramshackle beds and very little else. Janet pulled up the cover of one of them ineffectually. It could not disguise a disreputable straw mattress and the pillow rags. There was a heap beneath the cover of the other bed, heaving protestingly. Then a woman sat up.

No matter how unkempt, nothing could disguise the beauty of her pale hair, spun sugar in the candlelight, nor the perfection of her smooth pink body which she made no attempt to cover up. Candida's heart lurched. It must be Mary Paterson, it must be! But then the woman turned her face to them, and she saw that it looked old and so raddled with paint that it was impossible to make out its original features. She was frozen with horror. How could anyone think that she resembled her?

'What is it?' the woman spat out of a face of venom when she saw the two hooded ladies standing in the room with the uniformed figure of a policeman behind them. 'We've done nothing wrong! Get oot! Get the hell oot!'

Candida remained to the last, gazing at the heart-shaped outline of the woman's face, frowning, and committing it to her memory. She would draw it as soon as she got home.

Frank Clarke pulled her away. 'That's Mary Paterson,' he said. 'Beyond it, as usual. You won't get anything out of her tonight. Poor Mary!'

'Here's yer parcel.' Janet Brown thrust it into Frank's arms, and they made their way out past Daft Jamie to walk home.

'I wanted to speak to her,' Candida protested.

'A lady like you?' Frank snorted. 'Never! She would never speak to you. She would be too jealous of your fine clothes and your looks, Miss Candida.' He grasped her arm and Kitty's and guided them back to Princes Street.

A tall man stepped out of the shadows and watched them go with a grim look on his face. Ross Alexander Laing had not been long in Edinburgh before a word here and there soon elicited this address. His only surprise, visiting it for the first time, was to discover the previous callers. Then he, too, battered on Mrs Worthington's door.

'Take me to Mary Paterson,' he demanded, when Janet opened the door again.

There was a cold authority about him, even if what he was wearing was dark and nondescript and not at all the grand clothes of a gentleman, that put the shivers up Janet's spine. She did not dream of arguing. Up in the bedroom only his eyes were memorable, even remarkable. They were green, and as Mary saw, the kind that stripped the clothes off your back at a glance. She had not felt such a thrill for a long time.

'Who's askin'?' She drew the rags of her night flannel instinctively around her. This was one of the kind who would appreciate the unfolding of the layers, one by one. 'Ay, I'm Mary.'

'I've heard of you,' he said, sitting on her bed.

'Everybody has. I'm famous,' Mary simpered.

Janet Brown waited in the wings anxiously. She was sure this was not the right approach, not wi' this one, and she prayed that Mary would not burst into her favourite song, for she hadn't recovered from the effects of that bottle yet.

'How much for a good time?' Mary was asking the stranger.

'Anything you like,' he smiled pleasantly. Janet did not trust his smile, or the soft Irish in his voice. 'But it depends on age. I do not go with older women.'

'Old women?' Mary spat. 'An' how old d'ye think I am?'

'Twenty-four, twenty-five, perhaps?'

'Well, ye're wrong! I was nineteen a few weeks ago, on the 9th of November.'

'The 9th of November?' The tall dark man smiled, and tossed a few coins on the cover of Mary's bed. 'It was a pleasure talking to you, Miss Paterson.'

'An' goodbye to you,' she said, mystified, and then shouted after him. 'Ye missed yersel'!'

They heard him laughing on his way downstairs, but by the time he caught up with Candida and Kitty, escorted by Constable Frank Clarke, just arriving at No. 13 Charlotte Square, Ross was not laughing any more. By the light of one of the new gas street-lamps on the pavement outside the house, they could see that his expression was grim.

'Thank you, Constable,' he said crisply. 'I will attend to Miss Candida from here. You may take Kitty in by the mews.'

Before she had time to think, they had gone, and she was left alone with a man who was obviously in a towering rage, although what about, she could not tell.

'We cannot stand out here on this perishing night,' he said firmly. 'If I take you into your own house, there will be no opportunity to talk, and I am determined to have a word with you privately.'

'What about?' Candida asked. 'There is nothing to talk about that anyone else could not hear.'

'Oh yes, there is! We will go round the back, and up by the iron stairs into our rooms on the top floor.'

As they ascended the twisting staircase, the stony silence between them began to grate on her nerves with as much intensity as their shoes grated on the iron steps.

'What do you suppose this staircase is here for?' she asked nervously, clutching at the straw of something to say. 'Nobody ever uses it.'

'Fire.'

The curtness of his tone left her in no doubt that she was going to face an unpleasant interview. Why should she? she suddenly rebelled. She made a half-turn to go back down again.

'No, you don't!' He held her in a vice-like grip with one hand and unlocked the door at the top with the other. 'In you go!'

He propelled her into the sitting-room she and Mama had prepared last summer, only now it had been transformed. Alanna's hand had transformed it, of that there was no question. Ross turned up the lamps on each side of the mantelpiece, and the vibrant, clashing colours of the Indian rugs now hanging on the walls vied with the softer hues of Persian carpets heaped up here and there on the floor. He made no comment, and she was forced to the conclusion that Alanna had been making a collection for their new house, when they got it. Great urns were everywhere, some filled with peacock feathers, others with tall plumed grasses, and still more massed with the huge heads of dried hydrangeas, once blue but now turned purple like some poisonous wine. Candida felt she was drowning in a sea of colour. The room was closing in on her.

'What did you think you were up to tonight?' His voice stung like a whip-lash. It brought her back sharply.

'I cannot think what you mean! And, in any case, it is my own business.'

'I mean, what were you doing in one of the most notorious parts of Edinburgh in the first place? To say nothing of the fact that it was late at night, with only your maid for company.'

'Constable Clarke was with us.'

'Do you have any idea of how rough Leith Walk can be? It is on the way to the docks, you know. A man might be able to resist one attacker, or even two.' His green eyes flashed angrily. 'But what would have happened if a gang of foreign sailors had set about you? Which one of you would Constable Clarke have defended—first and last?'

The vivid room, and all these questions! For a fleeting second she wondered if the one caused the other; whether living in so restless a background inflamed his temper.

'It would have been Kitty,' he stated categorically. 'Naturally he would have saved his future wife, the mother of his children. And then what would have happened to you?'

'But I am nobody!' She was goaded at last into speech, and horrified by what she had said. Still, until she had proved her identity, it might as well be true. 'And I'm nobody's future wife, now,' she added. 'I am free. So what am I doing up here, to be harangued like this?'

Blue eyes blazed into green eyes, as they glared at each other angrily. There seemed to be no answers the one could give the other, they were on opposite sides, and they did not understand each other at all. But how could Ross understand? He did not know all she knew. She decided to answer one question, at least, and that might satisfy him so that he would leave her alone.

'I went to see Mary Paterson,' she said.

'I know. I followed you there.' He could not have said anything to bewilder her more.

'Why?'

'Why?' he echoed, so furiously that it aroused new depths of anger in her, depths she never knew were there. 'Why should I answer any of your questions, when you answer none of mine?' he blazed at her. 'What makes you think you cannot marry anyone—*now*? What has gone wrong with you—*now*, Candida?'

'You are asking me too many questions,' she spluttered indignantly. 'How can I remember any of them, let alone all of them? Besides, I do not have to answer, if I so choose!'

Ross totally ignored this last ditch of independence. 'Very well,' he said grimly, 'let us take them one by one. Why do you evade every question I ever ask you? That will do for a start.'

'I do not! I told you about Mary Paterson. I did not have to,' Candida said stiffly.

'We shall leave Mary Paterson for the moment.' He brushed the subject aside, reminding her of a bloodhound relentlessly on the trail. 'Much more important, what makes you think you cannot marry anyone? A few weeks ago you thought you could.'

'Ah! So now you have sniffed out the heart of the matter, Ross Alexander Laing!' Candida said bitterly. 'If it comes to that, it is the heart of me, the top and the bottom of me, everything!' She turned her head away momentarily, only to fling back again passionately. 'But it will get you no further than it has got me! The heart of it is a huge mystery. How can I tell you, when I don't know myself?'

She surprised herself with the depth of her passions. This conversation was only bringing to a head all her past suspicions, glimpses of something she dreaded to know —and yet had to know, or die. She hated him for making her face it. She hated him, she hated him!—and it showed on her face.

It made no difference to Ross. He studied her coldly for a moment and gripped her hands so tightly that it hurt.

'Then we shall try to get at it from another direction,' he said in a voice as incisive as a knife. 'Already you have told me that there is an unpleasant secret in your life, something that has upset you so completely that you are not the same Candida that I first saw on the 19th of September.'

'Yes, I have certainly changed,' she said, with a bitter twist to her mouth and tears in her eyes.

'Have you found out any more, Candida?'

'I can only tell you that it is a very old secret, one that I may never find out. If it has been a secret all these years—nineteen years, that I know of—why should it suddenly come to light now? I am up against a brick wall, but it is a wall of manners and feelings and emotions. That is what makes it so impossible.'

'Nothing is impossible,' Ross said positively, and Candida sighed. He simply would not let go. 'Then the secret is as old as you are. That, at least, is something to go on.'

Unless she diverted him somehow, he would worry away at it until he uncovered the truth. Now she understood why her parents had kept it so well locked away.

'Mary Paterson was not what I expected,' she said hastily.

'Mary Paterson.' He smiled shrewdly. 'The red herring.'

'She is *your* red herring, if you remember. You introduced the subject of Mary Paterson to me,' Candida reminded him coldly, pulling her hands away.

'But is she so much of a red herring, after all. I wonder? Did you speak to her, Candida?'

'She would not even look at me.'

Ross put his hands on her shoulders and wheeled her round to look in the heavy gilt mirror that now hung over the mantelpiece.

'Do you wonder?' he asked. 'Look at you, even if you are miserable and tear-stained, and then think of her. She is only nineteen, too, you know.'

'That woman could not be nineteen,' Candida cried. 'She had the face of an old woman!'

'She spoke to me,' Ross insisted. 'Her birthday is even on the same day as yours. She is nineteen, all right. Do you not think that is a strange coincidence?'

'While we are on the subject, I do not care to be followed wherever I go!' Candida deflected the conversation again, although Ross still looked thoughtful, as if a new idea had come into his head. 'You had no business to follow me,' she continued. 'You are not even remotely responsible for me. I can look after myself!'

'Nonsense, Candida,' Ross said, dragging his thoughts away from wherever they had been. 'Nobody else in the house knew you were out on the streets so inadequately protected, except me. What do you think another instinct of the male is towards the female—you who know all about instincts, if I remember correctly? It is to protect her.'

She stared at him. Inadequately protected—with Frank Clarke's massive bulk behind her? She had no doubt that Frank would take a gang of sailors or any other attackers and knock their heads together. Then she remembered Ross stripped to the waist, his muscular body. He was not as bulky as Frank. There was not a pound of extra weight on him. With a shiver, she realised he could probably knock the policeman to the ground with one blow.

'Furthermore,' Ross went on, 'you have been so upset lately that I never know what you might do next. Do you think I enjoy escorting a lady who darts off here and there into quite dangerous situations without any explanation? You remind me of a silverfish, these days, one of those silvery insects that dart about old fireplaces, impossible to catch.'

'You have caught me this time!' she could not help laughing.

His smile flashed for the first time, it seemed, in hours, and the sun came out again from behind the clouds that cold dark night in Edinburgh in front of the fire, and then his arms were round her, holding her close.

She leaned her head on his shoulder and wished with all her heart she could tell him her terrible secret, but that moment of weakness passed when his mouth closed over hers, and instead she felt a leaping response through all her body.

Dear God in heaven, she never dreamed it could be like this, the hot quickening in the blood, the longing to be closer to him still. She never dreamed she had been falling in love with him all along, until now. When at last he let her go, and she caught her breath again and her head began to clear, she realised that here was another complication in her life. It had been complicated enough already, but now it was worse than ever.

CHAPTER FIVE

'DID YE hear that, Janet?' Mary Paterson asked her friend after they had listened to the sound of Ross's firm footsteps fading away from Mrs Worthington's. 'I'm that well kent now that men pay just to speak to me!'

Janet watched her getting up out of the ramshackle bed and going over to peer in the brown-spotted mirror. She wondered if the effects of the gin were still distorting Mary's mind. Somehow, she had got the impression that the tall dark stranger had paid for something quite different. It was something he had found out.

'Ay,' she replied, frowning with the effort of trying to remember the conversation she had just overheard. 'Ay, ye're famous now all right, Mary.'

'Fancy him thinking I was through my twenties, though . . .'

Yes, that was it. Janet remembered it now. Mary had told him her birthday. But why should he want to know that, and be so pleased to find it out that he had even paid for it?

'It's the rouge, Mary,' she said aloud. 'It's all run. We'd better heat some water and wash our faces with the Windsor soap, and then put on some fresh paint.'

'I've half a mind not to,' Mary said, surveying her reflection half an hour later. Now that it was clean, her skin was clear and pure with only her natural colour glowing on her cheeks and lips. But there were dark patches under her eyes, and sags here and bags there, and funny lines between her nose and her mouth which were never there even a few months ago. That man with his challenging green eyes was right. God, it didn't take long to lose your looks in this game. 'Oh, to hell with it! Pass me the paint-pots, Janet.'

It was well after nine o'clock before they got to Swanston's, crowded with students, blaring with noise and thick with the fumes of tobacco and spirits. It was all the breath of life to Mary, and her own spirits rose accordingly as she led the way to a little table in the middle of the bar-room.

Janet bought the first drinks. If all went as well as usual, she would not have to buy any more. Sure enough, when she got back to the table with the glasses, Mary was chatting and laughing with a crowd of students already, and she tossed off her gin as if she were parched.

'Can I buy you another?' one of the students asked. He was tall and well dressed and spoke the New Town way, Scottish all right, but posh. 'My name is William Fergusson, by the way.'

'Is it, now?' Mary laughed, and sent out her signals. She ran her tongue over the red of her mouth so that the paint gleamed invitingly, and dropped her tippet from her shoulders to reveal plump young breasts scantily covered by the bodice of her red dress. William Fergusson flushed and grinned, and the other students sniggered and dug each other in the ribs. 'What about me calling you Billy, for short? Yes, I'll have the next few drinks wi' you, Billy, and anything else you fancy, long or short.'

Her meaning could hardly have been clearer, and all the students whistled and laughed. Tucked behind a table in the corner, two men watched the whole performance. One looked fearsome enough, but the other, bigger and darker, looked like the Devil incarnate, even more so now that he had grown a small black pointed beard.

'I'd like to get my hands over that one, Wull,' he said, staring at Mary.

'Sweet Jasus, an' how could we do that, William?'

'Easy! Ye can see for yersel'. Fill her fu' o' drink . . . We could have some fun wi' her first,' he added with his fiendish smile.

Wull compared her with the two drabs back home in Tanner's Close. Oh, for just one night with a woman like Mary Paterson! 'Nelly and Maggie would go mad,' he said despairingly. 'Of course,' he brightened a little, 'we could always send them out on a message.'

'She's leaving, anyway,' William growled, as Mary stood up, put on her tippet slowly and ostentatiously so that her next clients had every chance to admire her, and swaggered out with William Fergusson. 'And she's gone wi' the one that takes our subjects and pays us the money in Surgeons' Square.'

'Sure, an' he's the lucky one!' Wull said longingly, and then his eye fell next on Janet. 'We might get her friend along o' her as well. She doesn't look that bad, either. But it won't be easy. How can we arrange it?'

'I'm after thinking,' William said.

Liza took first Candida's umbrella and then Alanna's and shook them vigorously out of the front door. 'Oh dear, what weather!' she said, accepting Ross's hat and Finlay's. 'I'll take these to the kitchen to dry out. Lady Alison hopes you will all join her in the parlour for the four o'clocks. She is expecting you.'

Candida saw at once that this was quite a formal occasion, as she kissed her mother on her cheek. The oval table was spread with a damask cloth on which plates and cakestands vied with each other for room. Lady Alison presided over six tea-cups on the low table by the fire, with the silver teapot in her hand.

'Sit down, my dears,' she said in the gentle autocratic way she had when she expected no argument. 'Candida will hand round the cups, and with any luck Mr Forbes will arrive before long.'

'How is it you contrive to have so many different scones and cakes every day, Aunt Alison?' Alanna asked. 'Every time we take afternoon tea with you, nothing is duplicated.'

'There are receipts for over four hundred tea-breads in Edinburgh,' Lady Alison said, getting to her feet and handing round plates while Candida followed her with a cakestand in each hand. 'Help yourselves, do! It is not the tea which is so important today, anyway. It is the invitation from my brother Cameron and Lady Rosalie. Christmas is a family occasion here, and we always spend the festive season out at the Thistle Courts. This year is no exception, and we are all to go out as usual. You, Finlay, are especially welcome, along with Ross and Alanna. I do hope you can all come.'

Finlay Semple and Alanna exchanged glances. They seemed to heave a sigh of relief between them. Lady Alison chose to ignore it and sat down again, although Candida knew perfectly well that her mother was too clever not to have seen it.

'It is such a large house,' she continued, 'and there will be many other people coming—there always are. Their own family, if they can come, and us, and friends—especially Sir Walter Scott and Lady Scott, of course. Sir Walter is one of Rose's oldest friends.'

'I should be absolutely delighted,' Finlay said. 'Absolutely.'

Alanna murmured in agreement. They both looked quite dazed with pleasure.

'And you, Ross?' Lady Alison enquired.

'I only hope so,' he replied. 'But you know my commitments. They are quite pressing.'

The plate of Petticoat Tails that she knew were as crisp and fragile as eggshells, a mere sensation of sweetness before they melted in the mouth, suddenly weighed like lead in Candida's hand. Atholl Forbes could not have chosen a more propitious moment to enter the parlour if he had tried. His wife handed him the sixth cup of tea, and his daughter held out the silver cake-basket.

'It is the Paradise cake, Papa. Your favourite.'

'Paradise cake, is it? Ah, well! And that reminds me, you have told her about Paradise House, Alison?' Mr Forbes asked, settling himself comfortably.

'No, dear, not yet . . . Candida, a gentleman I have known for many years—almost thirty years, in fact, and who wishes to remain anonymous—has bought that house in Canaan's Lane you liked so well.'

'Ah, a mystery man! I do so adore mysteries,' Alanna exclaimed. 'Tell us more!'

'He has given me carte blanche to renovate and refurbish Paradise House in his absence. It seems he likes the style of this one.'

'You cannot blame him,' Ross put in quietly.

'It is quite bad enough that he has bought it at all, Mama! Why shouldn't we know who he is?' Candida asked, disappointment and irritation spiking her voice. 'It is adding insult to injury.'

'Perhaps he has a good reason,' Ross said reasonably.

'Of course he has, my boy!' Mr Forbes assumed his lawyer's voice. 'I have come across the sort of thing before, and there was always a good reason for it.'

'What can it be?' Alanna laughed. 'Shall we guess? Perhaps he is running away from his family? Or his wife?'

'Or it could be a surprise for the lady he would like to marry,' Ross joined in. 'Perhaps there is a good reason why he cannot tell her yet.'

'It can't be that,' Candida said crushingly, 'not at his age! At least you could tell us what he is like, this old gentleman, Mama?'

'What makes you think he is old?' Ross's eyes gleamed emerald in amusement.

'If Mama has known him for thirty years, he must be.'

'You heard that, did you, Ross?' Mr Forbes laughed. 'There she goes again! But that is an exceedingly good cake, Candida. Would there be another slice?'

She handed her father the cake-basket again, refusing to meet the laughter in Ross's eyes.

'In any case, I thought you and I could see to the house in the New Year, Candida,' her mother said. 'The chemistry class will be over then.'

'But we are going to the biology class next, Aunt Alison,' Alanna announced. 'It starts up in the middle of January, in the mornings, and we do not need gentlemen to escort us, which is just as well. Ross has his own classes in the mornings, and Finlay will be at business.' She smiled brilliantly at Finlay, and he smiled eagerly back. 'Candida and I can go alone, except for our maids.'

There were a lot of undercurrents in this conversation, Candida concluded. To begin with, Mama had adroitly avoided discussing the old gentleman. Mama could be very adroit when she liked, and when it mattered. He must be a very important gentleman. Obviously her mother was not going to betray his confidence, not even to her own family. And now Alanna appeared to be guiding Finlay firmly on the straight and narrow path of duty—on business bent, with a vengeance! What was more, he seemed to like it. Perhaps it was what he had been needing all along.

Worst of all, Ross was playing a cat-and-mouse game with her. Why? Would she get to the bottom of that before the walks to and from the chemistry class were over? And now, it seemed, he would not be spending Christmas at the Thistle Courts, either. Everything in the world was going wrong.

'Then it is all settled,' Lady Alison declared.

It was very far from that, Candida felt, in a sudden rush of rebellion. 'You will please excuse me, Mama,' she said, and fled upstairs.

On the 24th of December it was still raining, with a dismal persistence known only in Scotland, and on the east coast in particular. At four o'clock it was pitch dark, the rain suddenly stopped, and a malevolent cold gripped the air.

'It will freeze tonight,' Mr Forbes prophesised gloomily as he handed his wife and daughter into the dark green carriage. 'Mark my words!' But as the horses picked up speed into a rattling good pace he cheered up visibly, and with every mile that passed, his good humour returned.

'You are badly in need of this holiday, Atholl,' his

wife observed. 'And, for once, we have actually managed to get away on Christmas Eve! You have your golf-bag?'

Their gentle conversation went in one ear and out of the other, while the gloom outside reflected the gloom in Candida's heart. This year the excitement and the happy anticipation of packing their bags in Charlotte Square had completely passed her by. Even the Boxing Day gifts she had bought or prepared were of no interest. Not now.

'What are in all these?' she had asked Kitty idly, when all the boxes and bags were assembled and ready to go. Kitty described their contents right down to the last box. 'And this last one?'

'Perhaps the most important box of all, Miss Candida.' Kitty's tone was utterly reproving. 'It contains your presents for everyone. It is supposed,' she went on, warming to her theme, 'to be like the Three Wise Men taking their gifts to the baby Jesus.'

'Do you think I don't know that?' Candida retaliated. 'What is wrong with you, Kitty? The carriage will turn about and be back here for you and Liza and the others at six o'clock, the same as usual.'

'Yes, miss,' Kitty sighed. 'I dare say.'

'So that's it! You do not want to go . . . Because of Frank Clarke, I suppose?'

'It won't be much of a Christmas without him,' Kitty wailed. 'It won't be much of a Christmas for him, either.'

Candida put her arm round Kitty's shoulders. 'I know the feeling,' she said sadly.

And now it was intensified. Every rut in the road hurt her, when they had never hurt her before. Every bone in her body ached. Everything ached, including her heart. The moon came out, cold and brilliant, riding above the stairs, and the wind that had howled for weeks fell silent before its silver majesty.

'The trees are white with frost,' Lady Alison said. 'It is all so beautiful, Atholl. Always, out here, it is like fairyland, but never so much as at this time of year.'

It was true. The carriage slowed down almost to a stop, the horses wheeled sharply to the right, and they were passing the lights of the lodge. Then they were in darkness again as they wove a path through the trees with only flickering patches of moonlight dappling the way ahead with silver, until at last they left the trees behind and came out into a hollow sparkling with frost.

The Thistle Courts always tugged at Candida's heart-strings, always at first sight an enchanted castle, but now bathed in the cold moonlight and touched with hoary fingers it was a sparkling Palace of Ice. It was a once in a lifetime experience, and she should not be seeing it alone. Candida felt ridiculously alone, sitting there with her parents, and lonely. She had to hold back her tears.

But inside the house it all presented a very different picture. In the great hall the holly and the ivy had been freshly brought indoors, so that the visitors could smell the greenness before they even saw it. Huge swathes adorned the ingleneuk where the logs burned low and red, and above every doorway the rowans were twisted into the shape of the Cross.

'No witches here, Rose!' Lady Alison kissed her sister-in-law.

'No witches. No bad luck,' Lady Rosalie Kyle welcomed them. 'And Cameron is just about to make doubly sure.'

'I always wondered how you lifted the Yule Log in,' said Mr Forbes.

They watched as Sir Cameron and two men pulling a sledge dragged in the stump of a withered tree. Someone had roughly carved it to look like an old woman.

'Get everyone here, Rose,' he said. 'It is time for Christmas to begin.'

All the guests, with the household staff behind, assembled in the hall for the ceremony. There were people Candida had never seen before, young and old, and all smiling and laughing when the men heaved the Yule Log into the embers in the fireplace and the sparks flew up the chimney. The servants went round with trays of glasses and tiny bannocks cut twice crosswise into farls to symbolise the Cross, and Sir Cameron proposed the toast.

'To the Old Wife of Christmas,' he said. 'Blaze away!'

'Blaze away,' everyone echoed, including Finlay and Alanna standing close together. But of Ross there was no sign . . .

It was later in the evening and almost time for bed when the bangings started on all the doors of the Thistle Courts.

'The carol-singers,' Lady Rosalie announced, and Sir Cameron went to open the large front door. 'They are from the villages on the estate.'

The carol-singers stood at the open door, each one with a broom on his shoulder and sang the first carol. Then they 'swept the good luck in', and were joined by the others who had come in through all the other doors. It was Aunt Rose's idea to put a little crib by the side of the ingleneuk in the hall where everyone gathered round and joined in the carols. It went on till midnight struck.

'Now He is born,' Uncle Cameron said. 'Let us welcome Him.' After a short prayer, the carollers went away, and one by one and two by two the household went to bed.

'I have been downstairs already!' Alanna bounced into Candida's room on Christmas Day, dressed for once in white, with pink and pale brown trimmings. The delicate colours did not suit her. Her dress made her look almost drab. 'All the men are going out to golf. It is a glorious day!'

The frost had gone, Candida saw in one glance out of the window, and it was one of those curious spring-like days that often occur in the Edinburgh winters. 'It is the same every Christmas Day out here,' she said. 'The men play golf and the ladies go to the Kirk.'

'We will not even have lunch till two o'clock,' Alanna said. 'The whole house is being centred on Sir Walter

Scott. It seems he writes from six till nine in the mornings, breakfasts until eleven, and golfs until two. He will not change his routine even for Christmas.'

'We are used to it. He is upon the second edition of his *Tales of a Grandfather*', Candida said, selecting a pale green gown trimmed with a darker green splashed with a thousand scarlet spots.

'Oh, how beautiful, Candida! It looks like Christmas.'

'So Mama said.' Candida climbed into it dispiritedly. 'And, of course, we must all have something new for Yule. There is no news of Ross, I suppose?'

'He is always busy,' Alanna said lightly. 'Nobody has ever made head or tail of Ross! He comes and goes at a dizzy speed, and he always has half a dozen irons in the fire at the same time. Goodness knows what he is doing in Edinburgh today, I'm sure! Finlay Semple is much easier to follow, do you not think?' She cast an anxious look at Candida while she adjusted her gown in the oval pier-glass by the window. 'How did you get on with him?'

'Finlay Semple is a very nice young man,' Candida found herself describing him, now at this distance. 'You must remember he never knew his mother. I'm sure that if he had the firm guidance of the right woman, he would go far.' She touched Alanna's arm. 'You must not feel embarrassed to talk to me about him, dear Alanna. I never loved Finlay, and he never loved me. It was all a mistake.'

'Oh, Candida! But I love him! I love him so much . . .'

After they came back from the Kirk, they wandered down to the playing-field together to watch the boys and young men at the foot-races and the shooting and the hammer-throwing, and for the whole of that hour Alanna spoke of nothing else but Finlay Semple. She poured out her heart.

'It was so fortunate I did not waste my time on Paradise House, Candida. It would have been quite wrong for Finlay, and too far away from the business. And I have the feeling,' she laughed breathlessly, 'that the next house I go to view will be for him and me together! If I play my cards right, that is.'

'But what about Ross?'

'Ross?' Alanna exclaimed in surprise, as if they were speaking about a total stranger and not her brother at all. 'Oh, Ross!' She dismissed him with a wave of her hand. 'He will be going back to Ireland, of course, as soon as his studies are over.'

Lunch was a dreary affair for Candida. The football match in the afternoon was even drearier, but Alanna insisted they must go. 'Finlay is playing!' she enthused.

Candida watched him puffing up and down the field, and thanked her Maker for her many blessings in this life. She had been rescued from certain death in a shop doorway, brought up in luxury, kindness and in the fear of God ever since, and now, whatever happened, she had been spared Finlay Semple. She even became quite cheerful.

'Yes, I really enjoyed it,' she assured Alanna when, in the fading light, it was over at last. 'What now?'

'Dinner, I hope and trust, before I fall down and die with hunger,' Alanna replied characteristically when they left to go indoors to wash and dress for the occasion.

But neither Candida nor her maid felt very enthusiastic that evening.

'What shall it be, Miss Candida?' Kitty asked.

'I am only going to wash, Kitty, and you had better attend to my hair, if you will. I am not going to change my dress. There does not seem to be any reason to change, does there?'

'No, miss,' Kitty agreed dolefully.

Candida counted twenty-nine people at the dinner-table. There was a space two or three seats down from her on the left-hand side, but just now her cousin, the eldest son of Sir Cameron and Lady Rosalie, was addressing her.

'You've grown up in a hurry,' Jamie Kyle said admiringly at her side, while his little French wife Blanche beyond him nodded and smiled in agreement.

'And you have both grown younger!' She looked at Jamie's shock of auburn hair above his youthful face and then at Blanche. 'How can you both be thirty? Where are the children?'

'Upstairs,' Blanche told her. 'I do not know if I can stay long at the table. They are in a naughty mood. It's Christmas!'

'And, to prove it, here is the Scotch broth,' Jamie groaned ecstatically. 'There is not a great deal of it going about in France, you know, Candida.'

'No,' she laughed, 'I do not suppose there is,' Then she became aware of someone standing behind her chair.

'Move down one, Jamie darling,' Lady Rosalie said from the bottom of the table. 'Ask everyone to move down one place. I think Ross would like to sit beside Candida.'

While the shuffling and the good-natured bantering and the reseating was going on, she felt the blood in her heart congealing and then all of a sudden Ross was at her left side. She could not believe it! He was there; he looked handsomer than ever, lean and clean in dark green and white. Candida was aware that all the ladies eyed him approvingly, and she felt the forbidden tremors begin again.

'I had no idea you would come,' she said, caught so completely by surprise that she was unable to keep the pleasure out of her voice. 'I never thought I . . . that is, we never thought we would see you this Christmas.'

'But you are pleased, Candida?'

He was smiling, but she saw the pleading in his eyes, and in that single second time stood still for them, and she realised she had passed the point where she had a choice any more, for better or for worse.

'Yes, I am pleased,' she admitted. 'If only to have someone who understands to come and see Candlelight with me.'

'Now you are teasing!' As he served her with a slice of goose, his hand brushed her arm, and a delicious shiver ran through her. She moved quickly away. 'I like you to tease me, you know,' he said softly.

'You are the one who teases me, Ross Alexander Laing! No, only one slice of goose, but plenty of apples.'

'Do you think you should, Candida? They are soaked in rum! Perhaps its influence might allow you not to shy away every time I touch you.' Ross piled the apple stuffing on her plate. 'That would be very interesting. It was, last time, as I recall,' he added with a grin.

Her heart was racing with excitement, stirred by his words, and when his hand closed over hers in her lap she held on to his fingers. She could not let go, and she could not stop herself gazing up into those astonishing, astonished eyes to see her reflection there. She saw how the dark greenery of Christmas on the walls behind made a perfect frame for her pale green dress, and the bright halo of her hair. She was aware, that, in his eyes at least, she was beautiful, and sitting there side by side, the space between them dwindled.

'Did you really think I could remain in Edinburgh tonight, if it was humanly possible to be here? Oh, Candida, you do not know me at all, do you?'

'How much time is there for me to try? When are you going back?'

'Later tonight, unfortunately.'

The chilling thought entered her mind that perhaps it was fortunate, instead. She laid her fork and knife down carefully and precisely on her plate. What could he be doing in Edinburgh when all the colleges and the University were closed down for Yule? She did not know him, indeed. On the other hand, that was nothing compared with how much he did not know about her.

'I'm sorry,' she sighed.

'We are not going to be sorry, not for one minute of this whole night,' Ross said firmly. 'There may be plenty of time to be sorry in the future, but not tonight. This night belongs to you and me, Candida. Look, here is the hen and her eleven little chickens.'

'Aunt Rose makes them every year,' Candida said,

when the brandy was poured over the large plum pudding in the centre of the vast silver ashet and the eleven small puddings surrounding it, to signify the Twelve Days of Christmas. When a light was put to them, there was a glorious blue flame for a minute and then all the little sprigs of holly were swiftly stuck back on them again, for luck. 'I do not think I can eat any.'

'Corset or no corset,' he murmured in her ear, 'you are going to eat this tiny portion. With brandy sauce, furthermore. I know how to loosen your laces, if necessary.'

'Now you are being wicked!'

'I hope to become more wicked as the night goes on!' he promised.

When everyone had finished and they had all gone outside to watch Sir Cameron set the bonfire alight, it was still fine and even quite mild.

'A glass of punch, my dear?' said a voice in her ear, and Candida turned to find Sir Walter Scott with a tray of glasses in his hands. 'Yes, here I am again this year. It is the only duty Cameron and Rose allow me to perform all week. And you, sir?' he invited Ross. 'It is customary here. The fire to celebrate the Birth, and the punch to wet the Baby's head.'

At that moment the flames leapt up in a roar of yellow sparks.

'I am surprised the fire took,' Ross said, 'after all the wet weather.'

'Wet, yes, but green,' said Sir Walter. 'You know the old saying, do you not? "A green winter fills the kirkyard."'

'The kirkyards of Edinburgh were doing a brisk trade already, without this,' Ross replied, and a great shudder seized the whole of Candida's body, while Sir Walter hesitated for a minute as though to prolong the discussion before shaking his head and moving away.

'You are cold,' Ross said. 'We had better go back inside.'

'No. We do not dance in the house on Christmas

Night,' Candida pulled herself together to explain. 'It is always in the barn. Over there, where the little lanterns are lit all around.'

'Then drink up your punch and let's go. There is nothing like a barn-dance,' said Ross, taking her arm. She tingled from head to toe, and she knew it was not because of the punch. 'Everyone lets their hair down at a barn-dance. What about letting yours down for once, Candida?' He began to pull the ribbons out gently, one by one. 'It is something I have always wanted to see.'

Standing there with the muted light of the lanterns behind her, she could not know that the fair, almost silver, strands of the full glory of her hair shimmered like spun sugar. All she saw was a terrible sadness in Ross's eyes, as if he had seen something he had dreaded to see, before he led her silently into the barn where the heat and the noise met them like a wall.

Many dances later she was still disconcerted. She could not get that look out of her head. What had he seen? What was the matter? In the midst of all the laughing celebrations she felt like a ghost, insubstantial.

'You will have to tell me,' she said, when he took her in his arms for the first waltz of the evening. 'Why did you look so sad?'

Ross held her close, as if to comfort her. It was too close to be proper. She hoped her mother and her father could not see her in the crush of all these people, but the strange thing was, she did not care if they did. The only thing that mattered now was being in his arms, with his cheek on hers, with his mouth she ached to kiss only an inch away.

'Have you never felt sad, Candida, to see a beautiful flower? A perfect rose, perhaps? It can bring you almost to tears. And that is how I saw you; lovely, delicate and so easily bruised.'

It was a lie. She knew it was a lie, no matter how plausibly delivered in that soft Irish brogue. That was not what he had seen at all. Curiously, the knowledge lifted her spirits instead of casting her even further down. Now, and for evermore, she would always know when Ross was telling her lies. It gave added strength to a 'rose' who was very far from delicate. It gave her the insight to realise that if she had suspected him of hiding something all along, now it was confirmed. At first she had thought it was a body in a coffin, and she had been proved wrong there. But whatever he was hiding, it was connected with that body in a coffin, she was sure.

Then she was swept away into the magic of the dance, close in the arms of a man she knew was lying to her, and happier than she had ever been in her whole life. Ross had a reason for it all, she told herself, a good reason. Where had she heard that before, quite recently? 'A good reason.' Was it something about Paradise House? The question entered her mind, registered, and was filed away.

When midnight struck on the stable clock, Ross guided her discreetly out of the barn. 'Come,' he said. 'Here is your wrap.'

'Where are we going?'

'Over here.' He pulled her into the shadows, by the ivy, round the other side of the house. 'It is Boxing Day now, and I can wait no longer to give you this.'

He handed her a square box. In the shadow she could hardly see what was in it. She took a step out into the moonlight and saw the gleam of golden strands knotting together small pale stones.

'It is a bracelet! And the stones are the same as the large one in one of your boxes.'

'Yes,' he laughed, fastening it around her wrist. 'I thought you would not miss that. In fact, I hoped you would not. These are small opals to match that large one, and these are the gemstones to reflect your moods, Candida, not moonstones.'

'They are beautiful,' she said. Thank you.'

'Thank me properly, then.'

She lifted her face to his and went on a voyage of discovery. With every kiss he bound her to him with threads of gold. Each kiss was another new thread, tweaking the older threads as well. They were kisses to say No to freedom, and as she gasped for air she remembered she had a task to do, she needed freedom to do it in, and it should have been done before all this happened.

But his touch sent a thrill right down her body, from her scalp to the soles of her feet, yet it was in neither place. His fingers touched the pit of her neck and ran delicately up to her ear, then on to her hair. They were never still. The tips of his fingers strayed beneath the collar of her dress, raking the soft flesh of her shoulders, then down to the more ample softness below her collarbone. A convulsion seized her, making her feel empty and then congested. Its power both thrilled and frightened her, and she fought weakly with herself to move away. He must have seen the mounting panic in her eyes, for his hand was now caressing her neck. Relief overwhelmed her. He had not challenged her to surrender. She was safe again, and she raised her lips to his and kissed him with what felt like gratitude.

The moon came round to that side of the house, and in its light the bracelet gleamed on her arm around his neck. It was easy to see the opals sparkling subtly, managing even to outshine the diamonds that surrounded each one, and glowing a soft rose-pink.

That last week of 1827, that week between Christmas and the New Year when Ross had long ago gone back to Edinburgh, seemed never-ending to Candida. She was wasting time at the Thistle Courts when there was so much to do at home. She spent a lot of time with her sketchbook, and remembered to leave it always in her bedroom, so that it could be taken with her when at last they could go. It came as an extreme relief when Lady Alison said that of course they would all take in the New Year as usual at the Tron Kirk in the Royal Mile. Kitty had the bags packed before ten o'clock in the morning.

'Then you have stopped moping, Kitty?'

'Oh yes, miss!'

'We will not leave until eleven o'clock tonight, you know.'

'No, Miss Candida. I am seeing to it that we will not keep anyone waiting. We are ready to go.'

'You mean you cannot wait to see Frank Clarke again, Kitty! Will you see him tonight, do you think?'

'On Hogmanay?' Kitty looked scandalised. 'I should hope so, indeed! You are supposed to take the New Year in with your nearest and dearest,' she said indignantly.

The day dragged out into an eternity, until at long last the procession of carriages drawn up before the Thistle Courts was ready to go, the luggage finally stowed away, the steps folded up and all the doors slammed shut. Kitty and Liza sat on either side of Candida, facing her parents.

'I hope the three of you are not too crushed,' Lady Alison said anxiously.

'Oh no, my lady,' Kitty said enthusiastically and squeezed even further into the corner, while Candida smiled and shook her head.

She would have cheerfully sat on a tightrope, if it meant getting back to Edinburgh. As it was, Kitty and Liza wedged her in quite comfortably. She did not feel even one rut on the road.

They arrived at the Tron with half an hour to spare, half an hour in which to become infected by the mood of the lively, swaying crowd, to watch the hawkers with their trays of false faces and carnival hats, and feel the excitement rising as the hands on the four-sided clock above moved inexorably on. While the watch-night service was going on inside the Kirk, the Het Pint of mild ale spiced with nutmeg and laced with whisky was carried round the crowd in scoured copper kettles, and steaming noggins were offered to all and sundry. There was so much to look at and so many people to see that it came as a shock to find the hands of the clock suddenly pointing to one minute to twelve.

The crowd surged forward, sweeping Candida and her

maid away from the family group right to the front, and as midnight struck and 1828 began, she found herself face to face with the old woman they had bumped into in the Grassmarket a few months earlier.

'So it's you again, my poor lassie,' she said, grasping Candida's hands and gazing into her face with infinite sadness. 'Sooner or later we must talk. I canna go to meet my Maker until we do.'

Kitty fought her way to her mistress's side, and pulled her away. 'What did I tell you?' she demanded. 'I knew that woman was up to no good from the first! Oh, if only I could see Frank, miss.'

'Why, is he here somewhere?' Candida asked dully.

That was twice in the space of a week someone had looked at her with the same sad, almost pitying, expression, and nasty little fears and worries were beginning to form in her heart.

'He is bound to be,' Kitty said. 'If only we could find him, he would help us back to the carriage.'

But in the constant bombardment of young men, who for just this one night of the year had licence to kiss any lady they met, there was no uniform to be seen, and no Frank. So many people were wearing masks, some funny, some grotesque, that Candida recognised nobody. Yet, among them all, one tall figure stood out unmistakably. She grasped Kitty's arm, and pointed to him. Just then he was joined by another man, just as tall but very burly. They were both dressed in plain dark clothes and masks, and they passed by so close that they might have touched them.

Neither Candida nor Kitty could put out a hand, or utter a word. For Ross Alexander Laing and Constable Frank Clarke, far from being with their nearest and dearest on Hogmanay—or even seeing them—were in hot pursuit of two gaily painted ladies. One of them wore a red dress.

'Oh!' Kitty found her voice first. 'Did you see that, Miss Candida? Mr Ross and Frank were after Mary Paterson and Janet Brown! How could they? Oh, how could they? I'll never speak to Frank Clarke again!' She burst into tears.

For the next few days Kitty trailed about tearful and upset, refusing even to look at her beloved. Candida remained calm, outwardly at least. She was forced to be, in the sudden onset of her father's illness.

'It is a fever, certainly,' said the doctor, 'but what fever, it is hard to say just yet. I shall come back night and morning to keep my eye on him.'

At the very mention of the dreaded word 'fever', Lady Alison was thrown into a paroxysm of consternation and terror. Everyone in Edinburgh lived with the typhus fever just round the corner.

'He has never been ill before,' she wept. 'He has always been so strong . . . He has been working too hard, that's what it is! But I thought our holiday had done him so much good!'

'You will stay out of this room in the meantime, until we see what it is, Mama,' Candida said with new-found authority. 'I cannot have you both ill!'

'We will have to get in a nurse,' her mother insisted as she was being ushered out. She had never seen this side of Candida before. 'You cannot possibly know what to do, dear.'

'Somebody once told me that I had the makings of a first-class nurse,' Candida said grimly. 'Now is the time to prove it. This may only be the fever of a chill, and we do not want any strange nurses coming in here, perhaps out of houses which have had typhus. No, nobody else has to come near Papa,' she said firmly. 'We will take no risks.'

'But he could be ill for days! Where will you sleep?'

'In his dressing-room, with the door open so that I can hear him. Send Liza every now and then, and I shall keep you informed, I promise, dearest Mama.'

She closed the door firmly and went to smooth her father's sheets and straighten his pillows. He was certainly very hot. She wrung out a cloth in a bowl of cold water and bathed his face. She continued to do so until it was time to give his next powder.

For the next few days she threw herself into nursing, not surprised in the least to find she had a talent for it. Besides, the more she was able to help her father, the more she soothed her own wounded feelings which she was trying so hard to forget—as well as the man who had caused them.

'Here is the last of these powders, Papa,' she said on the third day, handing him a glass of water to wash it down. 'Although I am sure they might as well have been made of face-powder, for all the good they have done. It was staying in your bed and keeping warm which has cured you. I have a great deal more faith in herbs. They possess great medicinal properties. That is the next study I am going to make.'

'And how did you get on with your last study, Candida? The family tree, was it not?' Mr Forbes asked casually, but his eyes were very shrewd and watchful. 'How far did you get?'

Was she never going to escape from the problem? Could she not just go back in her life three short months to when she was eighteen, without a care in the world? These last few days has been so peaceful here with her father, with plenty to do and plenty to occupy her mind. It had been a holiday, an escape.

'Not very far,' she answered shortly, trying to avoid his gaze.

'But you made a start? Where did you start? How?'

Candida took a deep breath, on the verge of taking the plunge. She visualised what might happen if she gave him his answer: 'In the fly-leaf of the Bible, Papa.' Then she imagined the uproar there would be when her mother was brought into it, which was inevitable. No, with her father not fully recovered yet, it was unthinkable. She expelled her breath again in a deep sigh and retreated from the verge hastily.

'To tell you the truth, Papa, I did not even begin,' she lied. 'Something else happened, I forget what, and I just lost interest for the time being. I shall try again sometime in the future.'

'Hm,' Mr Forbes said. He even seemed disappointed. Then they heard Lady Alison's feet coming along the corridor, and he brightened up.

'Alison!' he greeted her. 'How much longer must I stay in this wretched bed?'

'Well, dear, you look a lot better to me! But we had better consult your nurse.'

'The doctor will be back later this morning, Mama. I think he will allow Papa to get up for a while this afternoon. We have escaped the typhus this time again, it seems.'

'You have done more than your share, Candida. I shall take over now,' Lady Alison said. 'Tell Kitty to get you a bath, and then have a long soak and afterwards lie down in your own bed for an hour or two. Alanna is itching to see you, for some reason, but she can wait until this evening when you are rested.'

'More than your share, indeed,' Mr Forbes agreed. 'If I am ever ill again . . .'

'Which God forbid!' Lady Alison sat on his bed and held his hand.

'. . . I hope you will be my nurse again, my dear,' he continued. 'She was always so cheerful, and so calm,' he was explaining to his wife when Candida made her way wearily up to her own room.

Calm, she thought with a wry smile when, an hour later, she lay in her bath and surveyed her jumbled feelings.

Afterwards, going to bed did not appeal to her. Going out into the fresh air after all these days cooped up in a sick-room did, no matter how cold and windy the day was outside. The brisker the better, Candida decided, and set Kitty to assemble her outdoor clothes. She was just about to put them on when Alanna knocked on her door.

'I heard you were back in the swim again,' she said, 'and that Uncle Atholl is a lot better. Oh, are you going out, Candida? I did so hope to have a little chat with you.'

'You may,' Candida told her, 'but outside. I am going out to fill my lungs with fresh air. Would you like to come with me, Alanna?'

'Well . . .' Alanna glanced out at the tops of the trees waving in the wind, and then suddenly made up her mind. 'Well, if you will wait until I run and put on everything warm I possess—yes, dear. It will do our complexions the world of good!' she said, and dashed off.

'Does she ever think about anything else but her looks?' Kitty groaned. 'If you told her coal-dust was good for the skin, she would be off hot-foot down a coal-mine!'

'Oh, Kitty,' Candida laughed. The laugh turned into a giggle when Kitty joined in, and then became uncontrollable. 'Oh, Kitty, I don't know what I would do without you!' She wiped her eyes at the end of it. 'You have made me feel so much better!'

'What have you been doing since I saw you last?' she asked Alanna as they clung together and battled against the wind in Charlotte Square.

'Talking to Donnie Lonegan, last Friday. I told him the chemistry classes were one thing, the biology classes will be another, but they are not really what we want, are they?'

'They are only scratching the surface,' Candida agreed. 'Now, after this scare over my father, I want more than ever to know about curing human beings, and we can never do that until we understand the workings of the body.'

'Well, we cannot get any further, not legitimately, at least . . .'

'But, Alanna?'

'But Donnie Lonegan may help us,' Alanna went on to explain.

* * *

They had been attending the biology classes for some weeks before Alanna told her one day in February that the way ahead was clear at last.

'Donnie will get us into Dr Knox's anatomy class on Thursday morning,' she said. 'Can you borrow men's clothing from somewhere?'

That afternoon Candida went along to the study as usual.'

'My dear child,' Mr Forbes said, 'I will say it again. It is a disgrace in a country so enlightened as Scotland that you are having to go in by back doors even to these Outside Classes. It is a disgrace that this University does not admit women. I have seen for myself that you might even have become a doctor, given the opportunity.'

'That is something, coming from you, Papa!' Candida seized her chance. 'Then I trust you will not disapprove of our latest efforts to become educated? I would rather do it with your knowledge than without it.'

'Do what?'

'Alanna and the Reverend Donald Lonegan have hatched a plan to admit us to one of Dr Knox's anatomy classes. He will obtain two pass-cards from medical student friends, if we can get ourselves up as men.'

'Your mother would take to her bed for a week if she knew of any such hare-brained scheme! And I am very suspect of Dr Knox's subjects. They worry me. You do understand that he will be dissecting a body, Candida?'

'I know, Papa,' she said, her heart sinking.

'But you will find coats and trousers and shirts in my wardrobe, and hats on the top shelf, since it is in a good cause.'

'Oh, it is! I love you, Papa!' Candida flung her arms round his neck.

On Wednesday night it was all arranged in darkest secrecy, with a lot of flitting back and fore by Kitty on tiptoe to Mr Forbes's wardrobe.

'The last thing is the hat, Miss Candida, always providing I can get your hair bundled up inside it.'

Kitty regarded her mistress critically as she stood

there in a pair of her father's cut-down trousers and coat.

'But will I pass, Kitty?'

'I hope so, I'm sure, Miss Candida,' she said doubtfully.

The next morning, Candida and Alanna slipped out very early and got into the cab that had been so carefully arranged the day before. Before it was properly light, the horses spanked along Princes Street, over the North Bridge and up to Surgeons' Square, where Donnie was waiting. Candida had not expected to see him in the company of Finlay Semple.

'Oh, Finlay insisted!' Alanna said. 'After all, it is a momentous occasion, and he said the more in our party the better, so that we can slip by the entrance more easily.'

Candida could see the sense of that, when Finlay and Donnie presented all the cards, and in the crush she and Alanna marched past boldly, up the stairs and in through the doors of the balcony.

'So far, so good,' Alanna hissed behind her. 'Now, right down to the front!'

By half-past nine every seat of the lecture hall was filled, and the roar of excited masculine voices all round was deafening as the students laughed and shouted to each other while they were waiting for the great man to appear.

The arrival of Dr Knox reduced them all to silence. He looked very urbane in his violet velvet suit and white ruffles, and his black eye-patch gave him a dashing, cavalier appearance. He was more than a little frightening. A tall young man stood a behind him, very much in his wake.

The trolley was wheeled on, with the body to be dissected. It was a naked female body, which was the first shock for Candida. The second was that it should be the remains of a young woman, with a very beautiful figure. She had expected that it would be someone old and ready to die.

Obviously so had Dr Knox, for he stopped in midstream and took a closer look. Candida was not the only person in the hall that morning to think with pity that the red dress never did justice to the curves and planes of her magnificent body. Her head lay on a block, and her streaming gold hair hung almost to the floor. But it was her face that came as the greatest shock of Candida's life so far. Cleansed of all the paint, and wiped clean by death of all its tell-tale lines, the dead woman's face was that of a young and lovely girl. The sharpened angularities had been filled in again, and the delicate features restored to girlhood. The ashen lips were curved in an innocent smile.

Candida gazed down upon her, and after long minutes of shock, when she almost thought she was looking into a mirror, and she had to hold on hard to the balcony rail in front of her to keep the buzzing out of her ears, she realised she was looking at Mary Paterson.

She was looking at Mary Paterson, and she was seeing herself, dead.

CHAPTER SIX

'OH, MY GOD,' said Finlay Semple, and slid to the floor.

His words echoing around the otherwise silent amphitheatre turned every head inquisitively towards the front row of the balcony, and after they had died away, a dropped pin would have seemed like thunder.

Dr Knox was the first man to come to his senses. 'Gentlemen,' he said, 'I shall not dissect today, especially not this body we see before us. Its perfection is such that I shall have it put into spirits to preserve it as long as possible.' He paused, while nobody moved a muscle. 'Our art students may come and sketch a model worthy of the best Greek art . . . Remarkable!'

As Candida saw, Finlay Semple was not the only man there to have this green and sickly look. Dr Knox's first assistant, William Fergusson he was called, as she discovered from her programme, had turned a ghastly colour and was swaying on his feet as he followed the great man marching off into the wings.

But Finlay Semple was the only one about whom Alanna was concerned. She gazed down at him, crumpled in a heap on the floor, her concern mingled with the same horrified realisation as Candida's.

Then Finlay, in common with so many other men here, had not been shocked merely at the sight of a naked, dead woman. The students saw dead bodies every day of the week, so it was far worse than that. It was the sight of this particular naked, dead woman that had horrified them so completely because it was so unexpected. Many of them had known it recently and intimately. Too intimately by far, to judge from all the reactions around them, and certainly Finlay's. Of course, that was why he had fainted. Or was it?

Even at such an untimely moment, Candida's brain

continued to work. It skated over the subject of Finlay objectively. So this explained how so many of his evenings had been spent when he was not with her, and she shuddered, and gazed down at him. Could an illness—a disease—have made him faint? Women in Mary Paterson's profession were 'dirty', according to all the whispers she had ever heard.

The audience began to come back to life, and the two girls could not help overhearing a young man in front of them.

'I cannot understand it,' he was saying. 'I was with her five nights ago, and she was in splendid health then. When I saw her there on the slab, I just could not believe my eyes.'

'Does the cause of death not worry you a little, in that case?' his companion asked. 'Especially when there are no signs of violence on her body?'

'Quick!' Alanna nudged her. 'Help me up with him, Candida!'

Before they had time to act, there was a movement behind them. The students had all filed out. Now a tall man stood in their place, and when Candida turned round to look up at him it turned her as sick as Alanna now looked, to see Ross's face, grey, devoid of all colour, staring down at them. The sight of it hit her like a sledge-hammer. She had been able to assess Finlay realistically. Finlay was no longer of the slightest concern to her. But it was an entirely different matter to see Ross's admission of guilt printed across his ashen face. That was very, very different.

Candida did not stop to debate or doubt the evidence of her own eyes. How stupid she had been on Hogmanay when she had seen Ross chasing after Mary Paterson, seen it for herself! Now that she had also seen Mary stripped of all her paint, she could not blame him. A shaft of pure green jealousy pierced her heart and resentment burned in her very soul, so that she was left breathless. It made no difference that Mary was lying there dead, none whatsoever, and she stared at Ross mutely, as if he were some hideous monster sprung up before her, with undisguised loathing and contempt.

'Leave him alone!' he said furiously, and lifted Finlay bodily back on to his seat, where he began to shake his head feebly to try to clear it. Ross's voice dropped to a hiss. 'I have never seen such a disgraceful exhibition in all my life! My own sister masquerading as a man!' His fury and contempt were vitriolic. 'And as for you, Candida . . .' Words failed him.

She gasped at his effrontery. Guilty as he was himself, how dared he criticise those innocently doing their best in the cause of medicine?

By this time, everyone was crowding to the doors. For the students, the show was over for today. It was only just beginning for the four from Charlotte Square.

'As for me?' Candida exploded. 'What about me? All I have done, as you say, is to masquerade as a man—a situation your sister and I were forced into, in this world which seems to have been created for men only!'

'Go on, Candida,' Ross goaded her. 'Say all you have to say, now that you have begun! Let us hear all the poison in your heart.'

'Poison it is! That is the word for it, when it is men only in the anatomy classes, men only that this whole world caters for, even down to that poor girl lying there! Poison it certainly is that the likes of her, earning her living as best she might in the service of "men only" even had to die for it!'

'And is there any more?' Ross asked out of bloodless lips.

'Yes, there is more,' Candida said recklessly. 'This morning has been a revelation. It has certainly given me an insight into why your face is as white as paper, for one thing!'

'And what might that mean?' Ross's eyes snapped a poisonous dark green.

'It means, sir, that I saw what you were up to on Hogmanay, you and Frank Clarke. Kitty and I both saw you. It explains why you look so wretched today, and why I have never seen you since! No doubt you have been otherwise occupied?'

'Indeed I have been otherwise occupied,' Ross stated in measured, contemptuous tones to underline her every bitter word. 'Occupied, as you have so accurately deduced, in chasing after Mary Paterson. I have been following her every movement for almost two months.'

How could he have the cruel gall to admit it? Candida almost fainted. Of course he could not know how cruel—he had no idea of these burning new feelings inside her. Then he further outraged her.

'Where do you get all this knowledge of the underworld from—you who have been brought up a lady? Is it perhaps another of your instincts?'

It was a challenge that stopped her in her tracks. It cut too near the bone. Of course she had no knowledge. She did not know how she could imagine the underworld of Edinburgh so vividly, but it was an imagination that would have appalled her mother and father in their strict and gentle upbringing of a beloved daughter.

'Furthermore,' Ross said with a perception which alarmed her, 'I respect your father, even if you do not. I respect his wisdom. Everything he has ever said about you is true. You jump to conclusions. You do not see the wood for the trees.'

'So what have I missed this time?' she flung back at him. 'Tell me one thing!'

'You saw Finlay; you heard the students talking, no doubt, and you drew your own conclusions. They were only the trees. What about the wood itself, Candida? What about Mary Paterson? Did you not see her face?'

Her face . . . Her face . . . Mary Paterson's face! Why was Ross so cruel? Why was he always making her look at things she did not want to see? Candida swayed a little, and gripped her hands so that the knuckles showed white.

'Of course I saw it,' she said.

'And you saw nothing else?' Ross persisted relentlessly. 'It did not remind you of someone?'

The fleeting vision of her own reflection in that poor waxen face she dismissed angrily from her memory. It was too momentous for her to comprehend. She would not listen to another word. She could not, and she turned back to Alanna, who was fanning Finlay with her programme. All together they heaved Finlay into the cab, which was back waiting for them, and in stony silence they arrived at the Semples' house in Moray Place. Without a word, Ross dragged Finlay out and propped him up until he reached the front door. A manservant opened it.

'Drunk again, is he, sir?' said James in a superior fashion.

'Nothing of the sort,' Ross said frigidly. 'He has had a very nasty shock. Put him to bed, man, and attend to him.'

James recognised authority when he heard and saw it. 'Yes, sir,' he said respectfully, and led his master inside.

Alanna did not seem disposed to speak when Ross climbed back into the cab. She huddled into her corner, a more dejected figure than Candida would have dreamed possible, for Alanna.

'Drive on, cabbie!' Ross said.

'A nasty shock indeed!' Candida flung at him. 'Finlay must wonder, as we all wonder, who was the last one to see her alive?'

At that moment, in her hasty words, a dreadful suspicion entered her heart. She had not given such a thing a minute's consideration until now. She should not have said it in front of Alanna, either. Ross's mouth was set in a grim line. He did not open it to reply, but his eyes looked stricken, and Alanna began to weep quietly in her corner.

From then on, Ross haunted the house in Charlotte Square, where Mr Forbes and Lady Alison welcomed him with open arms. Manners forbade Candida to ignore him, but her attitude was icily polite. If he was not closeted with Mr Forbes in his study at all hours, he was at the table for the mid-day meal or dinner in the evenings or invariably, as now, in the parlour for afternoon tea.

'Alanna is very rarely to be seen these days,' Lady Alison commented. 'What has happened to her? We miss her lively conversation.'

'She is "otherwise occupied" with matters of her own,' Ross said with a wry smile, 'and I am afraid her conversation is anything but lively at present.'

'Oh dear,' Lady Alison said. 'What has happened to her?' When nobody replied, she tried another tack. 'We should be otherwise occupied ourselves, Candida dear. We are into March already, and there has been nothing done about Paradise House.'

'No,' Candida agreed quietly. 'Otherwise occupied' indeed, she thought to herself. So that was why Ross was like a shadow at her back wherever she turned. He had not forgotten one word of their last terrible conversation. He was only waiting to pounce on her at the first opportunity.

'Would you like another cup of tea, dear?' Lady Alison turned in desperation to her husband. 'Here is Liza with some more hot water.'

'Ah, Liza.' Mr Forbes surrendered his cup, and Candida watched her mother's long, slim fingers first pouring the milk into it out of her favourite silver milk-jug, fashioned like a little cow. It had amused her since childhood to see the milk coming out of the cow's mouth.

Lady Alison's hands hovered next over the sugar-bowl. 'Sugar, dear?'

'Two,' Mr Forbes said, as he always did.

Lady Alison pursed her lips disapprovingly, as she always did, and put in only one scoop of the sugar spoon shaped like a little silver hand. It was all so much as usual, so everyday, when everything in the world was so upside-down.

'Is Constable Clarke in the kitchen?' Mr Forbes asked Liza, when she handed him back his cup.

'No, sir.' Liza was brevity personified.

'Why not? This is Thursday, is it not?'

'Constable Clarke has not been here for nine Thursdays now, sir,' Liza sniffed, and prepared to back out of the parlour.

'Wait there, Liza! Good God, Alison, what is this house coming to? Why is it that every woman in it —excepting you, my dear—has suddenly become a wet blanket? Candida is creeping round the place like a lost mouse. Ross says Alanna has fallen silent as well. Even Liza has lost her sparkle. What is the matter with Kitty, next?'

'She is not going to marry Constable Clarke now, sir.'

'Not going to marry Constable Clarke?' Mr Forbes was dumbfounded. 'Why not?'

'I'm sure I couldn't say, sir,' Liza said woodenly.

'I know why,' Candida put in. 'It is because she saw him chasing after bad women on Hogmanay!' She waited for horror and consternation to erupt. 'He was out of uniform, too,' she threw in for good measure, when it did not.

On the contrary, her mother remained calm. Mr Forbes looked at her and shook his head sorrowfully, and Ross smiled.

'Ah!' Mr Forbes said. 'I see. It is a well-known saying that men cannot live without women, and find it almost impossible to live with them. Is that not so, Ross?'

'Sometimes it is not easy,' he agreed, but Candida saw that he had stopped lounging in his chair. He sat upright, as if he was expecting something to happen after waiting for a long, long time.

'Well, I think I can put a stop to Kitty's vapours, at least,' Mr Forbes said. 'Go and fetch her here, Liza. Happy is the man with pretty women about him. Blessed is he with those that smile.'

'Really, Atholl, you make up these sayings as you go along! Bring another two cups with you on your way back, Liza dear,' Lady Alison said, and a few minutes later had them seated and both at ease as only she could.

'Now then, Kitty,' said Mr Forbes, 'did you know that Constable Clarke came to see me shortly before Christmas? He thought he knew the identities of two murderers.'

'He never told me, sir,' Kitty replied, with burning cheeks.

I never knew that, either Candida thought, struggling out of her numb misery to prick up her ears.

'He would not, since I swore him to secrecy for his own protection. He told me how worried he was at the disappearance of five people on his beat around the Grassmarket, three men and two women.'

'Five people?' Lady Alison was shocked.

'Of course there may be more by this time, my dear. The three men were lodgers in a house in Tanner's Close, and the two unfortunate women were last seen up at that end of the Grassmarket. My great interest in it is the remarkable explosion of bodies currently being supplied to Dr Knox. They seem roughly equivalent to the disappearances.

'So that is why you have been working so hard lately? You should have told me, Atholl.'

'There was no reason to involve you, my dear Alison, and except for the uproar in this house, there would have been no reason to involve any of the rest of you in so sordid a business. As it is, I must ask everyone of you not to breathe one word of this to anyone.'

'Of course not, Papa,' Candida said, hoping he would not pursue the subject of the great danger Frank Clarke was in. Kitty was looking frightened enough as it was.

'Your father is drafting the necessary legislation now for what he hopes will be the Anatomy Act, Candida,' Ross said.

'And what is that, Papa?'

'If plenty of bodies become legally available to the anatomists, there would no longer be this illegal trade in the Edinburgh underworld. Dr Knox does not seem to care where they come from!' Mr Forbes paused for breath and gave the absent Dr Knox an indignant glare.

'Unclaimed bodies should be allowed for anatomical dissection instead, or those gifted to medicine, as Ross's old soldier gifted his.'

'Indeed,' Ross said, with meaning.

'In the meantime, the terrible trade goes on, and Constable Clarke is convinced it is all the work of two men he suspects. He is determined to catch them red-handed. If he could, it would be a feather in his cap for him, and it would speed the Anatomy Act on its way for us.'

'Do you mean these two men are resurrectionists?' Lady Alison asked. 'The Body-snatchers?'

'At least the people had been allowed to die naturally before the Body-snatchers dug them up, my dear. No, it is worse even than that. These two men are murderers, and Constable Clarke is out even now trying to catch them.'

Kitty gave a little scream, and the parlour actually fell cold in the chill of these awful words. Then she seemed to pluck up courage to ask the question, vital to her. 'If you will excuse me, sir,' she said. 'I still don't understand. If Frank was trying to catch the criminals, why was he running after Mary Paterson and Janet Brown?'

'I shall send for him to come and see me this evening,' said Mr Forbes. 'I want to find out how he is getting on, anyway, in his desperate quest for promotion. It is, I understand, with a view to getting married. So do you think you could cheer up a little now, Kitty? Do you think you could bring yourself to speak to him, even? Then you could ask him that question yourself.'

'I will, sir,' said Kitty, with the first glimmer of a smile they had seen for weeks as she and Liza left the parlour.

Candida was well aware that disappointment showed in every feature of her face. It was too keen to disguise. Why did her father have to stop on the very brink of telling them the answer to Kitty's vital question? Whatever Frank had been doing on Hogmanay, Ross would have been doing the same thing. Her suspicions would have been confirmed by this time. As it was, she would have to wait and see what Kitty reported.

She was so busy with these thoughts that she scarcely noticed Ross getting to his feet. He was taking his leave. 'I have a very important meeting I must attend,' he said, 'and I cannot be late.'

It was a great relief when he left the room, and her shoulders sagged a little as she relaxed. Even if his eyes were not actually on her, she always felt he was watching her every move. She supposed Papa had been quite right, after all. If Frank Clarke wanted Kitty to know his business, he should tell her himself.

Suddenly she felt very tired. She would go up to her room, lie down on her bed and think about it all. What else did she ever do, she asked herself drearily, shutting the parlour door and wending her way upstairs.

The house was very quiet, and there was no sound from below-stairs. In half an hour, when there was no more likelihood of visitors, Liza would send up one of the undermaids to clear away the tea-things. After that, Papa would go into his study, Mama would go into her sitting-room or her bedroom beyond that, and a normal peace and quiet would descend, a rest for everyone before the evening activities began. Accordingly, the stair lights were turned down low, and Candida shuddered along the corridor to her bedroom. It was very cold, and the shadows made it seem even colder. She would be glad to get inside her own room, shut the door and sit for a while before her fire.

One hand closed over hers on the handle of the door, another closed over her mouth, and she was bundled inside.

'What took you so long?' Ross asked. 'I thought you were never coming! I am absolutely determined to speak to you, and there does not seem to be any other way.'

'You can't stay here,' Candida panted. 'You should not be in this room! I shall scream!'

'Scream away,' he said grimly. 'Nobody will hear.

You know that as well as I do, so you might as well be sensible and put an end to this antagonism—now.'

'Then why . . .' She collected herself sufficiently to ask the burning question. 'Why did you and Frank chase Mary Paterson and Janet Brown?'

'Why do you want to know?' he tormented her. 'Are you jealous?'

'Jealous?' she repeated, while jealousy pierced her heart with daggers and blazed in her blue eyes. 'Of course I am not jealous! Why should I be?'

'Why, indeed?' Ross echoed with a quiet smile. 'There was never any reason to be. I was helping Frank to watch the two men he suspects, that's all.'

'Chasing two women was a strange way to watch two men!' Candida said.

'Perfectly logical, when you consider that the two men were constantly in the company of Mary Paterson and Janet Brown, although always in public places. We dreaded that they would lure the women away from the bright lights, and for a much more sinister purpose than any of your lurid imaginings, Candida.'

That brought a flood of colour to her cheeks, and she wished she had never divulged her imaginings, least of all to Ross Alexander Laing. As he had already pointed out, they were far from ladylike.

'All your time and efforts were wasted, then, to judge from Mary Paterson,' she tried to cover up.

'She gave us the slip one night. Next morning, she turned up in Dr Knox's lecture hall,' said Ross. He looked as tired as Candida felt. 'I just couldn't believe it! I still cannot believe they got her, at last, after all the trouble we went to, to try and guard her.'

'But she died!' Candida cried. 'She wasn't killed! There was not one mark on her whole body. I saw it myself!'

'She was killed, Candida.' Ross's eyes bored into hers. 'Believe me, she was killed, even if there was not a mark on her! Suffocation leaves no marks.'

'Suffocation?' Candida drew back in horror.

'None of the bodies recently delivered to Dr Knox bears any sign of foul play. I have been watching, and I am a doctor.'

'Yes,' She bowed her head to that. 'But it still does not answer my question. Why were you interested in Mary Paterson above all other likely victims?'

'Ah, so now you have come to the crux of it, Candida, the most vexed question of all! Well, it was not for Frank's reason, for quick promotion. Not for your father's reason, to further the Anatomy Bill. Not for the reason you believed, for her charms. Not even out of medical interest—none of these.'

'Then what?'

'Mary Paterson fascinated me for quite another reason. She still does. It is because I believe she was the other side of the coin.'

'I do not understand,' Candida said tiredly.

'You do not have to,' Ross said coolly. 'Not yet.' The door closed on his receding back.

She was left with the enigma, dissatisfied and dejected. Yet within ten minutes she was asleep, dreaming uneasily.

'Leave me, Kitty,' Candida waved her maid away later. 'I am not coming down tonight at all.' Now that her short rest had taken the edge off her weariness, her mind began to run round and round like a squirrel in a cage. She lay for hours in a fury of regret for all the unforgivable things she had said to Ross Alexander Laing. How could she ever have said them?

The tears she shed on her pillow that night were different from all the other nights. Before, she had condemned him. Now, she condemned herself.

It had become Alanna's custom to go to see Candida first thing every morning. Now, after a lapse which had lasted a week, she came again next morning.

'I have decided to forgive Finlay,' she said. 'After all, the woman, Mary Paterson, is dead.'

'Yes,' Candida sighed.

'Not that there has been one word about her in the newspapers. I have searched the *Courant* every day. Do you not think that strange?'

'Very strange,' Candida agreed cautiously, after all Mr Forbes had impressed on them yesterday.

'But, of course, rumour is rife all round the town . . . Finlay has made several efforts to see me, Candida. I have been very distressed, you understand . . .' Alanna went on delicately, with the suspicion of a tear.

'Of course you have, dear.'

'But it has all turned out exactly as you said. It is plain to see that in the past he lacked guidance.'

Alanna had the air of a woman who could never stoop so low, if in fact at all, decked out as she was this morning in rather sorrowful shades of lilac, through to royal purple and into the severe midnight blue of her pelisse.

'I am sure you will change all that,' Candida said. 'Where are you going to meet him?'

'I have allowed a short meeting over coffee at Ambrose's.' Alanna actually smiled. 'After that, we shall see!'

Candida went to the biology class accompanied by Kitty, and when they returned, Lady Alison was in the hall.

'Did I remember to tell you that Mr Stewart, the master-mason, will meet us at Paradise House this afternoon, dear?' she asked. 'We should not leave it too late. Two o'clock, perhaps?'

By the afternoon, Candida, dressed in peach and white, was glad of her warm brown mantle. That, together with the tiny hot-water bottle Kitty had concealed in her amber fur muff, gave her some slight comfort as she and her mother set off.

Kitty was reunited with her Frank; Alanna would eventually allow Finlay back into her favour; but Ross might just as well be on another planet—which was exactly what she deserved. She brooded about it all the way to Paradise House, and got down with a sigh to shake Mr Stewart's hand.

'I have been over the house,' Mr Stewart said. 'The main building is quite sound, but I am afraid some structural alterations will be required on both the north and east walls.'

'Oh dear!' Lady Alison said. 'We should have had a man here with us. Men understand these things.'

'But there is a man here,' Mr Stewart said in surprise. 'He said he was waiting for you.'

'Oh, Ross dear!' Lady Alison said, as a tall figure strode round from the back of the house. 'So you managed to get away? I'm so glad. A masculine opinion would be most acceptable, since it is a gentleman who will live here eventually.'

'Candida,' Ross acknowledged her with a grave smile, his face tranquil. It made her feel more wretched than ever. 'I know we disagree about it, but I feel sure a lady will live here too, so your opinion will be as valuable as mine.' He turned to Mr Stewart, 'What are the problems?'

'The back premises are the worst, sir.'

'So I saw. I rode out this afternoon and went to find the stables. They are in a shocking state. In fact the whole of the back of the house is really bad.'

'Then let us begin there,' said Mr Stewart, politely escorting Lady Alison away.

Left alone with Ross, Candida's hands began to tremble inside her muff. She felt cold despite the hot bottle, she was still tired after a bad night, and she knew she did not look her best.

In this cat-and-mouse game with him, when, as she had found out, he knew things she did not—and she knew for certain she suspected things he could not possibly visualise—she would far rather have been in her full health and strength to deal with it. 'Ross,' she said in a low voice, 'I said things to you which were quite unforgivable. I'm . . .'

'Don't say it, Candida! Don't say you are sorry! You lashing out at me like a little gypsy is the only thing that has kept me going.'

After trying her best not even to see him for weeks, she looked at him squarely now, and what she saw gave her a little thrill of alarm. Ross had lost weight. Even his face was thinner, it was down to the bone, and his elegant donkey brown coat hung much too loosely off his back.

'What on earth have you been doing?' she asked.

'Working . . . day and night.'

His eyes had not changed, at least, and she longed to put out her hand to touch his cheek, in sympathy if nothing else. But of course it was too late for anything like that. It was her own fault.

'At nights, still?' she asked. 'What at?'

'Although we could not save Mary Paterson, Janet Brown is still fair game,' Ross said seriously. 'It may be her turn next. The only saving grace is that Daft Jamie seems to have transferred his affections to her, now that Mary Paterson has gone, and Jamie has the strength of an ox.'

'Ugh,' she shuddered. Edinburgh by night was full of shadows, terrors and tragedies. 'And by day?'

'Sometimes I attend another college in Clyde Street.'

'What sort of college?'

'Rather than explain all that now, I shall take you there one day soon. You would be very interested, I know.'

'And you are still attending Surgeons' Hall for the anatomy classes? Surely that is too much work altogether?'

'It is a lot of work, but it is only for three more months. After that I shall be a surgeon, I hope.'

Only three more months, and he would be going back to Ireland, then. Only three minutes ago she had dared to feel a little hope. She had dared even to feel happy, because he had come out to Paradise House when there was no need for him to do so. She should have known better.

It was still unnaturally cold in Edinburgh the following

morning, and Candida was awake shuddering under the covers long before Kitty came to her. There was a queer bright light in the room in spite of the brocade curtains, tightly closed.

'Would you believe it, miss?' Kitty drew them back dramatically. 'Snow! On the first day of May! What will they do now, all the girls who go up on Arthur's Seat to wash their faces in the May dew?'

'They won't even get to the foot of Arthur's Seat, never mind climb it, not in this!' Candida joined her at the window. 'So they will not see the faces of their future husbands in the dew, this year.'

All Charlotte Square was white and frozen, and the few tracks of carriages and horses shone polished and gleaming in the morning light. There was no let-up in the weather when she joined Alanna in the hall and they realised that they could not get to the biology class that day. It would be too dangerous for the horses, sliding and skidding along Princes Street.

'Shall we walk along to the coffee-house instead?' Alanna said. 'We might as well go out, since we are dressed for it.'

Her talk over coffee was all of the emporium. Candida gathered that nobody was happier about her reconciliation with Finlay than his father, Francis Semple, who had discovered that Alanna's claim to understand the world of business was no idle boast.

'I shall be giving up the biology classes before long,' Alanna said on the way back. 'I shall not have the time, since I have agreed to help Finlay to look for a house of his own—probably somewhere around the Meadows, so as to be quite near the emporium.'

'I never thought Finlay would leave his father's house in Moray Place,' Candida said. 'He's so comfortable there.'

'Too comfortable,' Alanna smiled. 'A house of his own was my idea.'

'Oh, Miss Candida!' Kitty met them at the door of No.

13 Charlotte Square, her eyes round and shocked. 'Your mother has met with an accident! She went out this morning and slipped on the steps. She has broken her ankle!'

'It is only a simple fracture,' Lady Alison said, minutes later, when Candida burst into her room. 'Of course your father is beside himself, so please, dear, don't you fuss too! One person fussing around is enough to put up with, as well as the pain.'

'Where did it happen, Mama?'

'On the top step at the front door, so of course I slid to the bottom. Goodness knows how I managed it! There must have been pounds of coarse salt laid down on those steps, but still I have broken my ankle. Very fortunately Ross was still here to set it. He has assured me that I shall be on my feet again in six weeks. My biggest worry, besides your Papa, is Paradise House, Candida. I am afraid you will have to carry on with it by yourself where I left off.'

'Then you need worry no longer, Mama. You know the work is proceeding according to plan, and I shall go out to keep an eye on it and report to you every day that the weather allows. Alanna is giving up the Outside classes altogether,' she added as an afterthought. 'She is going to look for a house for Finlay.'

'And you, Candida?' Lady Alison winced with pain.

'I too, Mama. I've found a house already.'

The month of May had come in like a lion. It continued more peaceably, and most afternoons Candida was able to go out to Paradise House. She became used to it. In fact, she missed the excursions when the weather was inclement. The builders did not seem to mind the wind and the cold and the eternal rain. The alterations that Ross had dictated on behalf of the old gentleman were growing apace.

Then, on the 17th, after all the cold and the rain, the sun beamed out and Candida could hardly wait to see the rhododendrons, from palest pink to deepest carmine, and the fresh yellow primulas, and the tips of the summer-flowering bulbs showing through. Their struggle to survive, almost choked to death by the weeds, brought hope to her heart. Good could transcend evil, ugliness could be transformed into beauty, and these gardens could be made the foil of the beautiful old house. The frame could enhance the picture.

It became her next enthusiasm, for long ago she had begun to play the game that the house was her house, and the old gentleman did not exist. She felt happy and secure in it, and she loved it with all her heart. What a pity she could not explore some of the further nooks and crannies of the gardens, but the paths were overgrown, and she came back to Mr Stewart, who was urging his workers on.

'I must engage gardeners next,' she said. 'The weeds are coming up as fast as the flowers. And what is this you are putting up now?'

'The conservatory, Miss. Dr Alexander Laing seems to think the lady of the house will want to bring the gardens inside, and so we are constructing this large window in it—a french window, it's called. As you see, it opens out into the garden to extend the dimension. It is an idea borrowed from the French. Of course, in France, there is the weather,' Mr Stewart finished rather disapprovingly.

'Oh, it is a beautiful idea,' Candida said. 'But expensive?'

'Very, by the time we get it draught-proofed in this windy city. But, according to him, only the best will do.'

She went upstairs to look at the room with all the windows again, 'the Captain's Cabin' as she had nicknamed it from the start. Somehow, it felt like the heart of the house. She felt comfortable here. It was her favourite room. Something had been added to it. A large glass-lidded case had been neatly fitted into one of the alcoves, and made by a craftsman out of the same mahogany as the rest of the wood in here, so skilfully that it blended in almost unnoticeably, as if it had always been there. The glass lid was locked, and inside on black velvet lay the large opal she had seen in Ross's boxes, along with other gemstones of great beauty to which she could not put a name. She spent a long time admiring the collection, and made up her mind to ask Ross about them at the first opportunity.

It came sooner than she could have hoped, and unexpectedly, next day at two o'clock. Ross was never home in the afternoons, but she met him now just as she was leaving the house.

'Where are you going, Candida?'

'Out to Paradise House. I go there on most afternoons.'

'Come to Clyde Street with me today instead.'

'But it is Thursday, Kitty's day off.'

'I know it is!' Ross smiled with the smile that lit up her heart, the smile she had missed so much. 'I worked it all out so that it would be a Thursday when I asked you. I want to be alone with you, for once.'

'I notice Alanna dispenses with a chaperon as often as she can. Is that the way it goes, in Ireland?'

'No!' he laughed. 'It is just that I allow her a great deal of liberty, and Alanna is sensible, and discreet. She knows when to take Elizabeth with her, and when she can leave her behind.'

'Well,' Candida said, as they got into the carriage, 'perhaps my mother's doctor would be considered quite proper.'

'More than adequate, I assure you!'

All she could see when they entered the college in Clyde Street was a confusion of skeletons: the skeletons of horses, dogs, cats, and even of apes. They reminded her of the human skeletons she had seen in Surgeons' Hall.

'Perhaps mad old Lord Monboddo was not so far wrong, after all,' Ross said, 'when a hundred years ago he suggested man had evolved from the apes.' He chuckled. 'Did you know that, whenever a child was born in his house, he would watch at the door so as to see it in its first state?'

'No. Why?'

'He was so convinced of his fantastic theory that he wanted to catch the midwives pinching off the infant tails!'

Ross took her to see what had been a stable at the back, but which was now a hospital for sick animals. There was a lecture-room, a library and a dissecting-room. Under this one large roof in Edinburgh was everything that Candida had been vaguely searching for all her life, and it was with shining eyes that she came down to earth again and held out her hand to the lady Ross wanted her to meet.

'This is Miss Mary Dick,' he said, and she found herself looking into the austere face of a woman of perhaps forty, but looking much older than that. 'She is the sister of Mr William Dick, who founded this Veterinary College.'

'Founded it, and funded it,' Miss Dick said grimly. But pride shone in her plain face. 'The Highland Society gave him a grant of £50. The other £9,950 came out of his own pocket. I know. I keep the books. But my brother is not interested in money,' she sighed, 'only animals.'

'But that is a disgrace!' Candida said, when they came away.

'He is one man with a dream,' Ross told her. 'A dream and an implacable determination to help sick animals. He is a visionary. He has certainly inspired me.'

'Tell me what you mean, Ross?'

'I mean that between Dr Knox's revelations of the human body and William Dick's inspiration I have at last found my true vocation. I will be a surgeon, but a veterinary surgeon, with God's help.'

Candida was silent for some time as the carriage bowled along. She found that she even had tears in her eyes.

'Of course,' she said at last, 'that is wonderful. But you will be very alone. There are so few animal doctors, let alone surgeons. And you will need premises, large premises, in which to practise.'

'I have it all thought out,' he assured her.

Somewhere in Ireland, of course. They were famous for their horses over there. At the races, Irish horses came in first so many times. And, as far as she had ever been able to glean from Alanna, they had premises and to spare on their huge Irish estate dominated by a real castle. Candida tried hard to dispel these gloomy thoughts, but they persisted all the way home.

Next morning she was still depressed, and No. 13 Charlotte Square did little to cheer her. Everyone was out except Lady Alison who was confined to bed, and Candida felt alone and lonely. There was nothing else for it but to go out to Paradise House, and once she and Kitty got there she felt her spirits soaring as they always did.

'I like it here, Miss Candida,' Kitty confided. 'It's so peaceful, away from the hustle and the bustle of the centre of the town.'

'Now that is very strange, Kitty, and you a town girl all your life, the same as I am myself!'

'Oh, I could spend the rest of my days here, miss, with the greatest of pleasure.'

'So could I, Kitty. But don't take off your cloak yet. I have never been right through the gardens of this house so far, and by the look of the ones furthest away neither has anyone else, for years. We will go exploring.'

They walked down the winding path, past the outhouses on the left and the tumbledown stables on the right, past the tree-bordered lawns until they came to a thick hawthorn hedge at the bottom.

'Over the stream to the left are the wild fields, and beyond them there is a pond nearly as big as a lake, Kitty,' Candida said. 'But what is round here, to the right?'

Long jagged tentacles of brambles had spread across the path, tearing at their clothes, obstructing their way.

'Follow me,' Kitty said. 'Tramp on them! Be careful of

the branches I hold up in case they get in your eyes.' She ploughed on, skirting the hawthorn hedge with Candida in her wake, until at last they dived out of the bramble patch and into a clearing. 'Oh, Miss Candida, look at that!'

They stood entranced at the sight of the little house tucked away in the corner. Its roof seemed intact, and its two chimneys were still whole. Even the windows appeared to have the glass still in them, and when they went nearer to inspect, Kitty rubbed a hole in the dirt on one.

'It must have been a gardener's cottage once,' Candida said, peering through the hole. 'It seems to have two rooms.'

But with Mr Stewart's help in taking the door off its hinges half an hour later, they discovered it had three rooms. There was a very small one in between.

'That's the usual for a servant's cottage in Scotland,' he explained. 'What do you want done with it, miss?'

'I am sure that Dr Alexander Laing will want to have it restored. A place this size will need servants, that is certain. Would there be a lot of work involved, Mr Stewart?'

'Not much,' he said after a brief examination. 'It has been protected from the weather by the trees and the hedges. There is not much wrong with it that soap and water could not cure.'

'Let me clean it, Miss Candida,' Kitty said at once. 'I could start tomorrow. It is Thursday, and I could get Frank to come and have a look at that well. There must be water there.'

The following afternoon Frank hacked a path through the brambles. 'This is only a makeshift job,' he told Candida and Kitty severely. 'These bushes must be dug up and burned, to do it properly.'

'Never mind that,' Kitty said. 'What about the well?'

Candida left them to it, and went back to the out-houses with a thoughtful air. There was so much that could be done with them, too. If only Ross would come, she could discuss it with him. She met him smiling, when like a miracle he appeared round the side of the house on his horse.

'Jet is sensible, and I took a nosebag with me for him. That should keep him occupied. I'll go and get him a bucket of water.'

Candida was stroking the horse's nose when he came back.

'You have had the gardeners in?' he asked.

'They made a start this morning, four of them,' she said, as they went for a tour of inspection. 'They said to clear the weeds alone will take at least a fortnight. From tomorrow onwards, they will work all day.'

'Very good. But once that is done, the flower-beds are going to look very empty, Candida. Have you any idea what you would plant in them?'

'I do not know what the old gentleman would like.'

'Neither do I, so we shall use our own judgment. We could go to the Botanic Gardens and choose between us.'

'But the money?' Candida asked anxiously. 'Before it is finished, Paradise House will cost a fortune!'

'I was speaking to your mother about that,' he said, with a gleam of amusement in his eyes. 'She said money was no object.' When they went on further to see the cottage, he did not seem very surprised. 'Yes, she also told me this small house was in the title deeds.'

Up in the Captain's Cabin he picked her sketchbook off the window-seat. 'You are almost half-way through the year,' he said. 'Let me see what you have been drawing lately.'

She opened her book nervously to find the page. This room had had a strange effect on her from the first time she had ever entered it with him. It was a feeling that drew her close to his side when the drawing of Mary Paterson she had made so long ago fluttered out.

'That face haunts me,' she said.

'I am not surprised.' Ross's face was suddenly expressionless with no trace of a smile on it. 'Where are your crayons?' He chose a stick of charcoal and began to feather out Mary Paterson's features. He did it very expertly so that only the outline remained. 'That profile . . . Whose is it, Candida?' he asked gently, while she gazed at it with the same horrified recognition as when she had gripped the rails at Surgeons' Hall that terrible day when Mary Paterson was wheeled in. 'Whose?' he asked, with the same sad look that had frightened her before.

Of course it had haunted her! Of course she saw it all in a flash, now.

'Have you never thought of the possibility of twins?' Ross asked, and caught her as she fell.

Her head was still whirling when they got back to Charlotte Square, and she was feeling very sick. Halfway through the night, when she had been stretched out upon her bed for hours, she woke up and began to shudder violently. What did it all mean?

Kitty rose from the couch at her side and pushed a hot brick covered in flannel at her feet. Its heat radiated out slowly, and after a few minutes up through her body. One gas light was on, turned down low, and in its subdued glow she smiled wanly at her maid and turned over, unable to speak to her. A minute later she heard Kitty's weary sigh as she lay down again, the rasp of blankets she pulled up about her, and then silence.

The truth had been there all along, staring her in the face every time she looked in a mirror, and yet she had not seen it. That was because she did not want to see it. From the moment he met her, Ross had done everything to point it out. 'You are one of the two most beautiful women in all Edinburgh.' He wanted her to know the sordid truth about herself. Why?

If he had any regard for her, he would try to hide it from her instead, as her mother and father had done. They could not bear to tell her even that she had been adopted, and it had taken Papa nineteen years to try. Even then, he had done it in such a tentative way that it had been a gamble whether she would ever look inside the Bible in the first place. Now Ross was asking her to believe something even more terrible, that the baby left in Candlemaker Row had had a twin. Mary Paterson. It always came back to Mary Paterson.

Her thoughts ran round and round in her head so that sleep was out of the question. Her parents loved her and wanted to protect her. Ross did not, and in only a few weeks his studies would be over and he would be going home. It would be better never to be alone with him again. Candida turned restlessly in her bed. The trouble was, she wanted to be alone with him again, to feel that excitement again she had only ever known with him, when he kissed her, when he held her, when he . . .

She smiled into the semi-darkness with a smile that would have done her dead sister proud. It was bitter, it was grim, and it belonged in the gutters where their mother had abandoned them both. In that moment she began to understand the life Mary Paterson had lived. She wondered if she had enjoyed living it for her brief spell. Candida had tasted wine and brandy and rum, and she understood that drinking too much of them could beguile a person into forgetfulness. Drink had been her sister's downfall and her death, when she had only been trying to earn her living as best she knew how. Her own twin sister . . .

'Oh, my God,' she groaned, and tossed about.

But Kitty did not hear her this time. At two o'clock in the morning, she was sleeping like a child.

The final steps taken at Edinburgh University after passing the MD examination were down the large college hall, to be granted the scroll entitling Ross to practise medicine at the highest level of the land.

Into the wavering sunshine of a June day that was almost mild, he emerged, grasping the precious parchment rolled up and tied with a red silk ribbon, and heaved the deepest sigh of thankfulness of his twenty-eight, almost twenty-nine years. He had invited none of his friends and relations to the public ceremony, to sit through the tedious speeches afterwards in the stifling hall. To him, it was merely the next step in the carefully planned campaign he had been working on since last September. The nineteenth, to be precise.

His cravat felt a little damp, but it was still as flawlessly white as the severely pressed pleats of the ruffles down the front of his shirt. He mounted his horse and set off bareheaded at a casual canter back to Charlotte Square. The ladies passing by on the North Bridge admired his figure, so perfectly turned out in black and white, and his seat on the shining jet black horse.

'How are you, Aunt Alison?' He ran a professional eye over his ageing but still beautiful relative.

'It is only thanks to you, dear, that I am so far advanced. I tried a few steps this morning, and there is very little pain.'

'Nevertheless,' Ross said, 'there is no use in running, and perhaps falling again, before you can walk.'

'You are a good doctor, Ross.'

'I am a doctor and a surgeon now, on paper at least, Aunt Alison,' he told her, handing her the parchment.

'My dear!' Lady Alison exclaimed. 'Oh, this is wonderful! I am so happy for you!' Then her joy diminished swiftly. 'Does this mean we are going to lose you? You are going home again now?'

'How can I go back yet,' Ross laughed into her eyes, 'when my most important patient—in fact, my only patient—is not even on her feet?'

'Ross, you are so like your dear mother Cornelia that it is uncanny! What are you trying to wheedle out of me now?'

'Now that I have a little more time free at last, may I escort you and Candida to the Musical Festival on Saturday night? Alanna and Finlay are going, and on to a late supper afterwards, and I thought it would be a welcome diversion for you.'

'Oh, Ross, it will not be like what it used to be when we were young, Atholl and I.'

'Time marches on,' he agreed. 'Nothing is ever the same.'

'And, besides, Atholl has invited his two dearest friends, Henry Cockburn and Walter Scott, for dinner on Saturday night. No, Ross. Take Candida along with Alanna and Finlay. That will be perfectly all right.'

'And we had thought, some time ago, of visiting the Botanic Gardens to find plants for Paradise House.'

'You have my blessing.' Lady Alison smiled, and then winced slightly as she turned her ankle upon the foot-stool.

'Show me where that hurt!' Ross bent towards her, a doctor again.

CHAPTER SEVEN

In Edinburgh, social events crowded thick and fast in the months of June, July and August, although even then there was no guarantee of good weather. After a day of chasing black clouds and thunder when Candida felt wildly excited one minute and depressed the next, the evening of Saturday the 27th of June turned out cool with a slight drizzle.

'I do not know what to wear, Kitty. If I had ever been allowed to possess such a thing, I would put on a red gown.'

'It is the thunder, Miss Candida. The next best thing would be your bright pink. Or is it that you don't want to go to the Assembly Rooms at all tonight?' her maid asked shrewdly.

'It is Handel's *Messiah*, Kitty. Every seat has been sold out for weeks. Of course I want to go.'

And Alanna and Finlay would be there, she told herself. Ross had got four tickets. Everything would be all right.

At seven o'clock the coach deposited them at the pillared entrance of the Assembly Rooms in George Street. The drive from Charlotte Square had lasted no more than five minutes.

'We could have walked,' Alanna said.

'You must be seen to arrive here,' Candida told her, 'and in the best possible style!'

'So I see,' Alanna said, gazing around at all the fashion and beauty of the day. 'How glad I am I chose my black!'

She had evidently persuaded Finlay to wear black, too. They stood there together, a tall and distinguished couple who turned many heads, Finlay in a black coat and pantaloons with a silver-trimmed white cashmere waistcoat, and Alanna wearing a daringly low-cut dress of black velvet bordered with white and silver lace, and a huge evening beret, a puff-ball of white and silver, at an angle on her head. Their outfits had been made to match, Candida could see, and were a striking advertisement for Semple and Son.

When they moved forward they found that the orchestra was opposite the door they had walked through, and the way ahead was carpeted in blue with a Greek key design in darker blue along its borders. Candida knew that at the interval the audience would promenade on the blue carpet and speak to their friends. She had been here before.

Alanna, who had not, was in raptures over the seating arrangements. 'What a wonderful idea to have one half of the audience facing the other, and on seats gradually elevated right up to the walls like this!' she said. 'Finlay and I will be able to see you throughout the performance.'

With that she swept off with Finlay in her wake to the left side, and Candida found herself being guided towards the right. Quietly dressed in pearl grey, Ross smiled and took her to their seats. She should have known he would manoeuvre the whole thing, she thought despairingly, as the concert began.

But bit by bit the glory of the music uplifted her, the fire and the spirit of the choruses made her forget her headache, and before she knew where she was it was the interval already, and time to go down to the middle of the hall to speak to Finlay and Alanna.

'Isn't it wonderful?' Alanna asked, while Finlay smiled behind her. 'Ross, will you and Candida be joining us for supper afterwards?'

'That depends on where you are going.'

'Upstairs, of course! I have been longing to be in the highest society in Edinburgh. This will be a splendid opportunity to break into it. Finlay knows so many people!'

'Yes, I thought you would be going upstairs, and of

course you will need the tickets to get in, Finlay.' Ross handed over two tickets. 'I dare say,' he looked at his sister, 'that you will manage to get through the evening with your virtue unscathed if we leave you two alone?'

'You are an angel, Ross,' Alanna laughed. 'You always were my favourite brother. And where are *you* going?'

'On an adventure,' he said.

'A man is entitled to at least one,' Alanna said, and kissed him on his cheek. 'Especially on his birthday!'

The Hallelujah was transcendent. The whole audience rose to it, and when it closed, their hearts were filled with devotion and reverence. Everyone who was leaving walked out of the Assembly Rooms exhausted and dazed.

'I am glad we did not go upstairs,' Candida confided when Ross helped her into a cab. 'This pink dress is not nearly showy enough for up there. Where are we going?'

'To find the sea breezes, to blow away the last of your headache in that pretty pink dress. I thought it was the best one there.'

'I did have a headache,' she admitted. 'How did you know?'

Ross laughed and took her hand in his. 'Oh, Candida, I watch you very carefully. After all, I am a doctor, and I would be a poor sort of doctor if I could not diagnose the strain in your face.'

'Of course you have been watching me!' Her irritation was plain. 'You would not have seen that dreadful resemblance between the drawing and me, otherwise. Of course,' she turned her head away, 'it was not the only cause of strain. Finding out that I was an adopted child was another, even greater, one.'

'Yes,' Ross said. 'How did you find out?'

'I don't suppose Papa would leave the family Bible lying around deliberately, but he did one day when I was alone in his study. I saw the entry almost by chance. God knows it would have been better never to have seen it, never to have known any of this!'

'That is nonsense coming from Candida Forbes, for a start!' Ross remained calm, and his hand holding hers was cool. 'Sooner or later you would have to know that you were adopted. Certainly when you got married, for example. Your birth certificate would have to be produced. Would your reaction have been any different then, do you think?'

'But I am not getting married now.'

'Not to Finlay Semple, certainly. But I wonder if your father began leaving the family Bible open for you, when it seemed that you might?'

She had never thought of that.

'Did it say how you came to be adopted?' he asked next.

'There was nothing else except the bare entry and the date. But I have this feeling from something Kitty said that I was found in Candlemaker Row. At first, they thought I was a kitten!'

'Newly-born babies are not much bigger.'

'Then you think I was newly born?'

'If a mother is going to abandon her child, she usually does it as soon as she is on her feet after the birth —perhaps before she becomes too fond of it. But why do you not discuss it with your parents?'

'I am trying to pluck up courage. I must speak to them soon, but what puts me off every time I try is the same old question. Why did they not tell me themselves, long ago? It must mean they have a reason for not telling me.'

'Perhaps they are wary of your enquiring mind, Candida, and dread what you might find out once you begin. Think of all your projects, all the things you are interested in, and how you do not leave go until you have found everything out you possibly can. No, your interests are not the same as other ladies' interests, sewing little bits of lace or learning new songs.'

'Except Alanna's.'

'Alanna?' Ross threw back his head and laughed in

genuine amusement. 'Alanna is the same as our mother before her. She has been prepared to go anywhere, take up anything, even the Outside Classes, so long as it led her eventually to a suitable husband.'

'Finlay,' Candida said.

'Finlay has already assured me of his prospects as heir to one of the most prosperous businesses in Edinburgh,' Ross told her. 'If he carries it on, he will become even more wealthy than his father, and if I know my own sister, she will see to it that he does.'

'You think they will marry, then?'

'If our father gives his consent; which of course he will, since Alanna has always been able to twist him round her little finger. I have advised Finlay to take a quick trip to Ireland, and he is considering it after the summer season is over. But it is not him or Alanna we are speaking about, except to warn you that you will find that Alanna's interests will narrow down now to a wedding, and a home, and a family. We were speaking of your interests, Candida.'

The moon had the effrontery to come out after such a day and smile down over the Firth of Forth, and a gentle breeze had blown away the drizzle. It also blew a strong smell of fish into the cab.

'Newhaven,' Ross said. 'We will soon be there.'

A few minutes later he had paid off the cab-driver and then guided her down to the little semicircular harbour where all the small fishing-boats rode idly at anchor. The breeze from the sea was cool on her face, and the moon made a silver path over the water.

'Perhaps the problem is that you want to know the truth about things, Candida, but you do not always like the truth when you see it.'

She had found that out already. 'No,' she sighed.

'First, you discovered that you were not the natural child of your parents, but adopted. You did not like that.'

'No.'

'Then you saw Mary Paterson for yourself, and

were forced to realise that two girl babies had been abandoned, not one. You did not like that.'

'Neither will my parents, if it is true.'

'It must be true, Candida. Her birthday was even the same as yours, the 9th of November.'

'How did you find that out?'

'She told me herself, once.'

'Oh,' Candida said, while jealousy streaked through her that he had been speaking to her at all.

'You did not like Mary Paterson. I saw it in your face just now.'

'How could I like her or dislike her? I never knew her.'

'But you knew her reputation. What is worrying you most? Is it that you resent being the twin sister of a bad woman like Mary Paterson?'

'It is not even that, Ross,' Candida said sadly. 'Blood is thicker than water.'

'You could not just leave it at that?'

'How can I?' She rounded on him, her eyes blue and passionate in the moonlight. 'Could you? I no longer know who I am. But you are quite right about one thing. I shall never rest until I find out. I can think of nothing else.'

'While you are finding out, remember one thing,' Ross said. 'There is good and bad in everyone, two sides to everyone—twin sides, if you like—and in spite of it all there must have been some good in Mary Paterson, too.'

His words hit the spot she had been trying to find. Mary's face could not have become so innocent, lying there on that slab, otherwise.

'Black and white are easy even for children to identify. But it seems to me that the older you grow, and the more shades of grey in between you can see and sympathise with, the wiser you become.' Ross laughed. 'I can tell you all that from the superior age of twenty-nine.'

'Perhaps it was not a coincidence, then, that on your red-letter day I really wanted to wear red. Mary Paterson always wore red dresses. I never possessed one.'

'You will, I promise you! The red dress is the best

thing, even counting the Hallelujah Chorus, that I have heard today!' He turned her round to walk back. 'How is your headache?'

'Better. In fact, it is gone, and it was not the sea breezes that chased it away. It was a doctor.'

'I intend to do much more for you than that before very long,' Ross said. 'But, in the meantime, over there is the inn where we shall dine. The Peacock.'

'Everyone in Edinburgh knows about the Peacock, famous for its fish suppers,' Candida said as they crossed the cobbled street towards its lights. 'But I have never been before.'

'I have the feeling it is only the first of many new experiences for you,' Ross promised.

Inside the Peacock it was spotlessly clean, with small red tablecloths cornerwise on scrubbed wooden tables. On every one sat a red candle in a scallop-shell, and nets hung all round the walls, decorated with the white and pink shells of giant crabs and lobsters. Candida could not decide if it was these colours that made her feel so hungry all of a sudden, or the delicious smell of fish, fresh from the sea, frying in the back.

'You realise that the decoration of Paradise House will be the next thing? How shall we decorate the dining-room?' Ross asked uncannily.

'I had not even begun to consider it.'

'Good. Then since you have no preconceived ideas, it will be in red and gold,' he said decisively. 'Red is always welcoming and rich. It gives you an appetite.'

Young serving-girls dressed in the picturesque costume of the Newhaven fishwives of fifty years earlier were running about busily with their striped skirts looped up in the traditional way, when an older, buxom woman came up to their table to greet them.

'Dr Alexander Laing, sir! Ye've come back to see us, then! And wi' sic a bonnie, bonnie lass,' she cried. 'Dinna be shy, lassie. Nobody's shy for long wi' Bella Claws. "Crabby Claws" they call me,' she wheezed, 'on account o' my celebrated suppers. Noo, what'll it be?'

'It cannot be some of your oysters, of course,' Ross said regretfully.

'Not without an "r" in the month! No, no! But I have prepared little pots of Mussel Ragoo instead.'

'And what is that gorgeous smell?'

'Rizzared Haddies,' Mistress Claws said. 'Fresh today.'

'The very thing, Bella,' Ross said, 'along with a bottle of your best white wine.'

Mistress Claws bent down and whispered in his ear.

'Oh, better still!' he exclaimed. 'I meant this to be a celebration anyway.'

'I should have given you a present,' Candida said when Mistress Claws went away to see to his order.

'It is still not too late.' Ross leaned over the table towards her and put both his hands on hers. 'Of course blood is thicker than water. Of course you are in a turmoil just now, because of it. It is not the time to tell you that from the first minute I saw you there was no competition, twin sister or no twin sister. It is not the moment to tell you much more than that, or to ask you a very important question. There are too many unanswered questions in your life already for me to pose another at this time. You are not ready for any more.'

'No, Ross, I am not. And there is something else.' She hesitated, not knowing how to put it.

'Until you are, you would rather I did not kiss you again.'

She was amazed at his perception, and she had never wanted him to kiss her more than she did then, sitting there with him in the inn in Newhaven. She knew perfectly well she could will him to do so with just one look, and she battled with herself while she kept her eyes firmly fixed on the red tablecloth.

'It is because, when you do, it isn't just flirting, to me,' she said, looking up at him at last with honest blue eyes. 'It goes a lot deeper than that.'

'Well, you have managed it, Candida!' Ross gave her hands a final squeeze and let them go, smiling. 'You have just given me my best birthday present, after all!'

One serving-girl arrived with two little brown pots in which the mussels were cooked with mushrooms in a thick cream sauce sharpened with nutmeg and decorated with a slice of lemon. Mistress Claws herself had a bottle newly opened and frothing and covered in a white cloth.

'I opened it in the back, sir,' she said, 'so that nobody else would hear it pop. But it's no' every day we get in a bonnie lassie like your lady, here.'

'It is her only bottle of champagne,' Ross said, pouring out the sparkling wine. 'We got it, thanks to you.'

'A happy birthday, Ross,' said Candida, raising her glass.

'It is,' he said. 'The best ever. Now drink with me to my thirtieth. Next year I promise you it will be even better than this.'

'In Ireland?' she said, when the haddocks arrived, plump and crisply brown on the outside and snow white inside, accompanied by fried potatoes.

'I am not going back immediately. Mr Dick has asked me to help him for a time at the Veterinary College.'

Candida's heart thudded with pleasure. It was as though the tide had turned. Perhaps, now, the good luck would begin. She could not have borne it if he had gone away. For the first time since she had met him she relaxed, and the little supper became a light-hearted affair.

On the way home she leaned her head on Ross's shoulder, tired, happy and utterly trusting. He smiled above it, and anyone who did not know him might have thought his narrowed green eyes were calculating, like a cat's eyes, and that he was waiting only to pounce when the time was right.

Samuel Devine pushed his barrow of flowers to the Rotunda on the Mound, as near as he dared. Sometimes after the performances the men bought their ladies a bunch of roses, and today he had some beauties, it being the month of July. He wished he could see only one of the performances himself some day. Folk said there were views of battles and famous cities, and all in colour. Perhaps he might go in the winter, at Christmas or Hogmanay. That was when he always made plenty of money, going along the middle of the streets with his barrow full of pure gold, crying, 'Fine Venetian oranges! Wha'll buy sweet Venetian oranges? Nane o' yer foreign trash! Oranges! Oranges! Real New Year oranges, three a penny. Bloods, a bawbee!'

But the pickings were poor at the Rotunda today. Nobody seemed to want roses. After an hour, he trundled along to Deacon Brodie's Tavern in the Lawnmarket, and stood there wishing he had the money to go inside himself.

God, what a man that Deacon Brodie had been, forty years ago, before they hanged him from the city's new gallows! And the joke of it was, they were the gallows he had designed himself! By day he had been so well respected that he was elected Deacon Councillor of Edinburgh, but by night he had been a gambler and a thief, a drunkard and a womaniser.

'A rose for the bonnie lassie?' He sprang to life when a couple emerged.

Other hawkers came out in the Lawnmarket at the darkening until soon it was like a Friday market with ribbons, fish, greens, gloves and even flowers, Samuel observed sourly, laid out on tables and orange-boxes. Still, he did a good trade, after all. He must remember Deacon Brodie's Tavern another day. He sold all his roses and made half a crown. Time to go down to the White Hart for something to eat and a dram or two.

Samuel ate two mutton pies, one after the other. On second thoughts, he went up to the bar and ordered another, and his third glass of whisky.

'Sure, an' I don't know where you put it all!' said an admiring voice at his side, and he looked into the smiling face of a fellow with sandy hair and a touch of the Irish brogue. 'And you so thin and small!'

'I could aye eat,' Samuel said, 'when I got the chance.'

'Things are dear,' the man agreed, 'terrible dear. You like a dram, as well?'

'This'll ha'e to be my last,' Samuel said sorrowfully, 'and me just gettin' my brains to work, now.'

'Och, stay and have one with me,' the man said. 'I'd like someone to talk to.'

So he sat and talked, and drank, with the Irishman. A real grand fellow he was. And then, just before closing time, he up and left. Samuel couldn't understand it. The man just disappeared. He was the last one to lurch out of the White Hart into the deserted Grassmarket with his head that muzzy he could hardly see. Another drink would have cleared it fine!

'Why, where did ye get to,' he managed to ask the Irishman, suddenly at his side again.

'It was a call of nature, as you might say,' Wull said. 'You look as if you could do with another drink, Samuel. Come along with me. It isn't much of a house, but my friend William always has a spare bottle.'

It wasn't much of a house, right enough, Samuel thought groggily. But then, neither was his own. Wull had gone to get his friend William and the bottle. In the meantime, the straw by the fire looked inviting, and he was that sleepy . . . He closed his eyes for the last time, and something soft and suffocating . . . suffocating . . .

Candida was out in what she called the Dispensary, a large airy outhouse she had asked the workmen to line and shelve and paint pure white. She was working at the bench under the windows. In *Materia Medica* there were instructions for translating the herbs she had found into healing balms and tinctures and the pills she was rolling now, when Ross came out to Paradise House on what were almost daily visits nowadays, however fleeting.

'And what will the old gentleman say about this?' he asked.

'Oh, I will clear it all away long before he gets here. This is a place I thought his housekeeper could use as a dairy, perhaps.'

'What is in this row of oyster-shells, Candida?'

'Ointments of various kinds. Everything has come from herbs out there in the wild land and the woods.'

Ross sniffed at the ointments. 'Hm! You did not waste your time at the Outside Classes, I see. Indeed, it is to be hoped that he will never destroy the wild land. But today I have a little time in hand, enough to pay a visit to the new Botanical Gardens in Inverleith Row. Have you ever been there?'

'No,' she said, beginning to take off the long pinafore she wore over her thin muslin gown.

She loosened its sash while he unbuttoned it at the nape of her neck, and she shivered at his touch, in spite of all her resolve.

'What is the matter?' he asked, with a smile lurking in his eyes. 'Are my hands cold?'

'I have always wanted to go to the Botanical Gardens,' she said, flinging her pinafore on the bench and ignoring his question.

'Then shall we go?' He smiled lightly and watchfully.

Still confused, Candida walked out of his grasp and quickly round to the front of the house, while the July sun beat down. She got into his carriage in her floating white gown, every curve accentuated, and Ross followed her, still smiling.

'It is so hot,' she said, trying to keep the conversation, at least, impersonal. It did not last long. They had not gone far when she discovered she had left in too much of a rush. 'And I have forgotten my hat. It was in the house.'

'Yes, I noticed you were in a hurry to get away.' Ross looked into her flushed face. 'Never mind. I shall buy you one at the gates. There is always a woman there selling straw hats—of a sort. But they are light and airy at least, and shade you from the sun.'

Why must she persist with her problem? she wondered unhappily. Why did she not let the whole thing drop as he had tried to persuade her? Why did she not just give in now, when he so obviously adored her?

Every day he was becoming harder and harder to resist. What would be the inevitable outcome if she did not resist?

She knew the inevitable outcome. But she could never marry him, if it came to that. She could never marry anyone with a mystery like this lurking behind her. Blood was thicker than water, and it was only commonsense to remember it—for the sake of her children, if she ever had any. Her spine became steel at the thought. She had to know her own forebears before she could ever contemplate such a thing as a family of her own. Her problem had become their problem. Her problem had become a quest.

Her expression was serious when they got down from the carriage, and Ross settled a wide-brimmed hat on her head.

'It is quite ridiculous,' he said. 'Everything you put on suits you, even this silly straw hat!'

'Don't, Ross,' she said quietly. 'Don't pay me compliments . . .'

'It is all right,' he tried to reassure her, taking her hand. The special tingles started up her arms and down through her body, and she looked at him with all the longing in the world.

'It is not all right,' she said with a quiver, and stood her ground.

'No,' he sighed, 'and the sooner you straighten everything out, the better.'

'How can I do that?'

'Something will happen. I cannot tell you what, or when. Life has a strange way of making things happen. When the time comes, you will know. However, Candida, just now we are here to look at the shrubs and the perennial plants, something to establish the old gentleman's garden. Tell me all the ones you admire, and I will take a note of them.'

'But my taste may not be his.'

'Let me take the blame. I will help you.' Ross took out his notebook and pencil so matter-of-factly that the heated moment passed safely.

He did help her. He seemed to understand the wild confusion of her heart and body, and gradually it subsided while they wandered through a fraction of the eight acres of the Gardens, round some of the hothouses and the frames, and discussed and argued between them what would be best in this part, or that corner, and which border of the Paradise House gardens, while they sat awhile in the dappled shade under the trees.

Candida's mind was still running on flowers when, bathed, cooled and resting, she lay on the chaise-longue in her room later that evening. All the windows were open and the scent of the roses was strong and sweet. But one perfume in the room was sharper and sweeter still. It came from a vase of white, yellow and pink dainty tubular flowers.

'What are these?' she asked Kitty.

'Freesias, I think Frank called them, miss. I do not know too much about flowers myself, but I can see I'll have to learn, for his sake. He said he grew them from bulbs.'

'How delicate they are,' Candida said, 'and what a scent! They are perfect.'

'They would be, if Frank had anything to do with them, Miss Candida. That is his hobby—flowers and vegetables. In fact, it is his passion.'

'You need not tell me that,' Candida smiled, eyeing the moonstone ring firmly back on Kitty's finger.

Kitty blushed. 'Oh, but it is, miss! He is passionately fond of growing things. It is a wonder to see those great stubby fingers of his so gentle with plants. They will be the ruin of him as a policeman, I say. But, Miss Candida,' reverting to her usual role of informer, 'did you know that Miss Alanna thinks she has found the perfect house? She saw it today!'

Lady Alison managed to accompany the party of four young people going over to the Old Town the following afternoon. They drove past George Heriot's Hospital and through the ornamental park of the Meadows.

'It is beautiful here,' Alanna said, her eyes shining.

Lady Alison told her that one of the landscape gardeners employed was Robert Burns's father, William Burness, and that Robert changed the spelling of his surname later in life. They drove on to the other end of the park, to the Hope Park district.

'And that is the house,' Finlay said. 'The house with the Dutch frontage. That is what took Alanna's eye.'

'Very elegant,' Lady Alison said, and they all got down to spend the next hour admiring it inside and out.

'Finlay is going to his solicitor now to put in a bid for it,' Alanna said. 'If you would drop us at the Tron?'

'What did you think of it, Candida?' Ross asked, as they went back to Charlotte Square.

'Very formal, and very elegant,' she replied. She did not dare to say 'stiff and stuffy'—not in front of Mama, to hurt her feelings.

'It should suit their future life-style as I imagine it, very well,' Lady Alison said. 'Rather stiff and stuffy,' and could not understand why Ross and Candida laughed so much.

'I hope Finlay gets it,' Ross said. 'I understand in Scottish law it is all done on a system of bidding?'

'By secret bids, if there are two or more interested,' Lady Alison said, 'and the solicitor must accept the highest offer. Of course,' she smiled at him, 'there was no problem in the case of Paradise House. The old gentleman was the only bidder.'

'I suppose that is why he got it for a song,' Ross said, and Candida had the curious impression that they were talking to each other over her head, but for her benefit. 'That is why he can afford to lavish money on restoring it now.'

'Ah,' Candida said, 'in that case, I shall not feel so badly. I was very worried that we were spending too much of his money.'

'You see, Aunt Alison, she worries,' Ross said, 'and her worries are her secrets. She tells nobody any of her secrets, and yet she wants to know all of theirs. She is a proper Scorpio.'

'She is indeed. I have often observed it. But that is one thing I do not believe she has pursued up to now—the signs of the Zodiac.'

'Birth-signs, Mama?'

'There is a very interesting Frenchman coming here at the end of the month to give a lecture about it,' Ross said. 'Would you both care to come?'

'It depends on the date,' Lady Alison replied.

'It is easy to remember. It is the last day of July, the 31st.'

'A Saturday, and that is the evening of "The Friends of Susan Ferrier". I have invited them all round to Charlotte Square."

'And who are they?' Ross asked.

'Sir Walter Scott, Henry MacKenzie—author of *Man of Feeling*, William Blackwood the publisher, James Hogg, the "Ettrick Shepherd", and a few others. Susan Ferrier has written two books. The first was called *Marriage* and the second *Inheritance*. She is our first Scottish lady novelist.'

Candida had read both of them, and had attended many such meetings. She would far rather have plunged into the signs of the Zodiac, and as usual she found the hardest thing to do was to disguise her feelings from her mother.

'But I will excuse you this time, dear,' Lady Alison said. 'I am sure the lecture on astrology will be far more educational.'

'People have always poked fun at things they do not understand,' Ross said on the way to Monsieur Garolin's lecture. 'And although they are fascinated by the stars and what the stars foretell, at the same time they are a little afraid of it all.'

Candida shivered. She did not know what to expect.

'They are afraid for the same reason that you shivered just then. They fear the unknown and what tomorrow may bring. They do not want to know the future unless it is good news, but at the same time they long to do so, as much as they want to know what happened in the past.'

'I wish . . .' Candida began, and then decided to keep it to herself.

'I do not know if what we hear tonight will help you.' Ross went on, as though he had not noticed, and helped her down from the cab. 'But I only hope it does.'

'Astrology,' Monsieur Garolin began in his broken accent, 'is the least regarded of all the sciences, although it was begun in 5000 BC to our certain knowledge.' He went on to explain its two branches. 'Natural astrology is concerned with the movement of the heavenly bodies and their calculations, which I do not suppose you wish to study tonight.' He paused, and looked around the packed audience with a smile. 'No matter where I lecture, the halls are full. It is the second branch, judicial astrology, which studies the influences of the stars and planets on human life and fate, that I shall discuss this evening.'

The audience clapped in appreciation.

'Whatever star we were born under, whichever of the twelve sun signs we were born under, influences the rest of our lives. In fact, it predestines our lives,' Monsieur Garolin stated categorically. 'Take the first sign of the Zodiac, for example. It is Aries. Those of us who were born between March 21st and April 20th have great qualities of leadership. Nothing on earth can change their direct, forceful manner. Nothing on earth can change their rashness. Nothing on earth can change their bravery or, once given, their whole-hearted affection.'

That was Papa, exactly. Candida sat enthralled as Monsieur Garolin went through all the twelve signs, while she mentally slotted everyone she knew into each one he described. She paid particular attention to Ross's sign of Cancer.

'Cancer's sign is the Crab, and there you have it. His soft heart is so full of sentiment that it often makes him feel too vulnerable. Then he crawls into his convenient shell. He craves security, and to that end acquires and stores up money. In fact he gathers everything around him he can under his shell—or his home. His home is of the utmost importance to him.'

Lady Alison's love of cleanliness and tidiness was described in the sign of Virgo, her appearance of tranquillity which often cloaked worry, her delicate features and her very clear eyes.

Towards the interval, Monsieur Garolin came to Candida's own sign, Scorpio. 'These are the hardest people to know,' he said. 'They hide their thoughts from us, and they can see right through everyone else. They love to investigate the shadows and sometimes wander into dangerous situations in their efforts to penetrate life, for they know no fear themselves, and respect fearlessness in others. Above all, they respect strength, and to those they consider strong, they are very loyal.'

'Well, Candida,' Ross asked, in the short interval. 'What do you think of it so far?'

'Fascinating, and not at all what I expected.'

'In a few minutes he is going on to tell us which birth-signs are compatible with which. In other words, which people would get on well together. It could be a recipe for marriage,' Ross said, 'and at the end, he will call for questions. Do you have any?'

'One,' she said, and told him.

'Exactly,' Ross laughed. 'I'll ask him myself.'

The Frenchman came back on stage again, and it was almost at the end of his lecture that he began to speak of the relationship between a Cancer man and a Scorpio woman.

'They will share the qualities of gentleness, loyalty, intensity of emotion and great imagination,' he said. 'Together, they can create all manner of marvellous things—a powerful love, a star-blessed child, or a great career. "Create" is the key word between these two.'

At question time, Ross stood up. 'Monsieur Garolin,' he said, 'have you considered the possibility of Free Will?'

'Yes indeed,' said Monsieur Garolin. 'Thank you for that question. We are all captains of our own ships, free to make our own choices in the shaping of our lives. But the stars predetermine how we do it.'

'We were certainly given a great deal to think about tonight,' Ross said, as they left the hall and got into another cab. 'Not least that we are utterly suited. Of course, we did not need Monsieur Garolin to tell us that.'

He put his arm round her quite involuntarily, and just as instinctively she clung to him. For a minute, before she broke away, she seriously considered what the future might have been with him, in different circumstances. A wonderful life.

'I hear you, dear Crab,' she said sadly. 'I really do.'

Some woman has come asking to see you, Candida,' Lady Alison said next morning. 'A Mistress McGuire.'

'I have never heard of her. What is she like? What does she want?'

'Goodness knows, dear. Liza says she is quite well dressed and about my age. Indeed, Liza got the impression from the way she spoke that she was from the Society for Fallen Women.'

'Fallen Women?' Candida was staggered.

'I thought it might be one of your latest interests,' Lady Alison said, 'although it was strange that you had not told me.'

'Of course not, Mama. I do not know any Fallen Women, except . . . and . . . there is enough to do, to mind my own business,' Candida finished in a rush.

'Perhaps you should give her a hearing?' Lady Alison said doubtfully. 'Why do I get this feeling that if I were in my sane senses I would never allow it?'

'Oh, Mama! It is only some lady begging for charity. Where is she?'

'Liza put her in the back sitting-room to wait. You had better take Kitty with you, dear. You never know, with strangers.'

'I had better take some money with me as well as Kitty. No, Mama,' Candida waved her mother's offer away. 'I have plenty upstairs.'

They opened the door of the back sitting-room, and Candida went in and round behind the table, while Kitty took up her position on a chair beside the door. Their visitor did not stand up at their entrance. She remained scowling on her chair, and as soon as Kitty saw who she was her face darkened and her lips stretched out in a disapproving line, while Candida recognised just as instantly the old woman from the Grassmarket who had been so determined to speak to her.

'Mistress McGuire?' she asked.

'It is,' the woman said, and clamped her mouth shut like a mousetrap.

Candida could see this was going to be a very difficult interview from the outset. 'You wished to speak to me?' she said.

'Alone!' Mistress McGuire jerked her head in Kitty's direction.

There was some pent-up excitement about the old woman that interested Candida. Whatever she wished to say, it was urgent. She could tell by the way Mistress McGuire's face was twitching. She even seemed on the point of tears, although they might be tears of rage, Candida suspected. She made up her mind. 'You may leave us, Kitty.'

'But, Miss Candida!'

'Leave us, Kitty,' she repeated determinedly, 'and wait in the hall.' As soon as the door closed, she spoke to the woman again. 'I understand you have come on behalf of the Fallen Women of this city?'

'You could put it that way, I dare say,' the woman said with the suspicion of a sneer. 'It's about one Fallen Woman I've known in me time, if not two.'

'Here it comes now,' every one of Candida's senses warned her, and just as Ross had forecast, she recognised it at once. In sone way, this old woman had the power to change her life. 'I am afraid I do not understand, Mistress McGuire,' she said.

'Then maybe this'll help you.' She pushed a letter across the tatable.

Candida picked it up, prickles running in the nape of her neck. Everything was strange about this interview, this woman, her previous encounters with her, but none so strange as now.

'But it is addressed to Mary Paterson,' she said, so revolted that she dropped it again, 'I am sorry to tell you that she is dead.'

'D'ye think I dinna ken it? Ay, she's dead! Murdered, she was! But you'd better pick that letter back up again, Miss Candida Forbes! It's about your mother—your real mother. The one in London. Dyin', she is!'

Candida opened it and read it in a daze. If Mistress McGuire hoped for a violent reaction or a denial, she was bitterly disappointed. The letter was from a hospital in London, written by a Sister Teresa. She asked Mary Paterson to come as soon as she could to see Biddy Mallone, who had met with a serious accident.

'I was present at the birth o' Mary Paterson,' Mistress McGuire's black eyes bored into her steady blue gaze. 'In fact, I delivered her. And then we discovered that Biddy wasnae having one bairn, but twa! The last thing she wanted was you! One was bad enough.'

The cruelty of her words was too immense for Candida to comprehend at that moment. The most important thing was to dig out the truth, and as many clues as she could.

'And what makes you think the other twin was me, Mistress McGuire?'

'You were born on the 9th of November 1809, were ye no'? A few months after that, Biddy wrote and told me where she'd left Mary Paterson. I kept my eye on her after that, and took up wi' her when she came from Gilmerton to live in Edinburgh. Yer mother was aye in touch wi' Mary. She wrote to her, and Mary even went to London awhile.'

'Why did she not stay there, then? She would have

made a better living in London, surely?'

'She was better kent here. She did a roaring trade here. She made a lot o' money . . . Although she never seemed to have any,' Mistress McGuire admitted. 'Biddy Mallone never gave you another thought. She took it for granted you were dead, and so did I, until I saw you that day in the Grassmarket. Then I knew!'

So her mother had always kept in touch with Mary, had she? And for her other baby daughter she had never spared another thought. It was very rarely that Candida got angry, but when she did there was a sting in her tail like a scorpion's. She unleashed it now.

'What is it you want from me?' she asked coldly. 'Money?'

'That, as well. For now!' Mistress McGuire snatched back the letter. 'This letter could earn me my keep for the rest o' my life.'

'And how is that?' Candida asked, dangerously pleasant. 'It is not even addressed to me.'

'You canna deny any o' it. And I'll make sure the word gets around Edinburgh—if I choose.'

'But you have not told me anything I did not already know, Mistress McGuire, and a lot of other people, besides. I already knew Mary Paterson was my twin, and we were both abandoned. I already knew I was adopted. I can even tell you something that you do not know. I was found in Candlemaker Row. Everyone who knows me, knows that,' she gambled.

'She only got as far as Candlemaker Row wi' you, did she?' the woman sniffed. 'It didn't take her long to get rid o' you, then.'

Candida swallowed hard and ignored that. 'I was fortunate enough to be found by very rich people,' she said, 'and money talks. It talks louder than slander or blackmail, which is what this is, Mistress McGuire. Money pays lawyers to put slanderers and blackmailers in prison!' She sat back and smiled at the old woman. 'Oh yes, I am very lucky. Shall I ring the bell? One of the maids will show you out.'

'An' what about this letter, then?' the woman's tone was truculent.

'What about it?' Candida asked, sensing she was on the winning side.

'I could sell it to you.'

'I do not really want it, Mistress McGuire. But I have three sovereigns with me. I was going to give them to the Society for Fallen Women. I could give them to you instead, and the letter, which I am afraid is of no value, could be my receipt. People with money keep accounts, you see.' She delivered her final sting and casually laid out the three sovereigns in front of her on the table.

'I'll tak' it,' Mistress McGuire said, and threw the letter angrily on the table.

Candida rang the bell, and Kitty burst in. 'Show this woman out, Kitty,' she said, and swept past her visitor. 'She will not be back.'

'Whatever you said in there was pure poison!' Kitty glared at the woman. 'I had you weighed up from the start!'

Mistress McGuire made as if to turn on her, but Kitty took her from behind and forcibly ejected her. 'Out ye go!' she said, with great satisfaction, and slammed the door.

'It was all very worth while,' Ellen McGuire told the caddies when she landed on the pavement, perhaps more suddenly than she had anticipated. She had got back into the rickety old sedan-chair before it struck her that if only she had followed Biddy Mallone that day she kicked her out with her babies, her own life might have been very different. She would have seen the one left in Candlemaker Row. She would have got on to her sooner—a lot sooner. She took one last look at No. 13 Charlotte Square, and sighed. That was how the great chances of this life slipped past you. 'Back to the Grassmarket,' she told the waiting men.

The caddies saw the gleam of gold in her hand. It was enough to make them lift up the old sedan-chair with a will, and patter off.

CHAPTER EIGHT

AN HOUR later, after she had read the letter over and over again, Candida was still angry, burning with anger. Then she did what she always did in a crisis. She went to see her mother.

'You saw the woman?' Lady Alison asked. 'How much did you give her for the Society for Fallen Women?'

It took all the wind out of Candida's sails. She looked at the lady who had picked her up out of the gutter, brought her back to life and made her a lady herself, and her heart filled up with a fiercely protective, fiercely loyal feeling that at all costs Lady Alison should never be hurt, least of all by her. Candida searched for the words to tell her the truth as gently as possible.

'Oh, Mama!' she said. 'If it matters at all, it was three guineas, and cheap at the price to get rid of a blackmailer! Mistress McGuire was not from any Society, except the Society for Mistress McGuire. But there is no need to worry. She will never be back here again.'

At the word 'blackmail' and the realisation of all her worst fears Lady Alison did not flinch, now that the moment of truth that she had dreaded so long had arrived.

'Well, my darling child, I can see that now you know it all. Three guineas was indeed a small price to pay, considering the price we have paid all these years to keep such knowledge from you. Your father and I have had a long-running argument about it for nineteen years. He always said you should be told. I always agreed with him. Yet neither of us could have the heart to do it.'

'I know you could not, Mama. But the midwife who delivered me could. She turned out to be Mistress McGuire.'

'That woman?'

'And by the look and the sound of her, probably turned all three of us out a week later, my sister and me, and the unknown woman who bore us. Unknown until now, that is.'

'Oh, Candida! My poor child! But there was another child? You had a sister, she said?'

'You will have to prepare yourself for a shock, Mama.'

'It is your Papa who fusses, you know. I am as strong as a horse, only he has never believed it since I lost both our babies.'

'I never knew you had two babies! Their names are not in the Bible. Oh . . .' Candida realised they could neither of them have been born alive. 'Oh, Mama, that was dreadful!'

'It *was* dreadful. It was heart-breaking, and one reason out of many reasons why we have loved you even more, Candida. Yes, to lose them both was one shock after another. But in this life it is nothing but shocks. What is it this time?'

Candida handed her over the letter.

'But it is addressed to a Mary Paterson!' A dawning horror came into Lady Alison's eyes. 'All the rumours were that Mary Paterson was that poor girl of the streets who was murdered recently.'

Candida decided not to mention that she had actually seen her dead body laid out on a slab in front of Dr Knox in Surgeons' Hall. Enough was enough, and Lady Alison still had another very difficult bridge to cross.

'She was, Mama.'

'Oh, poor child . . . But what has this to do with you?'

'Mistress McGuire did not deliver only me into the world. I had a twin sister, Mama. Her name was Mary Paterson.'

They struggled through the following days each in their own private misery. Lady Alison, her back as straight as ever was pale, quiet and withdrawn. Mr Forbes was outraged and bewildered.

'Twins?' he kept repeating to his wife. 'At the time we never thought of it! We never followed up the birth of any twins.'

He was so distraught that Lady Alison became more concerned for him than for all her other problems. 'Of course I shall get up today as usual, Liza,' she insisted every morning, her face pinched and white. 'Mr Atholl needs me.'

Up in her room Candida wrestled with the situation. The woman who had given her birth was dying. Sister Teresa had made that very clear without actually saying so. But why should she care? How could she care for a woman who had abandoned her? Had the woman ever given her another thought all these nineteen years since? Worse still, she had never lost touch with her other baby daughter, had she, not with Mary Paterson?

The answers always came back the same. No, no, and no. When Candida got down to the very bottom of her pit of unhappiness she faced the fact that in spite of it all, she was jealous of the woman's preference for Mary Paterson. Yet there was a sort of rough justice to it. Mary might not have been forgotten, as she had been forgotten, but Mary was dead, and she was still living. Candida got no satisfaction from that thought, and the woman in London obviously did not know any of it. The woman in London had tried to cling on to her own flesh and blood somehow and might be so overjoyed to find she had another daughter still alive that it would compensate for the death of Mary. It might even help her to recover. But the woman in London Candida could not call Mother, not if her life depended on it.

Lady Alison came out of her long trance, and No. 13 Charlotte Square sprang back to life on Sunday.

'What conclusions have you come to, Candida?'

'None. I do not know what to think, Mama.'

'I know you better than that. You do not want to go to London, yet you think you should. Is that it?'

'I was always the one who said "blood is thicker than water", but now I cannot accept it. I just cannot accept that woman in London as my mother. How can I? You have always been my mother, and you always will be.'

'My dear Candida, that will never change, no matter what happens,' Mr Forbes said. 'We adopted you. But it is not like you to be so incurious, that is the point. We believe you have not suggested going to London because you think it would hurt our feelings.'

'We also believe you should go,' Lady Alison said. 'Of course you should, before it is too late. You will only regret it for the rest of your life if you do not, no matter what your feelings are for this Biddy Mallone, poor soul. Think about it for a day or two.'

'If we are going to be man and wife, Frank Clarke, I hope you've learned a lesson,' Kitty blazed. 'I've never got over it! You canna keep important things like that from me—ever again!'

'Ho!' Frank scoffed, and admired her flashing eyes. 'Ye're that bonnie when ye're angry, Kitty! Anyway, it wasn't important at a'. Keeping an eye on Mary and Janet was only doing my job.'

'Well, I very nearly didn't take you back on account o' it. How was I to know? And on Hogmanay, too! After a whole week away from you at the time, as well?'

'Ay, ye've had that wee nose in the air ever since!' Frank put his arm round her and tickled her, to Kitty's utter delight, so that she giggled and screamed. 'Stop your screeching, lassie! So you missed me, after all? Well, after that you wouldn't let me see you for nine weeks. How would you like to go through the rest of your life without Frank Clarke? What about this?'

He kissed her soundly, and Kitty went absolutely limp. 'I couldn't live without you now, Frank. Those nine weeks were more than enough to find that out,' she said, melting completely. 'Anyway it wasn't a state secret you were asked to keep. You could have told me.'

'All right, then! I will the next time. How's that?'

'That's better!' She kissed him all over his beaming face.

'All the same, it's no' over yet, ye ken.' Frank held her at arm's length to warn her seriously. 'We still haven't caught them. And another thing: ye're not to go alone into the Grassmarket, even through the day.'

'Dinna worry. Who are these two men you suspect, anyway?'

'Murderers, and don't you forget it, lassie. Two Irishmen, and if I tell you their names ye've to promise me faithfully ye'll never repeat them to a living soul.'

'Not even to Miss Candida?'

'Oh well,' Frank laughed, 'I dare say Mr Ross has been put through the mill the same as I have. I dare say he's had to tell her, too.'

'So who are they, then?'

'William Burke and William Hare.'

'Two Williams,' Kitty remarked. 'Burke and Hare. I've never heard o' them.'

'Ye have now, and soon so will a'body else in Edinburgh. Oh, Kitty, I wish we could catch them tomorrow! We'd be married the next day!'

'I wish you could an' a', Frank,' Kitty sighed.

'Ross!' Lady Alison grasped his hands in the parlour two days later. 'She has made up her mind to go.'

'I expected it,' he said gravely. 'You knew she would not rest until she got to the bottom of it.'

'I do not blame her. It is only natural that she should want to see her real mother. If I were in her position, I should feel the same.'

'Then you do not resent it, Aunt Alison?'

'I may lose her altogether, you mean? Biddy Mallone spent the last nineteen years her way. I spent mine caring for Candida. I am prepared to take the gamble.'

'Well, she cannot go alone,' Mr Forbes declared, 'and neither of us can go with her. My wife is in no fit state, and I am tied up here with the Anatomy Act.'

'I suppose it would not be proper for me to accompany her?' Ross asked.

'Oh *no*, dear, although it is very kind of you to offer.'

'That is what I thought. But in any case I cannot very well leave Mr Dick for at least another month, except perhaps for a day here or there, so you will not be seeing much of me for a while. We are in the middle of a series of vital experiments at the Veterinary College. I wonder if Constable Clarke could be got off duty?'

'That is a brilliant suggestion!' Mr Forbes jumped at the idea.

'But not with Kitty in attendance,' Lady Alison warned. 'She has never been to London before. Liza must go instead. She has been with me so many times that she has some idea of the streets.'

'It is quite out of the question!' Mr Forbes thundered. 'I will not allow it! Liza will stay here with you and look after you!'

'I think Kitty could accompany Candida to London without any problem,' Ross said calmly. 'She is devoted to her, and on top of that she would go to the ends of the earth with the greatest of pleasure, if Frank Clarke were there also. We must never forget the power of love.'

'Absolutely,' Mr Forbes boomed enthusiastically. 'I myself have never forgotten it.'

'And as for the streets of London,' Ross dismissed them with a wave of his hand, 'which ones are we speaking about, anyway? Which hospital is it, and where will they stay?'

'The Linwood, I suppose, dear?' Lady Alison consulted her husband. 'They are used to us there. I shall have to drop them a letter very soon. And the hospital is the Royal Free, although I have never seen it.'

'Well,' said Ross, 'Frank Clarke has a good Scottish tongue in his head, has he not? When do they go?'

'On Saturday, dear,' Lady Alison said, 'and that is almost as worrying as all the rest of it. Candida has never been on board a ship before, and she is quite determined to go on the *Catherine*, sailing out of Leith at six o'clock.'

'Well, I cannot sit here any longer,' Mr Forbes said. 'If Constable Clarke has to be brought into this, there are a few strings I must pull.'

Thursday was one of the rare days that Ross was free.

'Do you think Candida could take me sightseeing?' he asked Lady Alison. 'So far, I have not visited one exhibition in this city. I have not even got so far as the Calton Hill.'

'That is a disgrace, Ross! You have been here nearly a year! Candida, you should go to the Raeburn Exhibition on the Mound.'

Leaving aside all the other famous people depicted there, even the self-portrait of Sir Henry Raeburn himself, there were paintings that drew Candida back and back again to gaze at them. The little boy with his rabbit, his glowing eyes innocent in his childish face, was so faithfully and lovingly captured, to stay just the way he was for evermore, that it was almost impossible to believe he was not looking at her in the flesh, and that all this before her eyes were only daubs of paint.

'I see that one is simply entitled, "A Boy with a Rabbit".' Ross came to stand beside her. 'But the catalogue says he was Raeburn's godson and favourite step-grandson, Henry Raeburn Inglis.'

'He must have loved him very much,' Candida said.

'You like these Raeburn paintings? It might be a good idea to buy one or two for Paradise House,' Ross said as they came out again upon the Mound. 'And now, where to?'

'We are supposed to be going from here to the Royal Observatory on the Calton Hill, according to Mama's itinerary.'

'By all means let us go to the Calton Hill. Perhaps there may be a seat to sit on, in this heat?'

'I did not really care about the Observatory anyway,' Candida said, after ten minutes of peace and quiet, when all they heard were the distant cries of children playing, and the birds twittering as they flew past. 'At least, not today.'

'I can see there are other things on your mind,' Ross yawned and lay back full stretch. He even appeared to be on the point of sleep.

'There are. I must go to London.'

'Why? That is a long way.'

His eyes actually closed, she could have sworn involuntarily. At this, the crossroads in her life, he was going to sleep. In fact, he was asleep. His breathing became slow and regular. He was totally uninterested. She got to her feet indignantly, and one lazy green eye opened.

'What were you saying? To London? Alone?'

'No.' She brushed down her skirts, smoothed them down and swept them across his head. 'Kitty is going with me, of course. And Constable Clarke.'

'Why?' he repeated, both eyes open now.

She had even been so weak-minded, so stupid, so trusting as to have considered confiding in him earlier this afternoon.

'There is someone there I wish to visit,' she said stiffly. 'A distant relative.'

'Distant in more ways than one,' Ross said as he got to his feet and stretched and yawned again. 'So it is a family visit, and all by yourself?'

'There is nobody else to go with me.'

'What a pity you did not warn me of this,' Ross said sincerely. 'But already I have made other arrangements with Mr Dick. When do you think you will go?'

'On Saturday, on the *Catherine*.'

'Not on Saturday! That is our busiest day of all! Otherwise, I assure you, I would not have allowed you to travel so far alone. Oh, Candida, I do not like it at all. You are a good sailor, I trust?'

He smiled so limpidly, so sincerely that she knew him well enough by now to realise that this was one gigantic lie he was telling her. He had not made any 'other arrangements' at all. He had other fish to fry on

Saturday, and she did not think they were in the Grassmarket, either. He simply was not interested in her.

One half of her felt completely rebuffed, the other half thankful and relieved. She had been battling with the feeling that what she would find in London was degradation of the lowest kind, the kind she had come from. Her pride insisted that Ross Alexander Laing was the last man she wanted there to see it.

'I shall be back in a week,' she smiled, calm and purposeful again. 'The *Catherine* sails back next Thursday, and depending on the weather, we should be back here by Saturday at the latest.'

'I shall be on Trinity Quay to meet you,' he promised.

'How very kind of you, Ross,' she said sweetly, and swept up the little steps of the carriage again.

If she had been very undecided before this afternoon, now she was utterly convinced she was doing the right thing.

'What are you in such a temper about?' Kitty asked her when she marched back into No. 13 Charlotte Square.

'A temper?' Candida snapped. 'I am not in a temper. I am too hot, that's all, and I cannot wait to pack our bags tomorrow!'

The drive down to Trinity Quay in Leith was one of the most uncomfortable of her life so far. The constraints were there, even without Frank Clarke so solemn and upright in his uniform, and Kitty beside him half adoring and half apprehensive, for her mother and father were more silent and gloomy than she had ever seen them before.

In an unhappy silence the luggage was taken off the carriage, up the gangway and deposited aboard the *Catherine*. Candida, with Kitty on one side and Frank on the other, stood at the deck rail, while Mr Forbes and Lady Alison stood on the quay, apart from everybody else seeing off loved ones, in their own little pool of misery. But at last to her thankfulness the hooters heralding departure went, and everybody waved good-bye. Everyone waved and waved, until Mama and Papa were only the merest specks.

It was still a beautiful warm August evening at half-past six when Candida surveyed their cabin. In it were two bunks, a washbasin clipped up to the wall, a round porthole and very little else, certainly no room to swing a cat.

'Unpack our night-things, Kitty,' she said. 'I am going up on deck.'

Nothing could have been smoother than sailing along the glassy Firth of Forth that evening. As they glided past, from Candida's position at the rail, the sea breeze was so cool upon her face that it reminded her just for a minute of a certain night in Newhaven. But now Newhaven was a long way behind. Edinburgh, with all its worries and horrors, was a long way behind. She stepped back a few paces to sit on one of the long wooden deck seats, and closed her eyes. Will this voyage into the unknown change my life? she wondered.

She opened her eyes briefly when somebody else sat down at the other end of the seat. It was only a man in a long black coat. His hat was pulled well down and the collar of his coat pulled well up over his face, and he lapsed immediately into immobility, with his head bowed. Perhaps he had worries of his own. In any case, he had disturbed her thoughts, and even the seagulls flew away, leaving no sound now except for the flip-flap of the sails and the mild protest of the waves splashing on her sides as the *Catherine* cut through them.

When they passed the Bass Rock the ship changed course and headed south into the North Sea. The breezes blew a good deal more strongly, and the ship began to rock a little. Candida sat there for another half-hour watching the sailors hauling down some of the sails and trimming the others. She and the man were the only two left on deck when the wind got up shrilly and she began to feel icy cold. There was no doubt that the *Catherine* was beginning to toss about quite alarmingly.

At first the uncomfortable pang in Candida's stomach was only a little pang, and stoutly she disregarded it. But as the ship heaved, the pang returned, and another and another, and her head began to spin. She would have to get up and go down to the cabin. She would have to lie down. When she got to her feet it was all a thousand times worse, and dizzily she staggered on the heaving deck. Then someone was behind her, two strong arms were supporting her and she felt herself half carried and half propelled down the steep companionway leading to the cabins, too sick and dizzy to care who it was.

Down there the wind was gone, the hard cold spray was gone, and the closeness of the atmosphere so unbearable that she gagged. The man did not stop to ask which cabin, and she could not have told him if he had. He seemed to know, and he kicked open the door and carried her inside while mists of sickness swirled before her eyes.

Kitty was nowhere to be seen . . . And she needed Kitty—*now!* Waves of sea-sickness broke over her. The man was still there, holding her head firmly over the wash-basin until it was all over. Candida was utterly mortified. It would have been bad enough with Kitty there, but with a complete stranger . . . She lifted her head from the basin, and the reflection of her face, a ghastly green, swam into focus in the mirror on the wall. But worse than that, behind her . . .

'*You!* Oh, no!'

'Yes, Candida,' Ross said. 'Come and lie down now.' He laid her down on her bunk beside the porthole.

'Oh, no,' she moaned again, while a thousand objections struggled through her mind. She felt too ill to deal with any of them. All she could do was roll over weakly with her back to him, rejection in every line of her body.

'That's right,' Ross said calmly. 'You are too tightly laced, as usual. But now I can loosen the fasteners on the back of your dress and then untie those laces.'

His hands were firm and knowledgeable, as if he undid ladies' clothing every day, and she was too weak to protest. But when he took her shoes off and put her feet under the blankets she stopped shuddering almost at once.

'If you could slip your dress off and get under the blankets altogether, you would feel much better,' he said.

She hesitated, but only for a minute. He was a doctor, wasn't he? And she felt so ill . . . Goodness knew where Kitty could be . . . She wriggled out of her dress, innocently revealing the petticoat underneath it. It was made of very fine white lawn and its bodice was décolletée—too décolletée by far, now that its strings at the back had been untied. She got under the blankets hastily and he pulled them up under her chin. The touch of his fingers on the delicate skin of her neck went through her like a current of lightning, shocking yet infinitely pleasurable, and Candida began to feel half alive again.

'What are you doing here?' she asked ungraciously. 'Why are you on this ship? Why did you not tell me?'

'You did not seriously imagine you could go to London, of all places, without me?'

For a second he looked as genuinely astonished as a small boy might do when wrongfully accused, and just as pained. A small smile flitted over Candida's face at the sight of it, wiped off immediately in the light of his next statement.

'I have every right to sail on this ship if I choose to do so.'

'Of course.'

'There is no law that says I must tell you my every move, either.'

'No,' Candida agreed coldly.

'As it so happens, I have business of my own in London.'

'Oh!'

'Besides, if I had told you, somehow your mother and father would have got to know, and Lady Alison expressly forbade it.' His eyes were dancing. 'I wonder why?'

'Oh, Ross, then you asked her? But I thought you could not leave Mr Dick at the Veterinary College?'

'Mr Dick understands that my business in London is much more pressing.'

By this time Candida had grasped many things. In spite of all his teasing, he was ruthlessly determined to accompany her. He was prepared to deceive anyone, even her mother and father, to do so. However, she still held one trump-card. He did not know that it was her real mother she had come to see, and if she died in the attempt he would never know that part of the mystery, and never set eyes on her.

'Of course you have a cabin of your own to go to?' she asked.

'Neither a cabin nor a berth.' His green eyes smiled down at her. 'I was too late to get one.'

'So that was why you were on deck! You cannot go back up there in this storm!'

'So what am I to do, Candida?' he asked mockingly, and when she looked agonised, he laughed gently. 'It would not be proper, would it?'

'Do you know everything I think?'

'Most of it!' He was serious again. 'So I shall go and see what Kitty has been up to, and fetch her back if she is able to walk. I dare say she has been a bit under the weather, too. Now, sleep if you can, Candida, and I shall sit here on her bunk until you do.'

She must have been sleeping for a long time when a knock on the door woke her, and for a minute she could not remember where she was. It was broad daylight, waves rushed past the porthole, and Ross had gone. At once, Candida was overcome with desolation.

'Come in,' she said hopefully.

But it was Kitty's white face that poked around the door, and once she had ascertained that her mistress was decently covered up in bed she opened the door a little further, to reveal Frank Clarke behind her.

'Kitty collapsed,' he said briefly. 'Mr Ross says she has not recovered yet.'

'Where is Mr Ross?' Candida asked.

'In my cabin,' Frank said, and marched off, leaving them to their own feminine devices for the time being.

'You had better lie down, Kitty,' Candida said. 'You look terrible.'

'I still feel terrible, miss!' Kitty smiled at her wanly. 'I never thought the first night I would spend with Frank would be like that! I wouldn't blame him if he never marries me now. I'm that ashamed of meself, Miss Candida.'

'What nonsense, dear! Nobody can help being ill. That is a thing everyone forgives and forgets when you are better,' Candida assured her, hoping against hope that this was true.

'How did you manage last night? I hope you weren't sick, too, miss.'

'A bit,' Candida admitted. 'But I managed. By the way, Kitty, did you or Frank know that Mr Ross would be on this ship?'

'Oh no, Miss Candida. I don't think he knew himself until the last minute. The poor soul has no cabin, and he was up all night in that terrible storm. He is lying down on Frank's bunk now.'

Candida got up and threw on her robe when a knock came on the door.

'Something to eat?' Frank held out a tray, and Kitty's face went a paler shade of green.

'What time is it?' Candida asked him.

'Five o'clock in the afternoon, and we have perhaps another night to go through. We lost time punching against the wind last night, although it has eased a bit now. If you will pardon me for saying so, miss, you had both better stay in your bunks for the rest of the voyage.'

'Just leave the tea.' Candida waved him away dispiritedly, bitterly regretting she had ever thought of a sea-voyage at all.

It was Kitty who woke first the following morning. 'We are here, Miss Candida,' she said. 'We have docked. Everything is standing still, thank God.'

A glance out of the porthole confirmed it. The ship was tied up and only gently swaying now, a few inches from the pier.

'I see Frank waiting for us at the foot of the gangway, Kitty. We shall have to wash our faces quickly and go.' They packed their bags as fast as they could and left the cabin. 'I wonder what has happened to Mr Ross?'

'There he is, miss, running down the gangway,' Kitty said, while Candida watched the smart carriage that had bowled up at the foot of it.

A young man jumped out, followed by a laughing girl, and from the deck they could clearly hear her words.

'Darling Ross!' She embraced him, and dragged him over to the carriage. 'I got here, after all, even if it was only by the skin of my teeth!'

The doors slammed, the carriage wheeled round, and then it was gone.

So he did know he was coming, and in time enough to warn whoever *that* was to meet him. Candida felt more dazed by this discovery than depressed. Then she felt angry, and when that receded a little she felt triumphant, for she had succeeded without even trying. Once again Ross would be 'otherwise occupied', well out of the way with whoever *that* was—which was just what she wanted in order to see her business through, and in private.

'Well, the last twenty-four hours weren't too bad, were they?' Frank smiled down at them. 'I have had time to look around, and there is quite a superior eating-house up the quay a bit. I think we could all do with some breakfast, don't you?'

He never understood, to his dying day, the anguished looks his beloved Kitty and her mistress as well, cast at him then.

'To the Linwood Private Hotel,' Frank directed the driver, and ushered the ladies inside the cab. Of course he had watched as Mr Ross dealt with Miss Candida at the height of the storm, when Kitty was already prostrate. He had not been in the least surprised to find Mr Ross on board. It would have been more surprising if he had not come on this trip, for Miss Candida's sake—and as for arriving at the last minute, well, men had to work, hadn't they?

And women must weep, judging by the fuss the ladies made over a cabin. He himself never expected to have one, but Lady Alison must have seen to that. He could just as easily have bedded down on the deck, and he was sure the same applied to Mr Ross. They had gone through too many hardships together lately in the Grassmarket to doubt it. He was a grand fellow, Mr Ross. Frank wondered briefly if he should call him Dr Ross, now that he was a surgeon—and an Edinburgh surgeon, at that. He would ask him later, for it did not do to become too familiar, and once again he went over all Mr Ross's directions in his mind.

On the whole it had been a very satisfactory journey, except for Kitty having been so ill. Now here was the next stage, he thought, gazing at them opposite him in the cab. He was not at all impressed by the streets of London. They were just the same as Edinburgh's, only longer, and just as dirty. Crawling with crime, most likely!

Kitty's face was recovering its colour. He could not say the same for Miss Candida's, and with her delicate colouring she could ill afford to look so pale. Too high-bred, he had no doubt. Just like her mother, Lady Alison. Such a delicate lady! Now, Kitty was a woman for you, with her dear, round face and her warm russet hair! He admired her all the way to the Linwood Hotel.

'That'll be arf a crown,' the cabbie shouted, shooting back the slot in the roof.

In his deliberate fashion Frank helped his ladies down, Kitty first, so that she could attend to Miss Candida, and then began to fish in his pockets for change.

'Not Londoners, then, are yer?' the cabbie said. 'A Londoner would 'ave 'ad the fare ready!'

'No, Scottish,' Frank said, 'and for that you will come down off your perch and get it, my lad, if you want it!'

He stood his ground, holding out the coin, and in the end the man got down, grumbling, 'All the same, you Scotch!' He grabbed his half-crown. 'Bloody prickly, the same as yer thistles!'

'Ay,' Frank laughed. 'Even our weeds are better than yours!' Still laughing, he lifted the bags and escorted the ladies into the Linwood.

It stood in a small neat garden, a grey stone house of solid dignity, with long shining windows. On the sills of every one were flower-boxes full of colour and trailing ivy, and from the white chimneypots of the house to the gleaming brass on its front door, there was a look of discreet luxury. It was a pleasure to walk over the thick grey carpets, past love-seats upholstered in claret-coloured damask, and the little skirted tables with bowls of roses on them. But it was no pleasure to look at the clerk's face behind the desk. Quite clearly, in his view, common policemen did not belong in here. Frank fixed him with his most authoritative glower, reserved as a rule only for Edinburgh's most heinous wrongdoers.

'You have been advised, have ye, of Lady Alison Kyle-Forrrbes's parrrty from Edinburrrgh?' He rolled and burred his 'r's in a truly terrifying manner.

The clerk's frown became a fawning smile at the mere mention of the name. A Lady, no less. That was more like it! He consulted his books. 'Certainly, sir. A suite of rooms has been reserved for Miss Forbes, two bedrooms and a parlour. There is a room on the floor above for your good self, Constable Clarke. You wish to stay until Thursday, I understand from Lady Alison Kyle-Forbes's letter?'

'We sail back on the *Catherine* at six that evening,' Frank agreed loftily from his full height, which was a good twelve inches above the clerk's.

They signed the register and the ladies went one way

and he another, guided by red-coated pageboys. Frank had never seen such a grand bedroom as the one he was shown into. The water in the ewer was pleasantly warm, and he took off his coat and shirt and gave himself a good wash. Then he went downstairs to wait for the ladies.

'It is the Royal Free Hospital that Miss Forbes has come to visit,' he informed the clerk, who had jumped to attention as soon as he heard Frank's heavy tread on the stairs.

'So I understand, sir. There are cabs waiting out in the street at all times, day and night.'

'What are the visiting times?'

'I took the liberty of finding out, sir. Three to four in the afternoons. The ladies have sent down for hot water for baths before luncheon, in the meantime.'

Frank wandered out for a walk in the sunshine. He had always heard they had plenty of public houses in London, and he believed the one round the corner and over the street had particularly fine beer. The Hangman's Noose it was called, so he had been told, along with the directions. A half-pint would go down very nicely . . . And, of course, you never could tell whom you might meet when you got there.

After the cabin on the *Catherine*, Candida's suite at the Linwood seemed almost palatial. She admired the charming wallpaper, the walnut furniture and the little tables scattered about. Even more, she admired the splendid hip-bath behind the Japanese screen. After the maids brought in the hot water and scented soap, she lay and soaked for a long time before she rubbed herself dry and began to dress in cool fresh underclothes.

'Ready, Miss Candida?' Kitty knocked on the door.

'Come in, Kitty. I think I shall wear the grey and white; it would seem the most suitable. By the way, Kitty, after luncheon—as they call it here—I shall go alone in a cab to the hospital. I am not going to allow you and Frank to waste your afternoons in London waiting for me while I sit at a bedside.'

'You should not be going alone, miss, and your relative so ill. Anything could happen!'

'Nonsense! A hospital is full of nurses and doctors. I shall not be alone for a single minute, and I shall come straight back again in a cab. Do you know how to get to Buckingham Palace, and the Tower and the Houses of Parliament? And all the parks, and the River Thames, and oh, hundreds of places to see?'

'No, but Frank will know,' Kitty said, her eyes shining. 'If he does not, he will soon find out.'

At two o'clock Candida set off. She had no idea how long it would take to get there and she did not want to be late. She was pleased to see that the cab coming forward for her was driven by an older man this time. He looked kind, and he stopped his horses gently.

'If anyone should know the Royal Free, I should, miss,' he said. 'Many a time I've been out there with Mr George Moore, who raised so much money for it and finally got it opened this year. A great gentleman he is—from Cumberland, he told me. You don't have to have a letter to get into the Royal Free,' he informed her. 'You only have to be ill. Going to visit somebody, are you?'

'Yes. How long will it take?'

'Gawd bless you, miss! I'll have you there long before three o'clock, don't you fret.'

At the hospital, the Sister looked through papers. Then she said, 'Biddy Mallone? She will be with the nuns, of course. Take a seat, and I'll get one of them.'

Now that the moment had almost arrived, Candida found that her throat was dry and the palms of her hands were damp. She wished she were anywhere else on earth but sitting on this hard slippery chair with panic steadily mounting every minute. Then along the corridor came a nun with a smiling face, who stopped in front of her.

'Miss Paterson?' she asked.

For a minute Candida was frozen. 'No,' she said, 'I am afraid Mary Paterson is dead. I am her sister, Candida

Forbes, also from Edinburgh. We were both adopted, you see, by different parents.'

'Oh! Biddy Mallone never spoke about another daughter,' the nun said doubtfully. 'I am Sister Teresa. It was to Mary Paterson that I wrote a letter.'

Candida thought quickly. It would be terrible to come all the way to London and be stopped now. 'Yes,' she said. 'Mary gave me your letter and asked me to take her place.'

'Well, follow me, my child.'

Surely this nun could not be much older than herself, she found herself thinking inconsequentially.

'So Biddy Mallone is your mother, too? I suppose you know that she is very poorly, Miss Forbes?'

At that moment Candida could not reply. They had stopped outside a door. She could not get her mind to concentrate on anything but the nun's snow-white coif, and her heart was pounding painfully.

'I'm after thinking you've never been in a hospital before?' Sister Teresa smiled into her terrified face. 'There's no need to be worrying. You will never be left alone in a room of death. When anyone is as low as this, one of the Fathers is always present, day and night. He sits behind the screen, so he does, and prays for the soul of the patient.'

'Oh . . . yes,' Candida said.

'Mistress Mallone may not be able to speak much to you, even if she does wake up. She comes and goes. But if you sit beside her, sure an' she might come round. You can never tell. I'll leave the door open and look in from time to time.'

Sister Teresa left, her long black skirts whispering along the corridor, and Candida entered the room. It contained a high narrow bed, a chair beside it, and a black fretwood screen in the corner. All she could see of the priest were his black shoes.

Candida approached the bed and looked down at last on the woman who had given her birth, her and Mary Paterson both. She was not at all what she had expected.

Her eyes were closed, which gave Candida the opportunity to see that there was not one grey hair among the brown spread out on the pillow; her face was the face of a woman not yet forty years old; and her hands folded on the coverlet had not been used to hard work. There was nothing at all remarkable about her. On closer inspection, Candida saw a light film of sweat on her pallid face, and her breathing was sometimes slow and sometimes shallow and fast.

'She is very damaged inside,' Sister Teresa whispered, on one of her visits. 'Poor soul, this is one of her bad days.'

'What happened to her?'

'Run over in the street, so she was.' The nun shook her head.

At four o'clock Candida rose stiffly off the chair when Sister Teresa beckoned to her, and left the room, bitterly disappointed that the woman had never opened her eyes all that time. She did not even glance at the screen. After a whole hour, she had got used to the idea that someone was there praying silently for Biddy Mallone.

At three o'clock on the following afternoon, Sister Teresa took her back to the room again. 'She's a bit brighter today,' she said. 'She's been awake and in her right mind all day, and I told her you would be coming.'

Yet Candida went into the room even more nervously than before. Biddy Mallone recognised her the minute she walked through the door, and now that her eyes were open and her face animated, Candida caught just a glimpse of the shrewish picture she had drawn of Mary Paterson.

'Mary, me darlin',' she said, and put out her hand. 'God, but ye're prettier than ever, an' dressed like a lady! You could fool anyone in that get-up!'

Candida put her hand in Biddy Mallone's, and said, 'I am Candida Forbes.'

'Don't be tellin' me! Sure you are. As soon as I heard the name I said to meself, "What's Mary up to, now!" I knew you'd come and see your old mother.'

'Mistress Mallone,' Candida tried again, 'you had twin girls, do you remember? I am not Mary Paterson. I am the other one, the one you left in Candlemaker Row. Candida Forbes.'

'Och, why be playin' this silly game, Mary? I never left anything in Candlemaker Row,' she flatly denied. Then her eyes went blank for a minute. 'Or if I did, I can't remember.' A wheedling note came into her voice. 'How much have ye brought me this time, darlin'?'

'What do you mean?' Candida asked.

'You've not come all the way here, and dressed so flash, without any money?' Biddy Mallone's tongue had a sharp edge to it. 'Ye've always seen to yer old mother ever since ye started to work! Always sendin' the money, or bringing it yerself, so you were.'

'I have money with me,' Candida said calmly. 'I will hand it over when I have heard what happened to that other baby.'

'What other baby?' she asked impatiently. 'I never had but the one. I told you.'

'No, you had two,' Candida insisted. 'Ellen McGuire said so.'

'Ellen McGuire!' the woman spat out the words. 'Sure, an' she always was an interferin' old bitch! All right, then. There were two, but one died, thank God. Oh, but I carried you all the way to Gilmerton, Mary,' she whined and grabbed Candida's hand. 'My, ye were that bonnie! Mr and Mrs Paterson begged me . . . Ach, but ye know that old story! I've told ye so many times.'

'Tell me all over again, then. There is half an hour yet before the time is up.'

'How much have ye brought this time, darlin'?'

'Twenty pounds,' Candida said. 'I will bring it tomorrow.'

'Me darlin' child. Which story d'ye want first?'

'The one about my father.'

She sat and listened while Biddy Mallone rambled, her stories all muddled and mixed, for the next half-hour until Sister Teresa came to take her out.

'Mind the money, Mary,' were her last words as Candida left.

'Don't be building up your hopes,' Sister Teresa said, as they walked down the corridor. 'They often get quite bright like that before the end.'

'I have no hope left,' Candida told her, with tears in her eyes.

'Go with God, my child,' the nun said, her eyes full of pity.

On the third morning, Candida was sent for to come urgently to the Royal Free Hospital.

'We are coming with you this time, Miss Candida, whatever you say,' Frank Clarke said. 'Kitty, get her things right away!'

But they were just too late. Biddy Mallone was dead.

'She passed away an hour ago,' Sister Teresa told them. 'She started to bleed again this morning very badly. She gave us only one name for her next of kin, Miss Forbes, and that was Mary Paterson from Edinburgh, as I told you.'

'Mary Paterson?' Frank said with a puzzled expression. 'But Mary Paterson is dead.'

'It is quite a common name,' Candida put in swiftly.

'Then . . . I'm sorry to say it, but Mistress Mallone's body will be unclaimed in that case.'

'We all know what that means,' Frank said gloomily, and Candida saw from his face and Kitty's that they had no idea of the significance of Biddy Mallone's death, and did not connect it with her at all.

'I am afraid I feel responsible for her, since I was her last visitor,' she said calmly. 'I have money with me, enough to pay for her funeral. Could there be some special dispensation to hold it tomorrow? We should like to attend before our ship sails at six.'

Sister Teresa was a long time finding out, but at last she came back and said that she had permission, and would she like to see her one last time? Inside the small room it was very cold, and the body on the bed was covered with a white sheet. Candida shuddered, and looked all round like a wild animal looking for a way of escape. Some part of her mind registered that it must be a different priest today, because the shoes peeping out under the fretwood screen were grey instead of black, and she could see that they were made of the finest leather with elegantly pointed toes. She had no time to dwell on how incongruous they were for a priest.

Sister Teresa pulled back the sheet, there was no escape from it, and Candida looked down for the last time on Biddy Mallone and felt nothing, absolutely nothing, no spark of affinity whatever. This woman had lived off Mary Paterson for at least three years. On the whole, she believed she had been a lot worse than Mary. Then she saw something the nuns must have missed, the little spots of blood on the snow-white sheet. She stared at them, blinked, swallowed back nausea, stared again and began to sway.

There was a rustle from behind the screen, and the next minute strong arms were holding her up. It flashed into her head that they were Ross's arms, that this had happened before, but then her head lolled down, everything was spinning round and round, and for the third time in her life she fainted.

CHAPTER NINE

FRANK MADE all the arrangements for Thursday. The funeral itself Candida hardly saw, except that it was in a churchyard, in consecrated soil. 'Ashes to ashes' a priest intoned as she and Kitty and Frank stood alone shivering in the rain at the graveside. All she could think of was Ross, and her tremendous relief that he had never seen Biddy Mallone alive. To a lesser extent she was glad that her mother and father in Edinburgh had never seen her, either. Except for them, she was all alone in the world, and by the time the service was over and she had considered everything, she thanked God for that.

Afterwards they got into the cab waiting to take them down to join the ship again, while the rain still lashed down depressingly. Candida stared out of the windows and thought no other weather would have been fitting, anyway, and although her eyes searched the decks and the passages on the ship, when they boarded her there was no sign of Ross.

After all this, the return journey to Scotland would seem very little, no matter how rough the trip. Candida and Kitty lay down on their bunks before the *Catherine* even got under way. They had learned their lesson. The wind remained obstinate. It still blew from the south, and this time followed them all the way back to Leith so steadily that they arrived at Trinity Quay up to time on Saturday morning. The carriage was there to meet them, and since there had been no sign of Ross on board ship, Candida concluded that Alanna must be inside it, waiting for the gangway to be lowered.

'At last!' Frank said, going down first with the baggage, with Candida and Kitty trooping behind him, so that it was not until they got to the bottom that they discovered that it was indeed Ross waiting at the bottom.

'How did you get here?' Candida wasted no time coming to the point.

'Oh,' he smiled easily, 'I came back on an earlier ship as soon as my business was finished. Besides, I promised I would be here to meet you this morning, didn't I?'

What business? It was no consolation to her that it had been over quickly, not when it had been with that pretty little girl who had whipped him away from the pier in London. Since she could not trust herself to speak, especially with Frank and Kitty facing her, Candida made a tremendous effort and managed to keep her mouth shut. She smiled faintly, then closed her eyes and put her head back on the cushions of the carriage, while the voices from opposite droned on.

'You have not told me how you found your relative in London.' Ross spoke into her ear.

'As well as could be expected, under the circumstances,' she replied, and closed her eyes again.

She was not going to be drawn into any discussion about London, about any of it, and especially not with Ross Alexander Laing. Why was it that she always forgot first impressions, when her first impressions never failed? She had never trusted him, right from the very beginning.

Lady Alison and Mr Forbes were in the parlour when they got home, and Candida went in alone to speak to them. Her first thought, when she saw them both sitting there, was that neither looked in their usual health. They both appeared to droop. They looked older than when she had left, and it was curious to see Papa holding Mama's hand like that, whether in comfort or for support, she could not tell.

'Well, Candida,' Lady Alison was the first to speak. 'What did you find in London?'

There was such anxiety in her voice, and such agony in her father's kind brown eyes, that she burst into tears.

Then she went over and knelt down and put an arm round each of them.

'Only that my dearest Mother and Father were back home in Edinburgh,' she told them, 'and sadly missed.'

'Oh, my dear,' Lady Alison said, with tears running down her face. 'Not so sadly missed as our beloved daughter! We have been so worried.'

'You came to no harm, Candida?' Mr Forbes trumpeted into his handkerchief. 'Are you all right, dearie?'

'Yes, I am all right,' she said, half laughing and half crying, and ten minutes later when they had all recovered and wiped their eyes, Lady Alison rang for some tea.

Liza brought it, all smiles. 'Kitty says it was a wonderful experience, miss.'

'It was certainly an experience, Liza.'

'Well, then,' Lady Alison said, when they were alone again, 'tell us all about it. Oh, what a week of worry!'

'Anything can happen in London!' Mr Forbes declared.

'A lot did, Papa,' Candida said, and for the next hour regaled them with the whole story, except that Ross was there in the background. She did not want to upset them any more. Anyway, she thought wryly, Ross had taken very little part in it. The tea was cold before she had finished. 'Right to the very end, Biddy Mallone refused to admit that I had ever existed, and even when I held out the bribe of twenty pounds, she still called me Mary.'

Lady Alison shivered. 'Now that your sister and Biddy Mallone are both dead, that part of your life can be buried with them, Candida. Nobody else need ever know anything about it, except those who have always loved you from the first minute they ever saw you.'

'It may not be as easy as that, Mama. Some day in the future someone may want to marry me. It will all have to come out then.'

'That is what I said,' replied Lady Alison. 'If he is right

for you, he will love you from the first minute he sees you, and then nothing else will matter.'

'It is going to be a race against time from now on,' Ross said on Monday morning when he came in on a flying visit. 'I mean in Paradise House. The walls have all been stripped and most of them repapered. All the woodwork has been attended to, and some of it painted. We shall have to turn our attention to the furnishing of it next, if the old gentleman is to take up residence at Christmas.'

'You will sit down and drink a cup of coffee, Ross,' Lady Alison said firmly. 'All you young people are dashing about too much.'

'Carpets and curtains and furniture for the whole of Paradise House?' Candida was aghast.

'Well, no. But the drawing-room, the library, the dining-room, at least one bedroom and the kitchens should be enough to start with. Just one cup then, Aunt Alison, and then I must go.'

'You have forgotten the most important room of all,' Candida said.

'No,' he said. 'That room has been locked up on the instructions of the owner. He has the key.'

What would happen about all Ross's beautiful gems? she wondered, but she had no time to ask.

'It is going to be a race against time from now on,' Alanna announced, bursting into the parlour in her usual way, in an explosion of marigold silk. 'What are you all laughing at?' She smiled her beautiful smile, and went on, 'It is no laughing matter, I can tell you!' She patted her most becoming hat, just a fluff of cream and golden feathers.

'Those were the very words Ross used, minutes ago, about Paradise House,' Lady Alison explained. 'What are *you* speaking about, Alanna?'

'Finlay's new house in Hope Park. He is coming with me to Ireland at the end of October, and it will have to be ready before that. It looks like seven weeks' hard labour ahead.'

'We will put our heads together over it,' Lady Alison said, 'and tell you later how we will set about it, Ross.'

'You are looking very dubious, Candida,' Ross said as he left. 'Remember what I told you before. We do not know the old gentleman's taste, so use your own. Pretend the house is yours.'

'I do,' she said. 'All the time.'

By the third week in September, carpets were down, curtains were up, and Alanna and Finlay, and Candida and Ross, were looking for furniture.

'Alexander Peter, the cabinetmaker's, is the best place to begin,' Finlay said. 'My father knows everyone in trade in Edinburgh. He will keep us right.'

As soon as they got there, Candida fell in love with a sideboard, characteristically Scottish in its fine superstructure with tiny thistles on the brass knobs.

'We will have that,' Ross said, 'and this serving-table with its brass rail, and green silk curtains for the dining-room. I particularly like its style.'

'It is of Adam design,' Mr Peter told them. 'So is the dining-table.'

'If we had chairs, that would be the dining-room well begun, Candida,' Ross said.

'I saw a set of chairs over there with their seats covered in red leather.' She pointed to them. 'Red is what you thought of, is it not?'

'That is a harlequin set of ten chairs,' Mr Peter said, 'and not only are they very smart in red, as you say, Miss Forbes, they are also easily cleaned. They are made up in pairs in the manner of Thomas Chippendale.'

'I suppose it will be the drawing-room next?' Candida asked Ross on the way out.

'I am much more interested in the bedroom,' he said, and grinned at her wickedly.

Candida blushed and sighed. If she did not take care, she would be back where she was before, with Ross. She had never been able to resist that smile of his.

The race against time went on in both the Hope Park house and Paradise House for another month before they were finished and before any of them had time to draw breath. When she did at last, Candida became very concerned for her maid.

'What is it, Kitty? Is something wrong?'

'It is Frank, miss. He is getting very despondent. They are no nearer catching the two Irishmen after all this time. He is out every night, trying. I hardly ever see him.'

'Did you ever find out their names?'

'Burke and Hare. That's their names, Miss Candida,' Kitty said, wielding the hair-brush and sprinkling on far too much bay rum and cantharides in her venom. 'Devils that they are! Has Mr Ross not told you?'

'I hardly ever see him either, Kitty, and when I do, he can speak of nothing but Paradise House. You would think it was his.'

'Oh, well, now that it is finished, he will come back,' Kitty comforted her. 'But he is such a quiet man! He likes to do things quietly, in secret.'

'Oh?' said Candida.

'My Frank says he never tackles things head on. He prefers to go roundabout.'

'Is that so?'

It was a possibility she had never thought of. If so, of course it was very clever. But she had never denied that Ross was clever: it showed in every move he made.

'I have been wondering about Frank, anyway,' she said instead. 'Perhaps we can help him.'

'How?' Kitty asked eagerly.

'Well, Mary Paterson is no longer here to tempt Burke and Hare. But I am very like her.'

'Oh, my God, no! No, Miss Candida!'

'Just calm down, Kitty, and consider it. We could enlist Janet Brown. You could get in touch with her, and I could dress up like Mary Paterson and go to her old haunts. You and Frank could be behind us somewhere. It might be the golden opportunity Frank has been waiting for. We will have to make things happen, if they are not happening themselves.'

'You cannot be serious, miss! Burke and Hare are murderers.'

'I am absolutely serious, Kitty. I want you to put it to Frank the next time you see him.'

'I can tell you now he will never agree. Never!'

Constable Frank Clarke laughed later that night when he and Mr Ross set off to prowl the High Street and then on down into the Grassmarket.

'Of course, if we ever allowed such a thing to happen in our wildest dreams,' he said, 'it would never work. It's just the sort of harebrained scheme women would think up.'

'No?' Ross's green eyes glanced away from him. 'But perhaps, because it is harebrained and devious and feminine, it might just work. Miss Candida is no fool, and she has a way of bringing things to a head. I shall think about it.'

On the 29th of October Finlay and Alanna set off for a month in Ireland, and on the morning of the 30th Mr Forbes opened the *Courant* with an exclamation of dismay. That was not unusual, but his expression of horror as he read the front page was enough to alert his wife.

'What is it, Atholl?'

'How long is it since we had the vaccination?'

'It must be twenty years,' she said, after consideration. 'Why?'

'There has been a case of smallpox found in Edinburgh. Everyone who has not had the vaccination within the last five years must go to the Vaccine Institution, where it will be done free of charge. It is compulsory.'

'Oh dear,' said Lady Alison. 'You have never had it done at all, Candida. You will certainly have to go. Do you understand about vaccination?'

'Cowpox is introduced into people, isn't it, for immunity? I know that Jenner discovered it.'

'Another Englishman who got his Scottish medical degree by post!' Mr Forbes said. 'However, there is not the time to discuss that, and no time to be lost. This entire household will go to the Institution either today or tomorrow. Make the arrangements, Alison, my dear.'

After breakfast, Candida went up to her room and found Kitty already there in a ferment of excitement and dread.

'Mr Ross and Frank have arranged it all for tomorrow night, Miss Candida. Hallowe'en night. The guisers will be out, all dressed up with masks on, so nobody will ever notice us, they say.'

'A few people had better notice me, Kitty! Did Janet Brown get me a red dress?'

'She got one from the Jew's shop in the Grassmarket, along with a mangy old fur tippet which she admired. I washed the dress, but there's nothing I can do about the tippet. She got clothes for me as well, and a mask.'

'And what about Mr Ross and Frank?'

'As far as I know, they will be as we saw them on Hogmanay,' Kitty sniffed.

'Well, never mind, Kitty. We will have a dress rehearsal later tonight. By the way, did you see my sketchbook lying about anywhere? I cannot find it.'

'No, miss. Now that you come to mention it, not since before we went to London.'

In the afternoon Liza, Kitty and the rest of the staff were bundled off to the Vaccine Institution, willy nilly.

'The rest of us will go tomorrow morning,' Lady Alison said. 'I know your father when he is in this determined mood. It is easier to give in gracefully.'

'Yes,' Candida agreed.

'Let us hope the weather is better than this tomorrow. It is so cold with the haar from the sea lying over Edinburgh as it has been doing all week.'

'It is almost November,' Candida reminded her.

'So it is! It is Hallowe'en tomorrow, already! This year has flown past. Are all you young people going out guising?'

'All of us, Mama. But we shall not go far, and we shall not be late.'

'Ross will be with you?' Lady Alison asked anxiously.

'And Frank Clarke, so what could be better than that?'

'I wonder if Liza has remembered apples and nuts for the children tomorrow night. There will be a steady procession to the door after dark.'

'Sit still, Mama! I shall go and see about it.'

In the showy but tatty red dress, Candida swayed down the High Street beside Janet Brown far more convincingly than Mary Paterson had ever done. At some distance behind Frank and Kitty, Ross could not keep his eyes off the infinitely enticing roll of her hips. She had been quite right. Even in that horrible dress, red suited her better than anything else he had ever seen her wear. His mouth set grimly. This would be the one and only public occasion on which she would ever wear it, that he swore before God. It was only one of many oaths he had sworn over the last year.

'Where is it?' Candida asked, thoroughly enjoying herself.

'Here, miss. Swanston's.' Janet shivered.

It had been from Swanston's that Mary had gone out and was never seen again. Janet looked around for her protector. Thank God, he was there. James Wilson had simply transferred his affections to her, once Mary had gone. Simple was the word. They could call him Daft Jamie if they liked, but what a body he had on him! She ought to know. She jerked her head to show him that Swanston's was the place, and followed Miss Candida inside.

There had never been a sudden hush like this in Swanston's, not even for Mary, not in all these years. Not while the drink was flowing fast. But there was now, as Miss Candida parted the crowd of men like a scythe cutting through hay and sat down in the middle of the bar-room at the same little table as Mary used to do. It was as if she knew by instinct.

'Jasus God!' Wull Burke swore, and choked. Then he crossed himself, with all the colour drained out of his normally ruddy face. 'It's a ghost, so it is! It's her, come back to haunt us!'

He waited in horror for the blood to stream down her nose and ooze out from the corner of her painted smiling mouth, as it had done the last time he had seen her.

'For Christ's sake, pull yoursel' together!' Underneath the table in the corner William Hare kicked him viciously on the shins. 'Mary Paterson is dead. We sold her long ago. That's not Mary Paterson, but it's a bloody good imitation! Jesus, it is! And that's Janet Brown with her.'

Wull shuddered so violently that he could hardly raise his glass to his lips to down the raw whisky, in an effort to cure his shakes in one gulp. He remained cold sober and speechless. There had been too many nightmares—fifteen or sixteen at least, before he lost count—and now here was one spilling over into real life. He was going mad. He always knew he would, before it was all over.

'Get up and get going!' William kicked him harder than ever. 'That's twenty guineas sitting over there, starin' us in the face! I would go myself, but for some reason folk are feared o' me.'

Another whisky brought Wull almost out of the jaws of hell. He tossed off another to make sure of it, and in a dream passed by the table in the middle, noted the drinks on it, ordered another round and sat down beside the two drabs.

'Have a drink on me,' he begged in his soft Irish, while he smiled into Candida's eyes—and, oh God, it was easy after all. She smiled back and winked. She actually winked. 'There's a fine booze goin' on at my house later, this being Hallowe'en,' he told them. 'And a bit of a dance, so there is.'

A dance! Janet brightened at the prospect now that a

few gins had bolstered her courage. Candida could see that she would have to keep an eye on poor Janet, and made her calculations. Kitty and Frank were waiting outside Swanston's door until they came out, and although she had not seen him so far, Ross would be out there somewhere as well. She decided to chance it. It was now or never.

'Lead the way!' She smiled boldly and wriggled her bare shoulders back into the fur tippet as to the manner born, and swaggered out. Janet prinked out behind her, doing her best to copy her. It was just like the old days!

It was a strange procession down into the Grassmarket minutes later. Candida and Janet linked arms hilariously with Burke and Hare. A little distance behind, Kitty and Frank in their masks shadowed them from doorway to doorway, and bringing up the rear Daft Jamie shambled along, trying to keep up with his Janet.

Down in the Grassmarket, away from all the noise of the guisers and the merriment of the Royal Mile, there was an eerie silence. Here there were no guisers. There was no money for any such frivolity, and the darkness felt cold and hostile.

Burke especially tried to keep their spirits up, chippering away like a sparrow, but behind his voice Candida's pricked ears made out the wail of some child behind a tatter-curtained window, the scrape of a fiddle somewhere else, and the little grating sound a swinging sign made outside a darkened tavern, the White Hart.

She tried to take her bearings, to peer at the street names. Burke and Hare rushed them past Crooked Lane and took them into Tanner's Close. She had no time to contemplate the dark void they were stepping down into before they were walking along a passage rank with filth. They stopped at a door, and Hare knocked on it three times. There were scufflings inside, and then a tiny old woman opened it.

'Me auntie, Mrs Docherty,' Burke said, by way of introduction, and put an arm round her. 'Just come over from Ireland on a bit of a visit. "Madgy", we call her.

Where are all the others, Madgy me darlin'?'

'Ned Brogan's gone out for some whisky, an' left me to peel the onions an' the praties.'

'That's it—ham an' onions an' praties. Nothing like it!' Burke rubbed his hands in anticipation, and Hare rushed about stirring up the fire and drawing the ragged curtains round the beds heaped up with straw that was none too clean.

There was more straw scattered about the floor, mixed with a litter of tealeaves. There were dirty, battered cooking-pots on the hearth, and another tattered curtain hung down despairingly at the side of a grimy window. Candida judged from the smell beside the window and the grunts outside that it looked out on to a pigsty. Above all else was the stench. She was glad when Mrs Docherty began to peel the onions.

'Sit down, sit down!' Burke set two stools for Janet and her beside the fire, and she tried her best not to look too much about the room, and not to wonder if it was in here that Mary had met her death.

Then in came Ned Brogan, a cheerful lad of about sixteen or seventeen, with the whisky and his fiddle. The ham began to spit in the frying-pan beside the onions, and Ned Brogan had only played a tune or two before the first knock came to the door.

Hare's face darkened even further when he opened it. A young couple stood outside, the woman holding a baby. Candida thought he was too furious to speak. Wull Burke came to the rescue.

'They've come down from the pauper's room,' he muttered to Candida and Janet, 'looking for food and drink.'

'Is it a booze ye're havin'?' the woman asked.

'Come in,' Burke said, shouldering Hare aside. 'Mr and Mrs Gray and the bairn, so it is! Och, it's not a great booze, just a celebration for Hallowe'en, and a bit o' a jig.'

More knocks came to the door and more people came in, the Laws and the Connaways, and the dancing began.

'I won't be a minute,' Mrs Gray said, rising from the bed she was sitting on. 'I'm just away up to put the bairn to his bed.'

Within half an hour the booze was in full swing. Ned Brogan sang old Irish songs, the lively neighbours joined in, and old Mrs Docherty was having the time of her life. Every time Hare filled up Candida's glass, she emptied it gradually and surreptitiously into the fireside straw.

She was up dancing with Burke when the door burst open and a terrible drab mean-faced woman stood glaring at the scene inside. Her eyes fixed on Candida in a way that scared her right down to her toes.

'Nelly!' Wull said.

'An' what's goin' on here, as soon as I turn my back? Who's this?' Nelly poked Candida viciously, and then began to shriek and curse and spit at her like a demon. 'D'ye ken he's my husband? The faithless pig!'

She turned on Wull next, and lashed him with her tongue until he could stand it no longer. He picked up a glass and threw it at her. It cut her eye and the blood began to flow. Nelly screamed bloody murder, and in the middle of it another woman rushed in, every bit as ugly as Nelly, but sullen and sinister with it. Without a word she came straight up to Candida and started to hit her. Hare came between them.

'Stop it, Maggie!' he said.

Then Maggie rounded on him. 'Some husband you are, William Hare! Always after taupies! Canna keep yer dirty hands off them!' she screeched, and began to kick and punch him and claw at his face with her hands.

Utter terror entered Candida's heart when William Hare fended off his wife with one arm, and his other arm closed like a vice around her shoulders, his fingers pressing into the soft flesh where the vaccination had gone in that morning. The pain was excruciating.

It had been a booze and a jig one minute; now it was a drunken brawl. Everyone joined in, and at the height of it Candida saw Janet Brown slipping out of the room. She tried to pull Daft Jamie away from where he stood at the door, but he kept on standing there and grinning, and Janet ran off.

It was then that William Hare lost patience. They had inveigled these two subjects here, and now one of them had got away. He had never wanted this booze in the first place, with all the money it cost to feed their faces and pour the drink down their necks like water. That was Wull Burke's fault! It was all going wrong. But better one subject than none at all.

His hands closed round Candida's neck, and she looked straight into the murderous eyes of the Devil himself.

'Not like that, for Christ's sake,' Wull hissed. 'Pull her over to the bed. They'll all think we're havin' a bit o' fun.'

The next Candida knew she was flat on her back on the unspeakable bed, and one of the filthy bed-pillows was over her face, shutting out the air, suffocating her, suffocating her . . . A red mist floated in front of her eyes.

Then the grimy window smashed in. Glass flew everywhere. A man's fist, covered in blood, crashed into Hare's face, and crashed again. There was the sickening sound of Hare's head hitting the stone floor. Then there was air in her bursting lungs again. She gasped and coughed, and the red mist began to move away.

'Help me,' Candida croaked.

Ross did not speak. He gathered her into his arms and carried her out, up the dark uneven steps and back out into Tanner's Close again. She clung to him. Her legs were unable to move.

'Don't leave me again,' she moaned.

'You know I will never leave you,' he said passionately, and in that evil place, dark as the grave, he bent his head and kissed her.

It was exactly the way she had always dreamed it would be, and she responded with a torrent of love and longing, shock and wild desire, until one kiss melted into the next and the next, and they both gasped for breath.

Candida's whole body was on fire for him when Frank in his mask rushed past them into the house in Tanner's Close, the light streaming around him when he opened the door. It lit up Janet, cowering round the corner.

'Where's Jamie?' she asked them anxiously.

'If he's still inside, we will get him out, don't worry,' Ross said. 'Come, both of you. A cab is waiting in the Grassmarket.' After he had put Candida and Janet into it beside a white-faced Kitty, he disappeared into the night.

Thank God Frank had come when he did! Candida berated herself. What on earth had she been thinking about with Ross? Had she not found out a thousand times that she couldn't trust him or his silvery tongue?

'What are all those stains, miss?' Kitty asked, when they crept into No. 13 Charlotte Square and took off their fancy dress. 'They look like blood!'

'It is blood,' Candida said faintly. 'Mr Ross's blood.' She was feeling very unwell.

All the Edinburgh newspaper were screaming the news: 'Daft Jamie Next!' 'James Wilson Disappeared!' Even the great Thomas Carlyle had something to say about it when he wrote for *Blackwood's Magazine*: 'There has been a dreadful piece of work at Edinburgh. We fear that "Daft Jamie", the poor creature who went about with his box begging snuff and asking riddles, has been murdered.'

Everyone in the town sat up and took notice at last. James Wilson had been young, a great giant of a man, and healthy apart from his twisted feet. He was hardly likely to die from natural causes. He had been one of the characters of the town, with all the bairns dancing around him and taunting him. But everyone had liked him. He was a simple, that was why, and Edinburgh took such of her children to her heart.

Constable Frank Clarke knew he must be on his mettle at this, the most important moment in his career in the

Police Force so far, and his biggest chance. If he could only find Daft Jamie, now, before anyone else did, he might also find hard evidence of Burke and Hare. The last time Jamie had been seen alive was down here in Tanner's Close, right on his beat. Frank was convinced Burke and Hare had killed him on that night of the drunken brawl. What had they done with the body?

He would begin now, this very minute, and search every nook and cranny of the Old Town, as well as his beat. Where could he be? Up a stair or down a close? He made a determined start at Mrs Worthington's.

All this time, Jamie's body was already unpacked and awaiting the inspection of Dr Knox.

'You will have to be careful with this one, sir,' William Fergusson murmured in his ear. 'It is Daft Jamie. Everyone knows him, and everyone knows there was nothing wrong with him. They will recognise his face and his feet.'

'Nonsense!' said Dr Knox. 'It is not Jamie! See that the feet are cut off, and the head. No one will be any the wiser.'

'Yes, sir,' William Fergusson said, and signalled to Dr Knox's willing and adoring band of students to come and help him. 'It shall be done.'

The hue and cry died down, but a lot of Edinburgh people could not forget it, Mr Atholl Forbes least of all.

'We are sitting on the edge of a volcano,' he told his wife. 'Soon it will erupt. This cannot go on.'

'We have a more immediate eruption upstairs,' Lady Alison said. 'An eruption of smallpox. Candida's vaccination has gone wrong.'

'Great God! Is Ross still in the house? Ross! Ross!' He went through the house shouting, and Ross came running down. 'It's Candida! Alison thinks she has taken the smallpox.'

'You cannot go into her room,' Ross said. 'Neither can Kitty nor anyone else until I see.' He went inside and shut the door. From the foot of the bed he looked at her flushed face, and then went round to the side of the bed and lifted her hand. 'You have a sore throat?' he asked, feeling her pulse.

'What a great fuss they are making! Yes, my throat is sore on the inside, and my neck is sore on the outside where that terrible man bruised it. Apart from that, I have a sore head and all my bones are sore. Not to mention my arm!'

'Yes,' he said, and his green eyes were soft and gentle. 'The vaccination has taken, there is no doubt about it. If you had never had the vaccination and really caught smallpox, you would have taken it very badly. These are only a few mild symptoms of what that might have been like.'

'Then I do not have smallpox?'

'No. But you may have started a nasty cold, so you will stay in your bed until further notice.' He pulled the blankets up round her and tucked them in.

'You mean that I should stay in bed until my own doctor examines me,' Candida retorted, her eyebrows raised coldly.

Ross's hands paused in the act of smoothing down the coverlet. 'Your own doctor would tell you exactly what I have told you,' he said calmly. 'That is, if I thought it would serve any useful purpose to call him in.'

'If *you* thought so? I shall demand to see Dr MacGregor! I trust him!'

'Ah,' Ross nodded his head, 'now we are getting somewhere. You trust him, but you do not trust me. Is that it?'

'How can I trust you?' Candida flung at him. 'I still do not understand what your business was in London. It certainly was not on my account. I saw that when you left the ship. But it was pleasant, no doubt?'

'Very pleasant,' he smiled, 'while it lasted. By the way, Amy sends you her apologies. She would like to have met you.'

'Oh, yes?'

'Yes. But in her usual impetuous way she had dragged

me halfway to Hampstead before she stopped to listen. We turned back, but you had gone.'

A love-nest in Hampstead next! How much more of this must she listen to? The fact was, she was not prepared to listen to another word, and she struggled to get out of her bed.

Ross clasped her arms and forced her gently back on the pillows. 'Amy is like Alanna in many of her ways,' he said. 'But, in looks, you would hardly take them for sisters, would you?'

'Oh . . . I did not realise you had a sister in London,' Candida said weakly.

'I have a sister, it seems, everywhere! There are six altogether, you know,' Ross went on, now that he had the advantage. 'Amy is the one married to Sir John Rollo in London, and they have two sons. You caught a glimpse of him, perhaps?' She nodded, feeling steadily worse. 'You will have to get acquainted with them all, sooner rather than later, Candida. I have two brothers as well. Raymond is married with two children also. In fact, they are all married, except Alanna and me, and that will be put right before very long, so help me.'

His hands slid up from her arms to her shoulders and then he was kissing her as passionately as he had done last night in Tanner's Lane.

'You were jealous,' he whispered exultantly, and kissed her over and over again. 'But I had better stop. I could make you hotter than ever if I carried on!'

He already had. Her pulse was racing and it was not because of the vaccination. 'I don't want you to stop, Ross, but you must.'

'I know you do not. This is the first time and the last time I shall be your doctor. Doctors must not have the sort of passion for a patient that I have for you.' He did not seem at all deterred by the sadness she could not keep out of her eyes. He looked happier than she had ever seen him when he left. 'I shall send Dr Liston in to see you. He specialises in these diseases.'

One sister married to Sir John Rollo! Alanna about to

marry the heir to one of the richest merchants in Edinburgh! His parents who lived in a castle! Oh, no . . . Candida Forbes would be out of the question!

She slid back down under the sheets unhappily. It simply would not work. She must put all thought of Ross out of her head completely, hope against hope that the torture of seeing him every day would soon come to an end when he went back to Ireland, and above all never allow him or anyone else to know how degraded her origins were. That would be for ever her own terrible secret.

Mrs Gray left her husband and her baby in the pauper's room and went down to see the Burkes and Hares.

'I've lost a shoe belonging to the bairn,' she said, 'and I canna afford to buy him another pair. Did I leave it here on Hallowe'en?'

She looked hungrily at the cold ham and the hot porridge. Burke and Hare and their women never seemed to go short.

For their part, Burke and Hare glowered at her. Filled her full of food and drink on Hallowe'en, so they had, her and that long drink of water she called her husband with her, and now here she was back looking for more, with the excuse of a bairn's shoe. Then they both got the same brilliant idea at the same time.

'Would you be havin' a bite to eat?' Wull asked. 'Sit down and eat something now while we're thinkin', and Nelly'll wrap up some ham and some bread for your man and the bairn.'

When she had finished, William fetched her a pipe of tobacco and she sat puffing it for a minute or two.

'It's funny,' she said. 'Daft Jamie never drank. He only ever took snuff. Yet they said he was reekin' o' drink when they cut him up.'

There was a funny cold silence in the filthy room. Wull Burke was the first to recover.

'Cut him up?' he asked incredulously. 'How do you know that, Ann Gray?'

'My James was in Swanston's and heard the students talkin'. Whoever killed him cut off his head an' his feet, but still they knew him right away.'

'We never . . .' Burke began indignantly, and then changed direction. 'Och, they're a' fou, these poors who get murdered! That's how they're so easy caught.'

'Where's old Mrs Docherty, your Auntie Madgy?' Mrs Gray asked Burke next.

'Auntie me foot!' Nelly said. 'She was just an Irish cadge Wull took a notion to. She was eatin' me oot o' house an' home. I had to kick her oot.'

Burke got up with a full bottle of whisky and started pouring it over the straw on one of the beds. My God, a whole bottle of whisky! Mrs Gray was stupefied. Then he emptied another bottle, sprinkling it all over the room and the sticks of furniture.'

'My God, is he fou?' Mrs Gray asked Maggie and Nelly.

When she got no answer, a great fear came over her. Nobody, not even a rich man, would just empty one bottle of whisky, never mind two, for nothing.

'I was sitting wi' the bairn over here for a minute.' She got up and went over to the bed which was now soused and reeking. 'Maybe his shoe fell underneath.'

'Don't touch the straw with that pipe in yer mouth,' Hare growled. 'Look on the floor, if you like.'

She scrabbed about on the floor under the bed, but there was nothing. Then, looking up through the wooden slats of the bed she saw the bent, naked little body of Mrs Docherty, hidden under the straw.

Ann Gray kept a cool head. 'No,' she said, 'it's not there at all. It must be out in the passage somewhere or on the stairs. I'll go an' look again.'

She even had the presence of mind to grab the parcel of ham and bread as she went.

Candida was recovering rapidly, with only her sore arm to contend with, and the longer she had to stay in this bed the faster she would become a vegetable altogether, she told herself mutinously. The sunshine outside on this November day, when there had been so little all through the summer, made her feel crosser than ever. It glowed behind the curtains of pale green watered silk, that her mother insisted must be drawn, so brightly that she did not need the little china clock on the bedside table to tinkle out the time to know it was two o'clock in the afternoon. She was very bored.

Mercifully, after a tap the door opened, and Lady Alison herself came in.

'How are you, dear?'

'Mama, I assure you I am better, and very tired of lying here.'

'Let me see your hair.'

It must have passed muster, because after pulling the sheet well up and patting it smooth, her mother smiled and went across and pulled back the curtains.

'You have two visitors, Candida.' Lady Alison dragged two other slender open armchairs over beside the one she sat down in beside the fireplace, and turned the handle on the brass bell on the wall at her side. 'It is Ross, with Mr Constable, the publisher.'

'Mr Constable, the publisher? Why?' Candida asked, and then fell silent when Liza ushered them in, and they sat down beside Lady Alison.

Of course, she had seen Mr Constable many times before, but she could not imagine why he should want to visit her, particularly. He was a pleasant man of about sixty, with a shrewd face and a fine healthy complexion. He was also very fat and very jolly, and for a while he and Lady Alison exchanged pleasantries while Ross listened politely and Candida wondered why all this was taking place. However, anything was better than lying here all alone with nobody to talk to.'

'Then you liked it, Archibald?' Lady Alison asked.

'Delightful,' Mr Constable said, taking Candida's sketchbook out of one of his voluminous pockets and having another look through it. 'Absolutely delightful! It will make a beautifully illustrated book for anyone to treasure, be it a man, a woman or a child.'

'Where did you get that?' Candida found her voice.

'It was lying about in Paradise House,' Ross said, 'and your year was completed. I knew you would never think of it, so I took it to show Mr Constable.'

'Of course it will have to be edited,' Archibald Constable said. 'That will not take long. Then it will go to the printers. Early in 1829 I shall publish it, if you will sell it to me for fifteen hundred pounds.'

'Fifteen hundred pounds!' Candida could not believe her ears. 'But I did not keep my diary with any thought of other people seeing it!'

'Then it is a mercy Mr Alexander Laing found it "lying about" as he says, and pushed the matter forward by bringing it to me,' Mr Constable said. 'You have given me an idea of what to call it, too, since there is nothing on it but your name. "Miss Candida Forbes's Diary".'

'Oh no,' Candida was horrified. 'I should not want to see my name on it at all!'

'"The Diary of an Edinburgh Lady",' Ross said firmly. 'And instead of the author's name, we shall use her initials. That should be sufficient disguise.'

'Excellent,' Mr Constable said. 'Congratulations, young lady! You have made me a very happy man.'

When Lady Alison got up to show the visitor out, Ross looked back on the threshold and winked at Candida.

'Oh, Ross,' she said. 'Please say I can get up!'

'I think perhaps you may. What about beginning with the four o'clocks? I shall send Kitty up.'

She was a real live author! A great surge of excitement splashed over her. And it had happened just by accident! Then her pleasure receded, and along with it the little pride she had allowed herself. 'The Diary of an Edinburgh Lady', Ross had called it. He believed she was a lady. What if he knew the whole truth?

She went downstairs with Kitty for the four o'clocks. They were on the last treads of the staircase when the news that shocked Edinburgh and all Scotland broke, and Mr Forbes dashed in with his coat flying open, waving the *Edinburgh Evening Courant*.

'They've caught them at last!' he shouted. 'Burke and Hare! Where is your Mama, Candida?'

'Here, dear.' Lady Alison came out of the parlour at so much noise. 'What is it?'

'A Mr and Mrs Gray fetched a policeman to the house of Burke and Hare in Tanner's Close. Mrs Gray had seen the body there of a Mrs Docherty. They have been arrested!'

'Which policeman, sir?' Kitty asked.

'Oh . . . A Sergeant Fisher, Kitty.'

Kitty's face crumpled, and she fled below stairs.

Kitty did not cheer up for the rest of that week, and every now and then Candida would come upon her weeping into a sheet or a towel or whatever came to hand. Nothing she could say or do had any effect upon her maid.

Then one day a letter arrived from Alanna, to say she and Finlay Semple were engaged to be married and they were trying to decide the date of their wedding. For some reason, the letter depressed Candida all the rest of that day. She felt as down in the dumps as Kitty looked.

So, the morning after, the shock was even greater when her maid bounced into her room bright-eyed and absolutely radiant.

'What has happened, Kitty?'

'Frank and I are to be married next week, miss. On Saturday.'

'Of course that is wonderful, dear!' Candida hugged her. 'I am so pleased for you! But how? What else has happened?'

'He is leaving the Police, Miss Candida. He has got a far better position.'

'What?'

'He is going to be the gardener and caretaker at Paradise House, and when we are married I am to be the housekeeper. The old gentleman sent word to Lady

Alison to engage a couple, and Frank jumped at the chance. We will live in the Cottage, miss, and now he can work with his beloved plants to his heart's content.'

'Wonderful, Kitty!' Candida hugged her again. 'How will you like being a housekeeper, though?'

'Ah, well . . . That depends on the mistress. Whoever she is, it will not be like working for you, miss. How could it be? I have been with you all my life.'

'I am going to miss you dreadfully, Kitty.'

'Liza will attend to you, along with Lady Alison, until a new maid comes. You will come and see me at the Cottage?'

'I shall probably be your first visitor,' Candida said sadly, 'and your most frequent one. I shall never be able to stay away. My whole heart is in Paradise House.'

CHAPTER TEN

'THE TRIAL of Burke and Hare has been set for the 24th of December,' Mr Forbes informed them at breakfast next morning.

'That is quite ridiculous!' Lady Alison said. 'It is Christmas Eve!'

Mr Forbes rustled over the next page of the *Courant* and imparted the next piece of information. 'Sir William Rae, Lord Advocate, is Counsel for the Crown. He will be far outclassed by James Moncrieff, Francis Jeffrey and Henry Cockburn for the Defence, of course, and he knows it. So what tricks will he try, I wonder?

'What do you mean?' Candida asked.

'Sir William Rae will try a short cut of some sort in an effort to outwit them, as well as keeping the proceedings as short as possible. We may not get out to the Thistle Courts even on Christmas Day, this year, Alison,' he peered round the edge of the *Courant*. 'I must be present at this trial.'

'Of course you must, dear,' she said, while Liza smacked down a letter on Candida's plate.

'Another one from Ireland,' she said briskly.

Lady Alison and more especially Mr Forbes seemed hung in suspended animation while she read it. He no longer trusted any communication from that country!

'Alanna and Finlay are to be married in Edinburgh on January the 3rd, 1829,' Candida told them, 'in the Kirk of St Giles. The whole Alexander Laing family will be here for the occasion.'

'But, counting Alexander Laing himself and Cornelia, that makes eleven at least! It is a large family!' Lady Alison exclaimed.

'It is worse even than that, Mama! Seven of their nine children are married, and two of those have children.

There will be twenty of them altogether, coming from all directions.'

'Anything Cornelia ever had a hand in spelt trouble,' Mr Forbes assured the world, while his womenfolk looked at each other in consternation.

'Of course, Cornelia and Alexander will stay here,' Lady Alison said worriedly, 'and we could take another four besides. Perhaps Alanna and Ross could accommodate one couple and their children upstairs. But that still leaves ten to be accounted for! There is nothing else for it, Candida. We shall go out to the Thistle Courts this very morning and discuss it with your Aunt Rose.'

For another fortnight the arranging went on, the worries over it and all the complications, the beds and bedrooms for everybody, the extra burden on the staff considered, and food, and incidental meals, especially for the children, until everything was in hand.

Towards the end of December Candida went out on an impulse to see her beloved Paradise House once more before the old gentleman came to take up residence. The gardens looked bare, with all the roses pruned back and the shrubs she and Ross had chosen together in hibernation. Nevertheless they were immaculate and looked now as though somebody loved them. It was exciting to think that underneath the caked soil were the carefully positioned perennials, which would break through in the spring and then flower in sequence all through the year.

The gardens were well begun. In another two or three years, when the plants spread, they would be a glorious riot of colour. There was still a lot of work for Frank to do, but the framework was there. She and Ross had seen to that, with so much argument, so much debate. Candida wondered if the old gentleman would be even interested.

There was a puff of smoke coming out of the chimneys of the Cottage, and she made her way towards it. Kitty in her new house . . . Her dear Kitty, lost now and gone for ever.

'Oh, Miss Candida!' Mrs Frank Clarke welcomed her in a welter of boxes and bundles. 'On your first visit I can't even offer you a cup of tea. Look at it!'

'I wish you would not be so silly, dear,' Candida said, handing her yet another box. 'Here is a hansel. May it bring this house nothing but good luck and health and happiness.'

Kitty tore it open and smiled. 'It shall have pride of place, once this place is square. I love it, and so will Frank. How many memories will it bring back every night, when our work is over and we sit and look at it, I wonder?'

They both looked at the little china ornament fashioned in the shape of a police constable with his night lantern in his hand.

'I love it, Miss Candida,' Kitty repeated. 'You are not going already?'

'I am going to take one last walk around the house, Kitty. Do you have a key?'

With the key in her hand she walked up the winding stone path, past the stables, all renovated and very much extended, past the Dispensary, long ago emptied and cleaned of all her medications, past the rose-garden and through one of the arches which led into the little paved area outside the long french window Mr Stewart had so assiduously constructed.

She unlocked it and then she was in the new conservatory, and through that into the drawing-room, and in there the miracle happened. The house held out its arms to her and enfolded her. There could be no other explanation of it, of why the cool green walls hung with so many of Henry Raeburn's paintings, the lemon-skirted easy chairs, the dark green carpet and the long windows festooned so carefully in lemon drapes seemed more like home to her even than No. 13 Charlotte Square. Sadly, longingly, she went through every room she and Ross had furnished together with love, the impressive dining-room, gold and red, the warm dark library with its shaggy rug before the fireplace on which she could picture a whole line of dogs panting and yawning and rolling over, all four feet in the air, through to the kitchens painted blue to keep the flies away, with the open-fire range only waiting to be lit.

Ross had said it was the bedroom he was most interested in. She climbed the wide, shallow steps of the staircase, uncarpeted and gleaming old oak, and walked past the Captain's Cabin to the bedroom next door. It was all white, with touches of silver and pink. She wondered if they had got the atmosphere quite right. It looked virginal, just waiting, and waiting, with only one dark mark in it.

It was a dark brown box, edged with white and gold lying on the white counterpane, a box in the Semple colours. Candida was nothing if not curious, but she felt like Pandora when she lifted the lid. She tore back the tissue and found a red nightgown, a gossamer thing, a dress for passion, for love, a dress for a woman in love to wear for a man crazy with desire.

She should not be looking at such a thing! She stuffed it back into its box. The old gentleman she had been visualising all this time was not such an old gentleman after all. Far from it!

Alanna's next letter contained two warnings: the first that she and Finlay and all the others would travel to Edinburgh so as to arrive on December 29th, and the second, which plunged Mr Forbes into the depths of despair, that she suspected her mother, Cornelia, would be in Edinburgh long before that.

Candida showed it to Ross, who was in the hall putting on his thin grey leather gloves and preparing to depart. He glanced at it, and coolly adjusted his grey top hat in the mirror at an even more rakish and devastating angle. He was completely devastating from head to toe, to her. There was nothing like pale grey and starched white for a man's daytime wear, she thought, and admired his long narrow trousers and the immaculate cut of his coat as much as she admired his clean-shaven chin and the scent of the gentleman's toilet-water he was wearing. It was faintly aromatic.

'That pink dress is very pretty, Candida,' he said. 'But, just for today, would you wear that white dress with the violet trimmings again? It was the first one I ever saw you in, and you have never worn it since.'

'Yes, if it matters,' she said, taken by surprise and at the same time detecting some excitement beneath his cool exterior.

'It matters,' he said, and opened the front door.

The carriage was waiting outside, and she watched him getting into it. Quite clearly, he had some important business to attend to, some meeting to attend.

At eleven o'clock Candida joined her mother in her sitting-room for coffee attired in the white dress.

'We shall just have it in here today, dear,' Lady Alison said. 'Your father has gone out on something connected with this wretched trial, so there is only you and me. It is not worth while to light any of the other fires yet.'

'I suppose we must attend the trial?' Candida asked. 'I would rather be a hundred miles away from it.'

'I have no intention of sitting all through it,' Lady Alison said, 'and I would not expect you to. But we must appear to be interested, for the sake of your Papa. He is so dreadfully upset about it.'

Liza knocked and came in with the coffee. 'They must have smelt it, your visitors,' she said.

'I did not expect any visitors, Liza. Who are they?'

'Well, in a way, there are two of them. Mr Ross and a lady.'

A lady, with Ross? Candida's heart almost stopped beating.

'Who is she, Liza?'

'I never saw her before, my lady, but she is very beautiful, and very fashionable.'

Candida's heart took another downward plunge.

'Well, we are totally unprepared for strangers, but I suppose you must show them in here, Liza.'

'Very well, Lady Alison.'

The next minute she was showing Ross in, escorting a very handsome lady of nearly sixty in a brilliant green dress under a matching pelisse trimmed with white fur. For a minute Candida's startled eyes thought she also carried a white fur muff, until a tiny pink tongue lolled out from the middle of it, and she realised that the lady was carrying a dog. To complete the picture she wore a green hat piled so high with feathers that they waved above Ross's head.

'Cornelia!' Lady Alison exclaimed. 'Oh, my dearest Cornelia! But we did not expect you!'

Mrs Alexander Laing disengaged herself and her feathers and her little dog from Lady Alison's embrace, and her powerful presence immediately filled the room. She simply took over. Now Candida saw where Ross got his emerald eyes from. Now she saw where Alanna got her personality from, and when Cornelia smiled, Candida was lost.

'I came on ahead,' she said unnecessarily. 'I thought it was long past time I met Candida, to judge from Ross's letters home.'

'Now at last you can, Mother. This is Miss Candida Rowena Forbes,' Ross said with pride in his voice.

'You were always very accurate, dear,' his mother said. 'This time, as ever. She is simply beautiful!' She enfolded Candida in soft arms, bright green feathers and a heady perfume. 'She is a credit to you, Alison.'

Ross seemed actually to sag in relief, and Candida felt she had surmounted some immense hurdle.

'You will take coffee, Cornelia?' Lady Alison asked.

'Oh, Alison, how wonderful to be back in dearest, dearest Edinburgh!' Cornelia sank into a chair with her cup in her hand, while the little white dog ran over to Ross wagging his tail, and Candida got the curious impression that Cornelia was only flexing her claws. 'But I have really come to see what Alanna and Ross have been up to.'

'Of course you have,' Lady Alison murmured. 'I always thought you would.'

'What did I tell you?' Mr Forbes bellowed, waving the newspaper triumphantly, and then looked over his shoulder and lowered his voice. 'She is not down yet?'

'If you are talking about Cornelia,' Lady Alison said reprovingly, 'no. She does not get up before ten. As far as I can gather, all that is in her head in the meantime is clothes for this wedding. She will be shopping all day and every day, by the sound of her. You will hardly see her.'

'Thank God for small mercies!' Mr Forbes said, unrepenting. 'As I was saying, it is all here in the *Courant* today. Hare has confessed. Sir William Rae has promised immunity in exchange. He has got Hare to turn King's evidence to put all the blame on Burke. Hare will go free, and Burke will hang. It is all a foregone conclusion. The whole thing could be over in half an hour.'

'That is one of your larger exaggerations, unfortunately, Atholl.'

'What time does the trial begin on Christmas Eve, Papa?'

'At ten o'clock in the morning, with only Burke and Hare arraigned. They have not even mentioned Dr Knox, who in my opinion is the blackest villain of the three!'

'Do not excite yourself, Atholl,' Lady Alison protested, as Liza came in with the morning rolls, crisp and hot under a white cloth.

'I am not in the least excited, my dear! I am only very angry,' he said, agitatedly spreading on the butter which immediately melted. 'I will have the marmalade, Candida, if you please.'

'You won't read the most exciting news of all in the morning paper, sir,' Liza announced. 'We heard it from the baker at the back door when he came with the rolls. Early this morning there was a riot. A mob on Calton Hill made an effigy of Dr Knox, marched it up the South Bridge and took it to his home in Newington Place. Then it was hanged by the neck from the bough of a tree, set on fire, and Dr Knox escaped by his back door. Nobody knows where he is hiding.'

'Justice,' Mr Forbes said, calm again. 'It was in the hope of seeing justice done that I ever took up Law in the first place. But Law unfortunately has a way of turning itself outside in, as in this case. However, you can always trust the man in the street to see the rights and the wrongs of any situation.'

'Especially the men in the streets of Edinburgh,' his wife said with a smile.

That Christmas Eve in Edinburgh was like no other, before or since. The people should have been at home getting ready their houses, their food, their clothes and their celebrations of the birth of Jesus. At the very least, they should have been intending to go to the Kirk for the Watchnight Service. Instead, every human being who could be packed into it was in the courtroom, while hundreds stood outside waiting for the slightest titbit, in spite of the bitter wind blowing from the north-east, straight from Siberia. They shuddered with every gust, but still they stood, huddling together, and it was somewhere in that crowd that a new song was born. Burke, Hare and Knox were judged and condemned before the trial ever began.

Up the close and down the stair,
But and ben wi' Burke and Hare,
Burke's the butcher, Hare's the thief,
Knox the boy that buys the beef.

Inside the courtroom it was anything but cold, and many of the ladies present were waving their fans. It was not only the press of people which raised the temperature, and not even the one crime for which the two Irishmen were being tried. It was the indignation and the outrage at so many others behind that. How many? God only knew, they told each other with a mixture of awe, loathing, and although none would have admitted it, salacious curiosity.

Mr Forbes came home at eight o'clock to tell them that Lord Henry Cockburn had been on his feet most of the day defending Nelly Burke, and making a splendid job of it. But Maggie Hare, vicious as she was, looked like going free, along with her husband.

'It will go on all night,' he said. 'I do not expect the jury to retire until tomorrow morning at the rate they are going. The Crown has called fifty-five witnesses, believe it or not. I hope you have kept my dinner hot, Alison?'

'Of course I have. Where do you want it?'

'Tell Liza I shall have it in my study, out of harm's way, and tell her I am in a hurry.'

'You are not going back, Atholl, surely?'

'Of course I am going back. You should all go to bed, and if any of you want to hear the verdicts, there are two spare seats allocated to me, and you should be there no later than nine tomorrow morning.'

Cornelia dragged Lady Alison off into the realms of satin and lace next morning, and so only Ross and Candida went to join Mr Forbes. By the time they had struggled through the crowd and found him and their spaces, they did not have long to wait.

At twenty minutes past nine the Justice Clerk, Lord Boyle, placed a black cap on his head and in a hushed courtroom delivered the jury's verdict. Burke was first on the list, and Burke should be detained in the Tolbooth until the 28th of January and then hanged. His body should be handed over for dissection. Then he turned to Nelly Burke, and told her that the libel against her was not proven. She was in tears when she looked up at her husband from under her dishevelled bonnet, and Wull Burke's face was pale but composed when he moved towards her in the presence of the guards. Everyone in the court heard his last words to her, and everyone was moved.

'Well, Nelly,' he said, 'you're out of the scrape.' Then he was led away.

Ross glanced at Candida's white face in the silence that followed. 'Shall I take you home?' he asked.

'No . . . If only the new owner was not coming today, I

would go out to Paradise House. I can think of no other place to comfort me now, after that.'

'You could do the next best thing. You could go and see Kitty.'

'Yes, I could.'

'I will get you a cab, then, if we can push our way out of here.'

Even as she got into the cab, the first snowflakes came out of the cruel wind, and five minutes later when they beat remorselessly on the windows she wondered what had ever possessed her to come on this hopeless errand. To see Paradise House would only depress her even further.

She could feel it was hard going for the horses to pull the cab up the drive to the house, and the driver had the money out of her hand and his horses wheeled about almost as soon as she descended into a perfect welter of snow. He had no desire to be stranded on the outskirts of the town on a day like this, especially Christmas Day. Of course the house was shut up, what she could see of it through the whirling snow, and even at that time of the day the sky was dark and heavy with much more snow to come. She would have to go round to the back and plough her way down to the Cottage. She only hoped Kitty and Frank would be there.

Kitty did not seem at all surprised to see her. She smiled, and took her sudden appearance on Christmas Day in the middle of a snowstorm quite in her stride. 'Well, you said to expect you at any time, Miss Candida. You are welcome under this roof day or night. But you are soaking wet and frozen! Come away in and let me see what I can do about it.'

She had not expected to see the Cottage so spick and span and so well organised in so short a time. All the boxes had gone, a table was in the middle of the kitchen, and two easy chairs sat facing each other at each side of the highly shined hearth.

'Sit down here,' Kitty put her into one of them, 'while I see what I can find to change you into.'

The china police constable had pride of place on the mantelshelf, flanked by two large china dogs. A large clock ticked loudly on the wall, its hands pointing to twelve noon, and there was no sign of Frank.

'Here we are, miss,' Kitty said, coming back. 'I must have the second sight. I took out one of your dresses, just in case. Your white, with the violet ribbons. We will get you into it right away before Frank comes in, and this dry petticoat. It is only one of mine, but it is new.'

Then Kitty appeared to be muttering something under her breath. It sounded like 'old, new, borrowed, but the blue?'

'However did you think of all this, Kitty? Where is Frank, anyway? And what is that glorious smell?'

'Chickens stuffed with thyme, especially for today, miss. Frank is very keen on growing herbs, and he had some dried. He will be here soon, don't you fret! He knows I've been making cock-a-leekie soup.'

Candida sat back in her chair again, warm and dry once more. 'You are very cosy here, Kitty, but I did not mean to intrude on you, today of all days! I really came to say goodbye to the big house before the new owner gets here.'

'There will be no new owner in Paradise House today.' Frank came in like a snowman and shook his coat out of the door. The wind howled in and a great flurry of snowflakes.

'Oh, shut the door!' Kitty cried. 'What is it like out there?'

'It is a blizzard. There are no more cabs running. We are going to be snowed in before the day is out.'

'Well, there is no use shovelling a path until it stops,' Kitty said practically. 'We'll all sit up at the table and have some soup while we wait.'

It was quite late in the afternoon before Frank went out to make a path through the snow and Kitty came back into the kitchen with some material over her arm.

'What have you got there?' Candida asked.

'It's the curtains, miss. I have never got them up yet.'

'Let me help you. Of course, I need not ask if the windows are clean, first?'

'Oh, get away with you, Miss Candida!'

'That was how you ever met Frank, as I recall.'

Kitty giggled and fetched two stools. 'Just thread the string through,' she said. 'They are all sewn and ready. I only hope they are the right length.'

Candida threaded her curtains and stood upon on the stool to hang them on the little hooks. Eventually she got the string taut so that the curtains hung down perfectly matched. She went to draw them, and then as she looked out she saw a tiny light moving about in Paradise House. It lasted only for a minute, and in that minute her heart stood still.

Frank came back in, his cheery face redder even than usual. 'There's a foot of snow, anyway,' he told them. 'All the grounds are like a white sea, with not a footstep to disturb it. Come and look outside!'

All they could see was a long, winding black path with wreaths of snow where Frank had dug it piled up at the sides. The snow had stopped altogether, and the moon came out. It made the gardens look like a huge white frosted cake someone had sliced down the middle.

'Oh, it is beautiful, and just in time for Christmas,' Kitty said. 'Isn't it romantic?'

Candida saw her chance. 'Much too romantic, to spend your first Christmas together with an unexpected guest. You are sure there is nobody arrived in the house, Frank?'

'Not a soul,' he assured her.

'Then I shall sleep there tonight,' Candida said determinedly.

Kitty did not argue with her. She knew her of old. 'I only brought the dress,' she said. 'I did not bargain for this. You will have to wear one of my cloaks, then. Your pelisse is still wet. And, Frank, you will have to go with her. She will never see her way.'

'Oh, what nonsense!' Candida said. 'It is as bright as day out there, and inside Paradise House the moon will show me where to go. Just give me the key, Frank, and I will see you both tomorrow.'

Frank closed the door behind her, and she was alone in the white wilderness. She flitted along the black path in Kitty's dark blue cloak, more curious and somehow excited than she was frightened. Whatever Frank said, she knew someone was in the house.

Thanks to Mr Stewart and his attention to detail, the key turned silently in the well-oiled lock of the french window. She had been right about the moon. It lit her way through all the deserted rooms downstairs and into the kitchen. She was not even surprised that someone had lit the wide open-fire range. The coals glowed bright orange and the long spit in front of the bars rotated emptily. Still, Candida felt no fear. Silver serving-dishes on the scrubbed table shone in the fire's glow, and so did the big silver covers for the ashets where she had hung them herself on the wall beside the pantry.

Then there was nobody downstairs. Whoever was here must be upstairs, and she had left all the doors closed up there. She would have to open each one in turn, no matter what the consequences, if she wanted to see who it was. She stole up the staircase and looked along the passage. Every door was closed, as she expected, except one, the door of the Captain's Cabin. Of course the windows in there looked out in every direction, including the direction of the Cottage, if a burglar wanted to keep an eye out for danger.

Then, and only then, did she feel a little thrill of terror. It must be a burglar, and he was after Ross's gems. What was more, he had the audacity to use a little light. She could see the dim glow of it round the door. It took every ounce of courage she possessed to enter the Captain's Cabin, and what she saw there made all her hair stand on end. A man was sitting at the far end on the chair beside the showcase of gems, and the dim light she had seen was coming from the candle sitting in a candlestick at his feet.

He did not speak, and she could not see his face. She

could only see his grey trousers and his grey leather shoes with their pointed toes. She had seen those shoes before. For a minute she stood frozen while she dredged them up from her memory. She had seen them last under the black fretwood screen in a hospital room. But what could a priest from the Royal Free Hospital in London be doing here in Paradise House?

Candida could not move a muscle. She had the same feeling as in a nightmare, when she wanted to run and yet knew her feet were pinned to the ground. Then the man picked up the candlestick and set it on top of the showcase, and at last she saw his face.

'I have been waiting here for you for hours,' said Ross.

Still she could neither move nor speak.

'Now that you have come at last, we can put the lights on and draw the curtains,' he went on in conversational tones, as if he had noticed nothing strange about her manner or about the situation, and his very matter-of-factness brought her back to reality more swiftly than anything else could have done.

'Why have you been sitting up here in the dark?' she asked, as he lit the lamps and set them both together in one of the windows while he drew the rest of the curtains. 'You should have lit them before, and then I would have been up here before, if only to see the old gentleman. I was so sure that he would come today! I felt it in my bones that he would come today!'

'Your bones told you no lies, Candida. So what do you think of him, now that you have seen him?'

'There never was an old gentleman! It was you all along, Ross?'

She took a deep breath and tried to smile. What did it matter what she thought? What did anything matter—now? She loved him, and she had lost him, and it was the worst thing that had ever happened to her through all the betrayals of this last year or in all her life.

'I didn't know it, but you were always there,' she said sadly.

'Always. I love you.'

'You were the one person who never, ever let me down.'

'Never. I love you.'

'That is the pity of it all . . . I love you,' she said with a sob. 'I really, really love you, but I recognise those grey shoes, you see. The last time I saw them, they were behind a screen in a hospital room.'

'So?' Ross laughed, and took her in his arms and kissed her. It was as though she drowned in that kiss. She was in dark waters, only to rise and sink again helplessly, happily. 'If I would not allow you to go to London without me, do you imagine I would allow you to go into a death-room alone, Candida?'

'But now you know it all, Ross,' she smiled bitterly. 'The whole sordid story.'

'You would not rest until you had found it all out. I could not rest until you had, either, and could settle at my side. It seemed logical to help you and speed things on. So now, at last, will you marry me, Candida, my love?'

She tore herself from his grasp. 'You do not understand, do you?'

'I understand everything,' he said, pulling her back into his arms. 'None of it makes the slightest difference to me. How could it? I loved you from the first minute I saw you. It is as simple as that. Will you marry me? You have seen that I can be as persistent as you. I shall just keep on asking you until you say Yes.'

'Yes, but . . .'

'Don't say another word yet,' Ross commanded, and released her.

He went over to the case with the glass lid and unlocked it and brought her back something in his hand.

'Now we are engaged to be married,' he said, slipping a ring on the third finger of her left hand. 'Oh, God, how long I have waited for you! What plots we all had to make when your back was turned! I got the size of this ring from the moonstone ring on Kitty's finger—so she and Frank had to be brought into it long ago. Then I had to lock the door of this room in case you saw it before I got a chance to propose to you.'

It was the large opal, now set in gold and surrounded by diamonds like the bracelet on her wrist, and its colour wavered from pink to turquoise.

'Before this night is out, I swear it will glow like a flame,' he promised. 'But just now you think you would need another hour to get over the shock,' he laughed tenderly, 'and have it all explained?'

Candida nodded.

'Well then, I shall leave you for a minute and go down to see Kitty and Frank in the kitchen. Oh, yes, they are here. Their signal to me was the hanging up of the curtains, which is why I was waiting in the dark. My signal to them was the lighting of the lamps in the window. They have brought up the chickens to finish them off here, and besides that, I have a message I want Frank to take to someone.'

Left alone, Candida twisted the beautiful ring on her finger and watched its colour changing. She should have sensed that all the time Ross had been watching her, it was only to protect her. She should have known he would never have let her go to see Mary Paterson, or to London, or into the den of Burke and Hare, without him. It was true. He really had loved her from the first minute he saw her, as she had loved him. But she had many more questions to ask.

'How did you manage to get behind that screen in the hospital?' she asked, when he returned and sat down with her, her hand in his.

'The Royal Free depends on donations, Candida. That first day you visited Mistress Mallone, I was arranging a very large donation. That ensured my place behind the screen for as long as it took.'

'Then you are not going back to live in Ireland?'

'I made up my mind about that, the very first day you and I were here together, my darling. Do you remember? Alanna had turned it down, and you had fallen in love with it. So did I. I bought Paradise House for you later that very day. Nobody else was interested. Of course, it is a very different matter now that we have restored it, but I hope you can see our children here as clearly as I can, and our dogs, and horses, and all our other animals.'

'So you will have your veterinary surgery here?'

'The stables are extended already. Your Dispensary is ready and waiting again, until such times as baby-carriages become your next passion.'

'I have not got over this one yet!' Candida wound her arms round his neck, and the next few minutes were lost to the world. 'What about Mama and Papa?' she asked breathlessly afterwards.

'I told your mother my feelings when I bought this house, and she approved. I never thought she would enter into the conspiracy of the "old gentleman" with me, but she did, and before I left your father today at the courtroom I asked for his permission to marry you.'

'What did he say?'

'He gave his permission for our first marriage, on the condition of our second.'

'Oh, Ross! What did he mean by that?'

'I do not believe in long engagements, Candida. Do you?' he smiled, and kissed her again. 'This one has lasted half an hour already.'

'No,' she laughed. 'I had one once. It was a disaster.'

'Then will you marry me today? Your father insists we get married publicly along with Ross and Alanna on the 3rd of January. Neither your mother nor mine would ever forgive us otherwise. Everything else about this story has been double. The wedding might as well be a double wedding, too.'

'How can we get married today, Ross?'

'Well, the wedding feast is nearly ready downstairs. Frank has gone to fetch the minister. You had not forgotten the Reverend Donald Lonegan? He lives on the other side of the road. Kitty and Frank are all the guests we need.'

'But . . .'

'No more buts,' Ross said firmly. 'There is no way of getting back to Charlotte Square tonight. There is only one bed in this house, and I refuse to share it with a lady who is not my wife.'

'That is another way of looking at it,' Candida laughed. 'But there are a lot more questions, yet.'

'One more, then.'

'Why did you leave no footprints in the snow when you came out here?'

'Because I arrived not long after you did, and the snow filled them in. Let me remind you I did not have any cock-a-leekie soup, either. The sooner we are married, the sooner we can eat. We can spend the rest of our lives playing questions and answers if you like, although that was not what I had in mind!'

'Darling Ross! Send Kitty up, then, and I will get ready.'

'I will give her two minutes. You are perfect as you are.'

'Oh, Miss Candida!' Kitty said. 'It was a good job I came to live out here as soon as we got the Cottage! I would have burst, otherwise, trying not to tell you!'

'I wondered what you were muttering about "old, borrowed, new, but what about the blue?" You will only have time to tidy my hair, Kitty.'

'I was determined you would have good luck. The old dress, the new petticoat, and the borrowed blue cloak. And, besides that, I wish you all the happiness in the world, Miss Candida!' Kitty flung her arms round her neck.

Down in the drawing-room Candida and Ross were married by Mr Lonegan, with Kitty and Frank for their witnesses, and after that they all five sat down to a hilarious wedding breakfast in the kitchen, while the fire glowed and Ross opened a bottle of champagne, and then another one, and later on a sudden flurry spattered outside on the windows.

'This is the happiest wedding I ever presided over,' Donnie Lonegan said. 'But it is snowing again, and I had better go.'

'So had we,' said Frank, and they all three left Paradise House.

'How do you feel, Mrs Ross Alexander Laing?' Ross asked between kisses.

It was taking them a long time to get upstairs.

'Wonderful, Ross . . . darling Ross . . . But . . .'

'What now?'

'I have no nightgown.'

'Yes, you have, in a brown box on the bed. It is red for the wicked streak I hope has not deserted you.'

'It is getting stronger all the time. It always does when I wear red.'

'That is why you are going to wear it only in our bedroom. Go and put it on, sweetheart. Then I can take it off again. Very, very slowly, to make the moment last.'

SPOT THE COUPLE

AND WIN A

£1,000

REAL PEARL NECKLACE

PLUS 10 PAIRS OF REAL PEARL EAR STUDS WORTH OVER £100 EACH

B

No piece of jewellery is more romantic than the soft glow and lustre of a real pearl necklace, pearls that grow mysteriously from a grain of sand to a jewel that has a romantic history that can be traced back to Cleopatra and beyond.

To enter just study Photograph A showing a young couple. Then look carefully at Photograph B showing the same section of the river. Decide where you think the couple are standing and mark their position with a cross in pen.

Complete the entry form below and mail your entry PLUS TWO OTHER "SPOT THE COUPLE" Competition Pages from June, July or August Mills and Boon paperbacks, to Spot the Couple, Mills and Boon Limited, Eton House, 18/24 Paradise Road, Richmond, Surrey, TW9 1SR, England. All entries must be received by December 31st 1988.

RULES

1. This competition is open to all Mills & Boon readers with the exception of those living in countries where such a promotion is illegal and employees of Mills & Boon Limited, their agents, anyone else directly connected with the competition and their families.
2. This competition applies only to books purchased outside the U.K. and Eire.
3. All entries must be received by December 31st 1988.
4. The first prize will be awarded to the competitor who most nearly identifies the position of the couple as determined by a panel of judges. Runner-up prizes will be awarded to the next ten most accurate entries.
5. Competitors may enter as often as they wish as long as each entry is accompanied by two additional proofs of purchase. Only one prize per household is permitted.
6. Winners will be notified during February 1989 and a list of winners may be obtained by sending a stamped addressed envelope marked "Winners" to the competition address.
7. Responsibility cannot be accepted for entries lost, damaged or delayed in transit. Illegible or altered entries will be disqualified.

ENTRY FORM

Name ______________________________

Address ______________________________

____

I bought this book in TOWN ______________ COUNTRY ______________

This offer applies only to books purchased outside the UK & Eire.
You may be mailed with other offers as a result of this application.